RESCUING DR. MARIAN

A MADE MARIAN LEGACY NOVEL

LUCY LENNOX

Cover Art: Najla Qamber | Qamber Designs
Cover Image: Michelle Lancaster
Editing: One Love Editing
Proofreading: Jodi Duggan

RESCUING DR. MARIAN

One kiss changed everything.

As sheriff, I'm the guy people call for help.
But when my solo Hawaii trip gets hijacked by my clingy ex,
suddenly *I'm* the one who needs saving.

My unlikely rescuer?
A gorgeous stranger who plants one breathtaking, reckless kiss
on me in the middle of a crowded bar—sending my ex packing... and stealing my carefully guarded heart.

Tommy Marian kissed me like he knew me.
Like he wanted me.
Like I was his.
Like he was *mine*.

But he's not.

He's a straight, ambitious city doctor—here in paradise for his own damn wedding.
And I'm going home alone, as usual.

Six months later, I land a dream search and rescue gig in Legacy, Montana.
One summer. A break from my coupled-up friends. Zero distractions.

Except guess who's freshly single… and bunking in my tiny cabin? The biggest distraction of my life.

Tommy Marian is still beautiful, still infuriating, and still everything I can't want.

He says what happens in Legacy stays in Legacy.
I say I'm not even tempted.
At least one of us is lying.

Because when Tommy disappears on the mountain, I realize I'd burn the world to get him back…
And maybe this time, I won't let him go.

AUTHOR'S NOTE(S)

Welcome to the next generation of the Marians! No, you do not need to have read any other books before diving right in. This is a brand new series, and each book is written to stand on its own. If you like what you see, feel free to go back and meet the older generation, starting with *Borrowing Blue*.

One of the main characters in *Rescuing Dr. Marian* is Tommy Marian. Many of you have asked what his relationship is to the original Made Marian series. We first met Tommy as a newborn in the book *Grounding Griffin*. He's Pete and Ginger's son. Again, you do not need to know any of this to enjoy *Rescuing Dr. Marian.*

Do not, under any circumstances, do any math related to character ages. I promise this will not end well for you. Don't make assumptions about what year certain events take place, or the relative age of parents, grand-parents, or great-aunts. Just *waves hand vaguely* enjoy yourself without thinking too hard about it.

Finally, thank you to all of the generous supporters of the Made Marian Kickstarter. Thank you especially to Beth for suggesting the name Jasper for use in the Made Marian Legacy series. I hope you enjoy seeing him in *Rescuing Dr. Marian*!

(For more author notes, check out the letter at the end of the book.)

1

FOSTER

THE EMERGENCY CALL came in just as I was locking up the sheriff's office for a long-awaited vacation.

Three hours later, I was rappelling down a cliff face to extract a photographer who'd gotten a little too creative with his angle shots. Three hours after that, we'd gotten him to safety, but I'd missed my flight to Hawaii and spent five hours driving through a blizzard to catch the next one. And eight hours after *that*, I'd made my final connection by the skin of my teeth, but my luggage had not.

So by the time my seatmate sloshed her vodka cranberry all over my chest, it was safe to say I'd lost whatever patience I might have had at the start of my hellish, never-ending day.

Fate was seriously fucking with me.

"And the wors' part is, I never saw it coming," the woman slurred, still waving her cup as she spoke, seemingly unaware it was now empty. "But then, I guess no one ever does. I thought he was The One. I thought he and I were the real thing. Like... like daisies in sunshine. Like kit... kin... *kinsmin.*"

"Kismet," a low, aggrieved voice muttered from the row behind us. "You mean *kismet.*"

I covered my snort with a cough. The guy in 9A had started correcting Miss Daisies and Sunshine's drunken mispronunciations under his breath, but the longer her drama went on, the less he seemed to hold back his commentary.

At this point, his comments were the only thing keeping me sane.

"Did you say something?" she asked, squinting at me.

I thumbed over my shoulder. "I think he said '*Kleenex.*' Speaking of which, do you have any tissues in your bag?" I gestured from the bulging carryall at her feet to the remains of her vodka cranberry trickling down my chest. "I could use one."

"Don't think so." She wrinkled her nose. "Oh, gosh, you spilled your drink!"

I sucked in a breath. "*I* didn't—" A travel pack of tissues suddenly appeared between us with a little waggle, and I glanced through the darkened gap between the seats to see a deep hazel eye smiling back at me.

Mr. 9A to the rescue.

"Thanks," I said.

"Don't mention it."

While I dabbed at my ruined shirt, Miss Daisies and Sunshine kept talking, ensuring everyone around us knew way more than we'd ever wanted or needed to know about the "cheating ass" who "din' *deserve* my love."

"And the wors' part is," she wailed, "I never saw it com—"

I jumped in to prevent her from starting again at the beginning. "Look, I know it doesn't feel like it now, but you'll move on from this. I dated a cheating ass once, too."

"Yeah?"

"*Matthew-don't-call-me-Matt.*" I rolled my eyes. "High-maintenance, persistent, terrible at karaoke, regrettably bad at monogamy. It sucked at the time, but I learned a lot of lessons about what I want in a partner. And the man had good taste in resorts," I added. "Hence my trip to Kauai."

She scrunched up her face. "Yer ex is gunna be here, too?"

"Oh, god no. The opposite. I ditched my ex, but I still love Hawaii, and the only time it's safe for me to visit is over New Year's. Matthew hasn't missed a ball drop in decades."

"Is that like..." Daisy Sunshine lowered her voice, but not by much. "...a gay thing?"

Mr. 9A snickered.

I pressed my lips together to keep from barking out a laugh. "Uh. No. It's..." I pondered this. "Well, come to think of it, there *are* a few gay men involved in that particular event."

This time, 9A snort-choked so loudly the woman beside him asked if he was okay.

Mercifully, the plane touched down at that exact moment.

"Know whut? I'm gunna take yer advice," Daisy announced as the people at the front of the plane began grabbing their things. "I'm gunna get a new man. I'm gunna find real love. Like poetry. Like Shakesgere." She frowned. "Shakes... Gere?"

"Shakes*peare*," came from behind us. "For god's sake."

"Brother to Richard. Obvs," I added, turning to grin

between the seats at the man who'd saved my mood if not my shirt.

He was clean-cut, with neatly trimmed light-brown hair, bright hazel eyes, and a knowing grin that made my stomach do something interesting.

I also noticed the equally attractive woman next to him, scrolling through her phone, and realized they were probably together.

Figured.

All the best ones were taken these days. All of my friends back in Wyoming had recently paired up, too, leaving me the sole, glaringly single target of my mother's matchmaking ways.

Hence, my hookup vacation in Hawaii. No mother. No snow. No work. Only me, the sun, umbrella drinks, and a plentiful Grindr app for the next ten days. Ringing in the New Year right.

Daisy turned around and beamed at 9A. "You know him? The poet?"

He bit his lip and nodded, eyes dancing as he glanced at me, inviting me to share the joke. "I know him well. Spent way too much time with him in high school, actually. Wordy fucker."

The seat belt sign dinged off, so Daisy turned and knelt up onto her seat to face him. She gasped. "Hey, wait, you're the guy from that commercial! With the dog and the thing!"

"Sorry, no. I—"

"You are!" Daisy argued, loudly enough to get the attention of all the passengers who were trying to collect their bags and deplane.

The woman sitting with him looked up from her phone and

shot him a teasing look. "I assure you, he's not that interesting. He's a physician in Manhattan. *Bor-ring.*"

The playful sarcasm in her voice suggested they knew each other well, and the way he rolled his eyes confirmed it.

Daisy set her jaw. "Be that as it mayyyyy," she said. "He's also in that commercial with the dog and the thing!"

A man craned his head around the people in the aisle to take a look at the handsome doctor like he was a bug under a magnifying glass. "You do look a little like him."

Another lady shook her head. "Too squinchy in the eyes. It's not him."

Someone behind us called impatiently, "Can we go, please? There's a fruity drink with my name on it somewhere."

Daisy pouted. "But I want an autograph and picture."

The crowd around us began to argue, some trying to get closer to the doctor to get a better look, a few saying they wanted an autograph and picture also, most just hoping to get off the damned plane.

The doctor blushed fiercely.

Suddenly, I had an idea. "Oh, I know exactly who you mean now," I told Daisy. "Wade, uh… Brown. Wade Brown. Yeah. But he died."

"What?" Her eyes went huge.

"Mmmm," I said solemnly. "Tragic. Even Kevin Bacon posted about it. They'd worked together a bunch. He played his guitar in a tribute song for the guy on social media." I laid a hand over my heart and cast my eyes to the ceiling of the airplane. "RIP, Wade."

"Ohmigosh! Now that you mention it, I think I did see Kevin

playing his guitar!" Daisy exclaimed. She turned to the doctor. "Sorry, bro. 'S too bad you didn't do the thing with the dog, though."

Others nodded and murmured, agreeing that it was sad for such a good actor to be cut down in his prime... and that this random guy on the airplane wasn't semi-famous.

The doctor shot me a look of incredulity and mouthed, "Thank you."

I winked back at him.

"So anyway," I said to the rest of the people around us, nodding and stepping out into the aisle before nudging others forward. "We'll all drink one to Wade tonight. I know I'm gonna."

"To Wade!" everyone added.

I didn't bother waiting for my bag since I already knew it hadn't made the connection. After filing an official lost-bag claim, I grabbed the first taxi to the resort and charmed the front desk lady into an oceanfront room, a toiletry kit, and a drink voucher.

The warm tropical air was a relief after the harsh Wyoming winter I'd left behind. I took a moment to breathe it in as I made my way out to the cabana bar by the pool. The rhythmic sound of the waves was soothing as I approached the bartender.

"Plate of whatever appetizers you have and a Double Old Fashioned, please," I murmured to the guy before scoping out a small table at the edge of the area where I could look out at the ocean. As soon as the drink was in my hand, I wandered over and sat down, enjoying the smoky citrus taste of the first sip.

Now, this was more like it. Warm, salty air. Quality bourbon.

Nowhere to be. Zero chance of a midnight call to a snowy accident on the highway.

"Mind if I join you?"

I looked up to see the handsome doctor from the plane standing beside my table with a slight smile. My stomach did that funny little thing again.

"Please," I gestured to the empty chair across from me. "I owe you a thank-you for the tissues and your sense of humor. And for not blowing my cover story about poor, departed Wade Brown."

He chuckled as he sat down. "As far as I'm concerned, you rescued *me*. That was quick thinking. I must look an awful lot like that guy, if she was that insistent."

"I have no idea who she was talking about, so I made up a name," I admitted with a laugh.

"Well, here's to my doppelgänger, the late, great, fictional Wade Brown," he said, raising his glass. "May he rest in peace."

I clinked my glass against his. "To Wade." I took a sip and then licked my lips. "You here alone? Where's your... friend?"

He smiled. "My cousin Ella. She had some work to catch up on." He reached out a hand to shake. "I'm Tommy, by the way. Tommy Marian. Boring doctor from Manhattan. Apparently."

"Foster Blake," I replied, enjoying the warm clasp of his hand in mine. "Boring sheriff of Majestic, Wyoming, currently on a much-needed vacation."

Tommy's eyes widened slightly. "Sheriff? That's not boring at all."

"You'd be surprised. It's a small town. Most of my job

involves breaking up bar fights and rescuing lost hikers. It's nothing like what you do."

He shook his head. "Rescuing people is important work, whether it's on the trail or in the hospital."

The bartender brought my appetizer plate and set it between us. "Help yourself," I offered, and Tommy eagerly reached for a pita wedge.

"Looks like you're not getting into vacation mode, Sheriff," he said, nodding at my jeans and the flannel button-down that still bore traces of my seatmate's drink.

I laughed. "*I'm* in paradise, but my luggage still has work to do." I explained the delays that had led to my nearly missed connection and lost bags, and he winced sympathetically.

I snuck a glance at his finely tailored pants and still-semi-crisp button-down, rolled up to expose sexy forearms. "Meanwhile, you seem remarkably put together for someone who just got off a plane. Where were you flying from?"

Tommy spread hummus onto his pita and took a bite, groaning appreciatively. "It was only a short hopper flight for me today. I was at a medical conference on the Big Island this week."

"What kind of doctor are you?"

He nodded. "Emergency medicine. I work in the ER at a busy trauma one hospital. Though..." He hesitated before adding, "I'm considering getting dual-boarded in anesthesia."

"You don't sound thrilled about it," I observed.

Tommy spun his glass on the table, his expression growing distant. "It's complicated. I prefer emergency medicine, but anesthesia's the smart career move if I want to settle down and have a family. More predictable hours, better pay. It's the path upward, and I've always worked hard to get to the next level."

"So you want to settle down and have a family?"

His eyes met mine, and I saw a vulnerable kind of yearning in them. "Yes," he said simply. "Family's everything to me."

My heart rate kicked up. He seemed as devoted to his as I was to mine. "Same," I murmured.

"So you know sometimes family means sacrifice," he said with a little shrug.

While he was right, I felt like if I agreed with him, I'd be condoning a choice that would damn him to a life of compromise. Achievement and stability at the cost of his freedom and happiness.

"If your family loves you," I hedged, "they'd want you to enjoy the journey, not just tick the boxes."

Tommy sighed. "I don't love living in the city," he admitted softly.

"I couldn't do it," I said. "It wouldn't be easy to have a dog, which is a dealbreaker."

His expression brightened. "You have a dog?"

"Not currently, but I'm on the list for a Search and Rescue dog. Hopefully, I'll get one by summer."

"You could find a pup and train him up yourself."

"It's a lot of work," I said. "I don't have time for that. Better if I get one already trained from the program. Otherwise, they wouldn't be ready for anything serious until summer after next."

Tommy dredged another pita through the hummus. "Well,

promise me if you get a dog, you'll name him after this dip. It's amazing."

I laughed. "Hummus? Very professional name for a SAR dog."

We continued talking as the evening progressed, ordering more drinks and appetizers.

I learned that Tommy had done a rotation in wilderness medicine in North Carolina, had a love for the outdoors that rivaled my own, and had a close-knit family who'd be arriving in the morning for a wedding. He also told me about growing up in San Francisco and the mountain lodge his family owned, where he'd spent summers hiking and climbing.

I shared stories about my family, too, of course, and the experience of being sheriff in a small tourist town. When I told him about some of the more interesting rescues I'd been involved in, he'd leaned in like he was hanging on my every word.

Hours passed, and I realized I was having more fun talking to Tommy than I'd had in a long time. His sense of humor, which had gotten me through the longest travel day ever, had me laughing out loud more than once, and there was something about his warm hazel eyes and genuine interest in what I had to say that made me feel seen in a way I hadn't experienced before.

I started to think maybe I didn't mind fate fucking with me after all. Not if it had led me here, with him.

As the night wore on, the bar began to fill with more people. A karaoke setup was wheeled out, and the first brave souls took to the makeshift stage.

"Oh no," I groaned as an off-key rendition of "Don't Stop Believin'" started up. "I should have known there'd be karaoke."

Tommy grinned. "Not a fan?"

"My ex used to drag me to karaoke bars all the time. He was terrible, but he loved the attention."

"Matthew-not-Matt, right? The high-maintenance one who was bad at monogamy?"

I was surprised he remembered. "That's him. He—"

I stopped mid-sentence as a familiar voice came over the speakers. "Don't we all have that special someone, the one that got away? Foster, wherever you are out there in this big, beautiful world, this one's for you!"

My blood ran cold as I slowly turned toward the stage. There, swaying slightly with the mic clutched in his hand, was Matthew. The opening notes of Katy Perry's "The One That Got Away" began to play.

"Christ, no," I muttered, turning back to Tommy with what must have been pure panic on my face.

"No way!" Tommy leaned forward, humor dancing in his eyes. "Is that—?"

"In another life..." Matthew crooned off-key.

"He's supposed to be in New York," I hissed, slumping down in my chair, wishing I could disappear.

Tommy's expression shifted from amusement to concern. "What do you need?"

"A hole to crawl into? A time machine?" I ran a hand through my hair. "I can't deal with him right now. Not after the day I've had."

"Omigod, Foster? Is that you?" Matthew called from the stage, squinting into the crowd. "He's here! It's kismet!"

"People need to stop throwing that word around," I groaned.

Tommy reached across the table and took my hand. "Do you trust me?" he asked, his voice low and intense.

I looked into his eyes, feeling inexplicably drawn to this man I'd just met. If anything felt like kismet tonight, it was the feeling of his hand in mine.

"Yes," I said instantly.

"You good with a little PDA?" he asked, eyes crinkling with laughter and scheming.

I gave him a once-over. *I* already knew I was attracted to the man, but I wanted to make sure *he* knew. "With you? Absolutely. With Matthew? I'd rather be coated in syrup and lobbed into the Everglades."

The warmth of Tommy's chuckle relaxed me. He moved his chair closer to mine and put his arm around my shoulders just as Matthew finished his song and hopped off the stage, making a beeline for our table.

"Foster? Is that really you? What are the chances?" Matthew's eyes were wide with excitement but quickly narrowed when he noticed Tommy's arm around me.

"Slim, but not as slim as I'd hoped," I muttered.

Tommy chuckled under his breath.

I shifted closer to him, grateful for his solid presence beside me. In a normal tone, I said, "Matthew. This is a surprise. Thought you claimed there was nothing better than New York at New Year's."

He shrugged. "Got into a bit of a disagreement with my brother, so I decided to come to Hawaii this year. And now that I've seen *you* here, I'm thinking I made the right—"

"Babe?" Tommy's fingers began playing with the hair at the nape of my neck, sending shivers down my spine. "Aren't you going to introduce me?"

Babe? I knew he was pretending, but my heart thumped wildly anyway.

"Uh. Yeah," I said quickly. "Tommy, this is Matthew. He and I dated for a little while a few years back. Matthew, this is Tommy. He's..."

"Foster's boyfriend." Tommy extended a hand to Matthew.

"Boyfriend?" Matthew's smile faltered.

Tommy's eyes melted into mine. "It's only a matter of time until we make it official."

Matthew gave Tommy an assessing up-down. "Really. Because you don't seem like Foster's type. He's all Carhartt and woodsy, and you look..." He tilted his head. "Actually, you look really familiar."

"Like Wade Brown, from the commercial with the dog?" Tommy asked innocently. "'Cause I get that a lot."

I rolled my lips to hide my smile.

"No," Matthew said seriously, reminding me that he'd never had much of a sense of humor. "Like a guy at my gym on West Fifty-Fourth."

"Oh." Tommy hesitated. "That... might actually be me."

"Tommy's a doctor in New York," I explained. "He came out to Majestic for a vacation last summer, and we hit it off on the trail."

"Foster used a cheesy pickup line on me," Tommy said, squeezing my hand. "Said he was going to have to arrest me for public indecency if I insisted on flexing my biceps."

I stifled a snort as Tommy held out his free arm and flexed, causing his muscles to tighten his shirt around his upper arm and show off impressive forearms.

"That sounds like me," I agreed, biting back a grin. "Always joking about false arrest."

"Hold up. So you live in New York?" Matthew folded his arms over his chest. "And you're okay with that, Foster? Because when I left Majestic, you said you had no interest in moving away from that backwoods town and no interest in a long-distance relationship."

"I don't," I blurted without considering that I might be torpedoing our story. My cheeks heated.

"Foster means we didn't set out for this to happen." Tommy shrugged easily. "But of course, he's not giving up his career. His work is vital. Do you know how many lives he's saved? The sheriff's department in Majestic handles some of the most challenging wilderness rescues in the region."

Matthew looked taken aback, probably as surprised as I was by Tommy's passionate defense.

"That doesn't mean we're not serious about our relationship, though." Tommy's thumb traced circles on the back of my hand. "When you find The One, you hold on to him and find a way to make it work."

Matthew narrowed his eyes, pointing and waggling a finger between us. "And Foster is... The One?"

"Oh yeah. I knew right away that this was real. Like daisies in sunshine. Like poetry. Right, babe?" Tommy's hazel eyes twinkled at me as he quoted my former seatmate, reminding me that even the worst situation was better when you had someone to share it with. "Foster's the real deal. And I find authenticity incredibly sexy."

The way he said "sexy" with his eyes locked on mine made my blood thrum. I'd known this was pretend, but something in Tommy's gaze seemed genuine, making me wonder if he was still acting.

Maybe if I could ditch my ex, the two of us could figure it out, preferably back in my room.

"But," Matthew began.

I felt a flicker of anger. My history with him was years in the past, and I had no interest in giving oxygen to the fire he was desperately trying to light.

"There were a lot of reasons you and I didn't work out, Matthew," I reminded him, surprised by how little I gave a shit anymore. "It's hard to be serious with someone who fucks your best deputy."

Matthew flushed.

Tommy's eyes lost their twinkle. "He slept with your deputy?" His face darkened.

I could tell he was gearing up for a response, likely something equally protective and passionate, and maybe that's why I did what I did.

Or maybe it was simple greed. Basic hunger. A desperate desire to get closer to the man who'd intrigued me for the past few hours.

I'd meant the kiss to be brief. A performance. A middle

finger... with tongue. But the moment our lips met, something surged—hot and wrong and absolutely right.

Tommy stilled. Then surged forward like he'd been starved.

My world narrowed to the weight of his hand on my neck, the burn of his mouth.

This wasn't pretend. This was a detour to a future I didn't dare believe in.

Everything around us seemed to fade away—the bar, the music, Matthew's shocked expression. All I could focus on was the softness of Tommy's lips, the warmth of his touch, and the surprising rightness of it all.

Under the table, I guided his hand to my thigh, needing more contact, more of this unexpected connection. His fingers tensed against my leg, then gripped firmly as our kiss deepened. I felt his breath hitch, matching the sudden leap of my pulse.

When we finally pulled apart, both slightly breathless, Tommy blinked at me in shock as if the man had never been kissed before. "Oh," he breathed.

Oh was right. His palm still rested on my thigh, burning through my pants like a brand. If I had my way, there was going to be a whole lot more of that as soon as I got Tommy back to my room.

"Fine, whatever." Matthew sniffed. "You've made your point."

"Take care," I murmured without taking my eyes off Tommy, surprised to find I almost meant it. After all, Matthew's presence had led to this.

He flounced off just as the bartender appeared with our bill.

Tommy blinked rapidly for a beat before clearing his throat. "You can, um… charge it to mine. To me. To my room. Mommy Tarian." He squinted. "Tommy Marian. Room… something. It has a number. I think it starts with a two?"

I tilted my head at him before glancing at the bartender hiding a grin. "Room 428. Foster Blake. Thanks."

I was surprised to find that my voice sounded normal and unaffected when I felt anything but. Kissing Tommy Marian had realigned every molecule of my body. Not one single normal part of me remained.

As soon as the bartender walked away, the breath escaped Tommy's open mouth on a strange sigh as his eyes and mouth opened in my direction. "Fuck. Sorry. I just…"

Somehow, Tommy's hand had ended up in mine, and I clasped it firmly. "It's okay. It's kind of nice thinking I have that effect on someone."

I glanced out at the water and away from the people in the cabana bar. As much as I wanted to get him upstairs, I didn't want to rush this. Tonight, with him, I wanted to take my time. "Want to walk down to the beach? Maybe get some air?"

Tommy nodded, his eyes still a little wild. "Yeah," he managed. "Yeah, okay."

We left the bar area and followed the sandy path between swaying palms. The music faded behind us, replaced by the rhythmic crash of waves. Away from the bar area, the night felt cooler.

Neither of us spoke as we walked to the water's edge. The

moonlight laid a silvery path across the dark ocean, and I felt more of my stress fade with every step along it. Tommy's quiet company was easy and welcome.

"Thank you," I finally said, turning to face him. "We're making quite a habit of rescuing each other."

Tommy shrugged, his profile sharp against the night sky. "It was nothing."

"Hell of a kiss to be referred to as nothing," I said with a soft laugh.

His eyes met mine then, and the intensity I saw there made my breath catch. Without thinking, I stepped closer, wanting to touch him and possibly kiss him again, if he was up for it.

"I, uh…" He pursed his lips together as if unsure what to say. "Yeah. That was a hell of a kiss." He let out a nervous laugh. "Not sure I've ever had a kiss like that."

I closed the remaining distance between us and reached for him.

This time when our lips met, there was no audience, no pretense. Just desire, raw and honest. My hands moved to his waist, slipping beneath the hem of his button-down shirt to touch warm skin. He shuddered against me, his own hands coming up to grip my shoulders.

We stumbled slightly, moving deeper into the shadows of a cluster of palm trees. My back hit the rough trunk of one, and Tommy pressed against me, our bodies aligned from chest to thigh. The kiss grew hungrier, messier. My fingers traced the ridges of muscle along his back as he made a sound low in his throat that shot straight through me.

"Wait—" he gasped as I nipped at his jaw. "I can't—"

I pulled back, brushing my lips closer to his ears. "What do you need?" I breathed against his skin, not wanting to put any actual distance between us. My stomach tightened with want, and my heart thundered with excitement.

"Foster," he whispered. The way he said my name—reverent but conflicted—made me pull back and cradle his face, searching for an explanation in his expression.

His eyes were dark with desire but also swimming with confusion. I wasn't sure, but I thought maybe there was some guilt in there, too. Whatever it was, it clearly meant kissing time was over for now.

Fuck.

My stomach dropped. Until that moment, I truly thought he was like any other attractive man I'd flirted with in the past few years—the kind I could enjoy, then walk away from fairly easily. But sitting here in the face of his rejection, I realized I really liked this guy.

Really liked him.

"Hey, sure," I said stupidly. "No, it's okay."

"I'm sorry," he whispered.

"Do you want to talk about it?" I was desperate to keep this from ending completely. I'd loved the fuck out of kissing the man, but I'd also enjoyed getting to know him. "You could come back to my room—just to talk, I mean."

Tommy's expression looked both pained and conflicted. "I, um... I can't. I mean, I want to, but... I... shouldn't."

The rush of euphoria I'd experienced simply being in his

presence and wondering what the night ahead of us held suddenly changed course, like the world's most powerful vacuum had decided to suck my happiness away.

"Why?" I asked. "If you don't mind my asking."

He reached over and gripped my forearm. "I'm... I'm straight."

I watched him carefully. "Not a dealbreaker, Tommy," I said softly, breaking one of my own rules. Nothing good ever came with hooking up with "straight" men, and I knew it from personal experience. But there was something about this guy that made me want to throw the rule as far out into the deep, dark ocean as I could possibly fling it.

His cheeks, already flushed pink from the kiss, darkened even more. "It... I... I just can't. I'm sorry."

I pasted on a grin I definitely didn't feel. "Understood. My loss. But I really enjoyed hanging out tonight. And thanks for being a great wingman. That was very cool of you, all things considered. I wouldn't have kissed you if I'd known you were straight."

He nodded a little erratically. "Yeah, no, uh. It's all good. I have a lot of gay and bi uncles and cousins. And one of my sisters is gay."

"And you grew up in San Francisco," I joked, suddenly feeling very awkward.

His hand tightened around my arm. "Foster... will you come back to my room and let me give you a clean T-shirt? I have extras, and you don't have anything clean to wear until your luggage gets here."

I put my hand over his and squeezed. This time, my smile

was genuine. "Now, that sounds like a proposition too good to pass up."

Thankfully, the awkwardness passed when we walked back past the bar and shared a laugh at the sound of Matthew's even more drunk voice crooning about something that rhymed with heartbreak. As we continued along the path toward the building where Tommy's room was—thankfully, nowhere near my own—we fell into easy conversation again.

Tommy pulled a faded T-shirt from his suitcase—soft cotton worn thin from years of washing.

"From my family reunion," he explained with a slight smile. "Annual Marian madness in Montana. Fair warning—it might smell like mountain air and nostalgia."

I laughed. "My favorite." I shucked my shirt off and quickly donned his, trying not to see the gesture as something more intimate than it was—an offering of something personal, something that had touched his skin.

The shirt fit better than I'd expected, stretching over the extra inches in my bulkier frame.

"Well," I said with a smile of thanks, clutching my flannel in my hand and feeling awkward again. "Guess I'll be going. Nice meeting you, Tommy Marian."

I was tempted to stick around and talk to him a little longer. But he'd already put the brakes on anything more than friends, and I hadn't come to Hawaii to make friends with a straight doctor from New York. Besides, I already had the world's stupidest crush on the man, and that was more than I could handle.

After returning to my room, I took a long, hot shower and

indulged in a very short session with my hand before falling into bed naked. Even then, sleep eluded me for a long time. And when I did finally fall asleep, images of a smiling Tommy Marian followed me into my dreams all night long.

Little did I know that particular affliction would end up lasting my entire life.

2

TOMMY

My heart thudded painfully as I watched Foster Blake walk away from my hotel room.

The dim lights in the outdoor passageway threw shadows across his shoulders, stretched wide across the soft cotton of the T-shirt I'd given him. His ruined flannel hung from one hand as he strode away.

I wanted to call him back. My entire body vibrated with the need to shout his name, to beg him to stay for just a little longer.

To talk to me just a bit more about his life in Wyoming. About search and rescue. About his snarky little sister and his meddling mom.

To keep the big, handsome man in my orbit a few more minutes because when he was with me, it was hard to think of anything we'd done together as the life-altering calamity I knew it was.

I'd never kissed a man before tonight. Not like that. Hell, I'd never kissed a *woman* like that before. Not in the kind of way that took charge, that dominated...

That owned me completely.

Breath sawed in and out of my lungs as I returned into the room and closed the door behind me. "Fuck," I whimpered. "Fuck, fuck, fuck."

I was in so much trouble. So. Fucking. Much. Trouble.

It hadn't just been the kiss that had taken me by surprise or the fact that Foster was a guy when I'd honestly figured I was a hundred percent straight.

It was that I'd wanted to say yes when he'd asked me back to his room. Wanted to go *anywhere* with him, just to stay close to him and find out what else he had to say.

And then when he'd unbuttoned his stained shirt to slip on the tee I'd given him... well, I'd found my gaze lingering on him longer than it should have.

Medical school had prepared me to understand the human body as a collection of systems working in harmony, and years of examining bodies had made it commonplace. But there was nothing clinical about the way I'd noticed his shoulders— broad and strong and gorgeous—as he'd pulled my T-shirt over his head. And nothing in my studies had prepared me to have my own pulse quicken and my mouth go dry as I'd watched the play of muscles in his arms, mentally tracing the path of veins visible beneath his skin.

I'd recognized these symptoms all too well. The rush of chemicals that turned rational thought sideways, the slight elevation in body temperature, the focus that narrowed to one person in a crowded room.

I *wanted* Foster Blake. And knowing the biological basis for attraction didn't make it any less powerful.

I squeezed my eyes closed. "This is normal. Cold feet. Jitters."

But it was not normal. Not for me. And not with another man.

So, I did the only thing I could think of when faced with something this potentially life-changing. I grabbed my key and ran down the hall in the opposite direction from the one Foster had taken.

My cousin Ella answered her door on the third knock, barefoot and wearing pajamas festooned with tiny rubber ducks. Dark strands had escaped her messy topknot to wave around her face, probably because she'd been tugging at them while working on her project.

"Bro, you suck at relaxing—" she began. But when she saw my face, her eyes widened. "Tommy? Are you alright?"

"Not really, no." I walked into her room without waiting for an invitation, not that she'd expect me to. "I did something, Ella." My voice sounded thready and panicked to my own ears.

"Take a deep breath," she instructed, closing the door behind me and wrapping an arm around my shoulders. "Whatever it is, we'll fix it, okay? Aunt Tilly once gave me a whole rundown on hiding a body... though I think she figured Uncle Teddy was the Marian most likely to commit a felony, not you."

I shot her a look. "Not helping."

Ella squeezed my shoulder. "You *are* okay physically,

though, right? Because you kinda look like you were mauled." She waved a hand at my wrinkled-as-fuck button-down and raised an eyebrow in a silent question.

Thinking of the answer to that question turned my blood to liquid fire—*Foster's big hands yanking up the fabric, the warmth of his palm at the small of my back, the flex of his fingers like he was as greedy for the contact as I was*—

"I'd guess you and Kari were pre-gaming the wedding night," Ella went on. "Except your bride isn't due in until tomorrow, along with the rest of the fam. And, frankly, I can't imagine Kari ever getting hot and heavy." She snorted lightly.

My bride.

Hearing her say those words was a cold dose of reality, reminding me why I'd had no business kissing anyone earlier and no business fantasizing about it now.

I was supposed to be getting married in three days. The perfect Hawaiian wedding of Kari's dreams.

"Fuck." I stumbled over to the bed and threw myself onto it, face-first. "Christ, how am I going to tell her?"

"Tom." Ella sat beside me and placed a comforting hand on my shoulder. "Whatever you've done, I'm sure she'll forgive you. I mean, if you took a job at a hospital that wasn't prestigious enough, or accepted a speaking opportunity in a country not on her list of pre-approved travel destinations—"

"Worse," I breathed. "So much worse. We're in the cone of silence, Ella. Swear to me."

"Babe," she said, dropping the joking tone. "What is it?"

I turned my head and met her eyes. "I kissed someone." Just saying the words set my cheeks on fire again.

She gasped dramatically. "Holy shit! Tell me every single thing. Start with what kind of special magic this woman had to make you cheat on your fucking fiancée literally three days before your wedding!"

My hands were shaking, and, honestly, it felt like the rest of me was, too. "Not a woman. And it wasn't actually cheating. At least... I don't think."

I ran a hand over my face. If cheating included emotions, I was at least slightly guilty.

"Not a woman?" Ella jumped slightly, making the bed bounce. "Omigod, I owe Alex so much money right now. I said you never flinch when I show you hot guy pics, but he said given the number of queer people in our family, there's no way you wouldn't have considered—"

"Ella!" I squawked. "Can you be serious? My life is imploding right now. Everyone is arriving tomorrow for *my wedding*."

"I am being serious. He must have been something special for you to cheat on Kari. For real."

"I didn't cheat," I insisted, feeling like I doth protested all over the fucking place. "I... look, I was at the bar by the pool, talking to Foster, the guy who was sitting in front of us on the plane—"

Ella sucked in a breath. "*That* guy? Oh, Tom. He was so hot, and *so* nice, and so... so..."

"Yeah." The word came out like a sigh, one that encompassed all the wonder of Foster Blake. "We just talked. For, like, hours, El. It was so easy. He's into a lot of the same stuff I am. He goes rock climbing and hiking. He's a search and rescue guy and trains tracking dogs. I could have listened to him talk all night."

"And then?"

"His ex-boyfriend showed up—remember the asshole he was talking about on the plane?—and I pretended Foster and I were together, just to get his ex to go away. Then to sorta seal the deal, Foster... kissed me." My entire lower abdomen clenched, and I whispered, "I didn't know it could be like that."

She let out a startled laugh, then paused, then laughed again. "Hold up. You kissed a stranger to make Foster's ex jealous. On a family wedding week. At a hotel bar."

"Uh, yeah. That's what I—" I suddenly realized why she was laughing. "It's not the same," I argued.

Ella hooted and smacked my shoulder lightly. "It is! My dad showed up to a family wedding, saw his shitty ex-boyfriend, and whined about it to a random guy at a bar, so the random guy pretended they were together. Now, decades later, he sometimes jokes that maybe it's time they stop pretending." She rolled her eyes, but her voice rang with love and pride. "Their first meeting is family legend."

"Yeah, well... this isn't like that, okay? There's no happy ending here." My stomach burned, and I found myself close to tears... for all the wrong reasons. "After the second kiss—"

"Second kiss?" she squeaked.

"Yes," I admitted. "After his ex stalked off, Foster and I went down to the beach. I was still feeling some kind of way after the first kiss... and then he kissed me again." I sank back into the pillow, covering my eyes with my forearm.

"Oh, honey. Was it just as good as the first?"

"Better," I groaned. "El... it's a disaster. I don't *think* it was cheating, since I wasn't the one who initiated the kiss... well, kisses. And I stopped him before it went further. But god, I didn't want to stop." I pulled my arm away from my face. "What does that say about me? About my relationship with Kari?"

"It says you're not ready to marry her," Ella replied simply.

I knew she was right, but the part of me that had planned out my whole life in careful stages and hated letting people down wasn't quite ready to hear it.

"*Or* it says I'm just panicking about the wedding," I countered, but the argument sounded weak even to my own ears.

"When he touched you," Ella asked carefully, "how did it feel?"

I swallowed hard, remembering the sensation of Foster's hands on my bare skin, of his lips on mine. While he'd been touching me, it hadn't occurred to me that it should feel strange because Foster was a man. I'd been too consumed with how *right* it all felt.

"Like waking up," I admitted quietly. "Like breathing mountain air after years in city smog."

She was silent for a long moment. "You need to call it off, Tommy."

"The entire Marian clan is flying in tomorrow. Kari's family, too. The venue is booked, the flowers ordered, the—"

"All of that matters less than marrying someone you're not in love with. Or, at least, not in love with the way you deserve to be."

I closed my eyes, feeling tears threaten again. "Mom and Dad spent so much—"

"They'd spend twice that to keep you from making a mistake you'll regret for the rest of your life. You know that."

"I love Kari," I whispered.

"I know you do," Ella said carefully. "She's been a part of your life since college. She's familiar, and the two of you make sense on paper. But sometimes that kind of love isn't enough. Sometimes you need the mountain air."

When she spoke, her voice was softer and more gentle. Ella and I were the closest in age in our large group of cousins, but the reason we were so close was because she was an incredible listener and an all-around loving human.

But I still wasn't quite ready to say out loud—or even in my own head—that she was right.

"You know..." I kicked off my shoes, propping my feet up on the bed. "Foster asked me why I wasn't thrilled about anesthesia."

Ella seemed to accept this conversational sidestep easily enough. "Because it's boring as fuck when your patient is half-dead?" she scoffed. "Because you're not passionate about anesthesia, and your heart is in emergency medicine?"

Memories of wild nights in the ER flooded my head. Challenging situations and the need to react on the fly. The adrenaline rush of saving someone, working as a team with others, and celebrating a job well done. Alternatively, sharing in the loss of a patient after doing our best to save them. But then having to jump right into the next challenge before processing the last.

"I do love emergency medicine." That much I could admit.

"I know."

I scowled. "But I *can* still practice anesthesia in the ER," I said, feeling the same defensiveness I'd experienced when I'd told my mom I was considering going into anesthesia. "It's a valid choice. A choice that has a lot more opportunity for career advancement."

"True." I could tell she was humoring me just like Mom had.

I threw my legs over the far side of the bed and sat up, running my fingers through my hair. "Besides, there's no real money in emergency medicine. Still less in wilderness medicine."

"Also true." Ella threw herself down in the spot I'd vacated as I stood and began to pace. "And god knows we Marians could use the money."

I ground my back teeth together. Our uncle Jude was a world-famous country music singer who'd made enough money to set up trust funds for all of his kids, nieces, and nephews. None of us needed to worry about keeping a roof over our heads or going without the basics.

I'd never been money-motivated, but I was competitive and high-achieving.

Winning was a rush. Doing the right thing, being the best— *those* things motivated me.

"Is this just cold feet?" I demanded, turning to face her. "Maybe it's situational anxiety about all the big changes happening. Getting married. Double-boarding in anesthesia. And if so..."

"Tommy, do me a favor." Ella sat up, her top knot listing precariously to one side now. "Don't think about what you've been planning to do, or who you're planning to marry, or who you want to kiss, or what gender anyone is. Put all of that out of your mind. Instead, tell me what you want your life to look like and the qualities of the person you want to share that life with. What are your ideal traits in a partner?"

I tried my hardest to do what she'd described, ticking each one off on my fingers. "Honesty and loyalty. A hard worker who understands my demanding career and unpredictable hours. Kind. Empathetic. Loving. Someone who likes to go on adventures and doesn't mind my big, nosy family."

"Hey!" she squawked with a laugh.

"Someone who wants kids. Someone who shares my sense of humor. Someone who's passionate about things but who can also sit quietly with me and just *be*. Someone who likes *The Great British Baking Show* but also likes..." I stopped and wondered if my long-standing obsession with Captain America and his spandex suit meant something different than I'd always thought. "Superheroes," I finished lamely.

The view out of the hotel window caught my eye, and I walked toward it. The bright moon laid down a wavering stripe of light across the water, and a couple sat side by side in the sand watching the waves.

"I want someone who can tell when I'm unsure of my path and helps me talk it through without pressuring me," I admitted softly. "I want someone who doesn't pretend to be someone they're not in order to impress people and who doesn't expect me to be someone I'm not."

Despite my best efforts, I'd been thinking of my discussion with Foster when I said that last bit. But when Ella remained silent behind me, I realized what I'd inadvertently admitted about my current relationship.

We both knew Kari had encouraged me to pursue anesthesia because her mother was the head of a thriving anesthesia practice. We also both knew that Kari had once convinced me to leave the hospital short-staffed rather than miss an appearance at a charity dinner. And if Kari enjoyed sitting quietly together, she'd never expressed it. She hated activities that felt like "wasting time."

I swallowed. "Maybe I want to figure out myself before sharing my life with anyone at all," I said, trying the words out for the first time.

They weren't new words. In fact, my parents had used similar ones many times when I was in high school, and again when I was in college. And again when I'd told them that Kari was ready for us to get married.

At every turn, I'd rejected them. "I know myself," I'd insisted. "I know what I'm doing."

But did I really? When was the last time I'd considered whether all these things I was achieving were what I truly wanted?

I'd gone into medicine because of experiences I'd had on the trail or while climbing. The first had been when my cousin Cami had fallen down a hillside at my grandparents' place in Montana. The second had been when my uncle and I had come across a man having a heart attack on the side of the trail leading to one of our favorite rock-climbing sites.

I'd become a doctor to help people in their scariest moments.

Ella made a soft, sympathetic sound. "I know it sucks, but I think you're right. You owe it to yourself *and* to Kari to figure it out."

I stared at the moonlight streaming through the window for another moment, thinking about Foster's warm hands on my skin, the look in his eyes before we'd kissed on the beach. Then I turned to my cousin. "I'm going to call it off. First thing tomorrow."

I expected the words to feel heavy, and in a way, they did. I dreaded facing Kari in the morning even more than telling my family the wedding they'd flown all this way to attend was canceled. But they were freeing, too.

"If you want, I'll be your personal bodyguard when you tell everyone," Ella promised.

I gave a half laugh and walked over to the bed to wrap her up in a fierce hug. "How about you and I get spectacularly drunk afterward instead?"

"Deal. I love you, Tommy. No matter what, okay?"

I nodded. "Love you, too," I said. "And thank you."

After I left Ella's room and returned to my own, I sat in silence for a long moment, letting the reality of what I was about to do sink in. Then I moved to the hotel desk and pulled out a notepad. I needed to leave some kind of message for Foster. An explanation for my strange behavior tonight.

But after nearly an hour, I was still staring at a blank notepad.

What could I possibly say that would explain why I'd kissed him like he was oxygen and I was drowning, then pulled away and claimed to be straight? That would convey that our time together had meant so much to me, I was about to upend my entire life based on that brief connection?

In the end, I kept it simple:

Foster,

Thank you for tonight. For the conversation. For the kiss. For more than I can say.

It changed everything. You changed everything.

Please take care of yourself,

Tommy

I sealed it in an envelope with his name on the front and took it to the front desk. "Can you make sure this gets to the guest in room 428? Foster Blake."

The desk clerk nodded. "Of course, Dr. Marian."

I hesitated, then added, "And could you please have a bottle of your best bourbon sent to his room? Put it on my tab."

"Certainly, sir. Anything else?"

I thought about what else I could leave for Foster—some token of what our chance meeting had meant to me—but nothing seemed adequate. "No, that's all. Thank you."

As I walked away, I wondered if I'd ever see him again. Wyoming wasn't that far from Montana, where several of my family members lived, including Ella. Maybe someday, our paths would cross again, when I'd figured out who I really was and what I really wanted.

For now, though, I had a wedding to cancel and a fiancée to face.

3

FOSTER

I woke up the next morning in a foul-as-fuck mood, with a head that felt like it had taken a solo ride down the Majestic River rapids without benefit of a boat or a helmet.

After being unable to fall asleep, I'd discovered a delivery just outside of my door of the world's most seductive bourbon... and a cagey, piece-of-shit note from the world's most alluring man.

The combination of the two had seduced me right into a pitiful midnight drunk the likes of which I hadn't experienced in years, if ever.

After fumbling with the in-room coffee maker and throwing down a cup of black coffee, I showered and dressed in my clothes from the night before, then headed to the front desk to inquire if there was any news about my lost luggage.

In the lobby, I stopped short. There, looking even more unfairly beautiful than I'd remembered, was Dr. Marian himself. I opened my mouth to call out to him when I noticed several things at once.

First, that he was surrounded by his friends and family, staring at the ground and looking profoundly uncomfortable.

Second, that the moment I stepped into the lobby, nearly everyone *but* Tommy turned to look at me and did a double take.

And third, but most important... that he was wearing a black satin sash across his shirt with the word *Groom* emblazoned on it in sparkly silver letters, and standing next to him was a striking woman with olive-brown skin and shiny dark hair, wearing a matching sash that read *Bride*.

My stomach dropped and wobbled sickly.

Tommy had mentioned being here for a wedding. He hadn't mentioned it was *his own*.

Jesus fucking Christ. I'd kissed a man who was about to be married.

As I stood there, stupid and frozen, an elderly, female voice from behind muttered, "What the actual fuck am I seeing, Irene? Let's get him out of here!" and I suddenly felt myself being yanked back the way I'd come by a trio of white-haired ladies.

It said a lot about how the last twenty-four hours of my life had gone that I didn't resist.

Just before they pulled me around the corner, I locked eyes with Tommy. His flared wide in surprise as he recognized me and possibly the old lady platoon attempting to abduct me.

My kidnappers muttered curses and fussed as they frogmarched me away from the scene and shoved me into an empty conference room.

"You got ten seconds to tell me how you got that shirt, Muscle Muffin," the leader of the trio hissed, grabbing the front of my tee. "'Cause I don't remember seeing you at the last reunion."

I scowled down at my shirt—Tommy's shirt—which read "I want to be" in a scripty font above block letters that spelled out MADE MARIAN. "A friend gave it to me last night."

"A friend." Her blue eyes narrowed in her wrinkled face, and her hot pink lips pursed. "I've heard that one before."

The tallest of the trio shook her head in disappointment. "We should have anticipated this. I remember the day Tommy saw a picture of that vampire from *Twilight*—"

"Irene, Jesus," the shortest of the three said. "Tom's as straight as they come. He lost his virginity at the prom, for fuck's sake. No self-respecting gay man would have held out that long."

The leader shook her head at them and glared at me. Her fist held fast to the shirt fabric over my chest, pinching a chest hair or two in the process. "Which friend, Captain Deltoid?" She tilted her head toward the lobby. "The pretty doctor out there or somebody else?"

"Who wants to know?" I shot back.

Her eyes widened in surprise. "I'll be asking the questions, Shoulders. You'll be answering them. *Capisce*?"

The little one darted closer as if to intimidate me. Her walker banged my knee. "Yeah! Answer her questions, asshole."

I put my hand over my mouth to hold in a sudden urge to

laugh when Tommy appeared. "For god's sake, leave him alone, Aunt Tilly."

My stomach lurched at the second sighting of the "Groom" sash.

"Tommy," I said blandly, as if I hadn't tasted the back of his throat last night with the tip of my tongue. "You left out a few details when we were… talking last night. It seems congratulations are in order. Who's the lucky woman?"

If I accidentally put too much emphasis on the word "woman," maybe I could be forgiven just this once.

"Knew it," the leader—Tilly—said, shaking her head. "For fuck's sake."

The tallest of the three shook her head again, but this time, it seemed to be in wonder. "Thomas Marian. What a dark horse you turned out to be."

"If dark horse is code for 'dumbass who thinks with his dick,' I agree," the littlest one spat.

"Hey," I snapped, stepping between Tommy and the woman. "Nothing happened. So whatever you're upset with him about, you can stop now. And you can sure as shit stop with the name-calling."

If anyone was going to give Tommy hell about last night, it was going to be me.

Tilly put her hand on the feisty little lady's shoulder and squeezed. "Take a breather, wildcat. I got this. Why don't you and Irene go out and tell anyone who asks that the big guy here is with Jett, then find Jett and loop him in." She turned and gave me an assessing up-down. "They'll buy it. Jett likes 'em muscle-bound and bossy."

Tommy's nostrils flared. "Absolutely not! Foster's not with Jett." His cheeks heated. "I mean, he's not with *anyone*. You're all overreacting. Foster lost his luggage, and I loaned him a shirt. That's all."

I bit my tongue and stared at the ground to keep from spouting off. *Yeah. Nothing to see here. Just a loaned shirt.*

Tilly barked out a laugh. "You've been a bad liar since infancy, Tommy. Tell me you didn't kiss this man. Tell me right now, and swear on my..." She paused and gave me that up-down look again. "Actually, scratch that. Tell me you *did*, 'cause life's too short, and Chesticles seems like he'd be a hot piece of—"

"Tilly!" Tommy snapped. "Please go back out to the lobby and tell K—" He stopped and swallowed. "Tell Kari I'll be right there, alright? I need to talk to her."

Tilly's face softened into something like empathy. "Fuck. This isn't a prank, is it, kiddo? I almost wondered if you and your parents were pulling one over on Blue and Tristan with the shirt."

He shook his head, looking acutely miserable. "No. Please go. And leave Foster alone. It's not his fault. None of this is his fault."

"Hmph. Have it your way. But I've got my eyes on you, Beef-cake." She jabbed two gnarled fingers at her own eyes, then at mine.

Once Tommy and I were alone, an awkward silence fell, so different from our previous easy connection.

He was visibly, wildly unhappy, and my chest went tight

with the urge to wrap him in a hug and reassure him it would all be okay.

But I wouldn't. No fucking way.

I had no right to touch him the way I wanted to when he was engaged to someone else... and he had no right to let me.

And the truth was, it *wouldn't* all be okay. That instant connection I'd thought I'd felt with him had been a lie. The man I'd thought I'd been kissing didn't exist. And I was a fucking idiot who'd once again gotten starry-eyed for a guy who didn't think the concept of loyalty applied to him.

"I don't entirely get what's happening right now, but you probably want this back." I yanked up the hem of my borrowed shirt and reached behind my head to pull it off, but Tommy darted a hand out to hold the shirt down.

Even that small touch—the barest brush of his knuckles against my stomach—caused goose bumps to prickle over my body. The shampoo and soap scent of him made me want to lean in closer for a better sniff, preferably one close enough to stick out my tongue and feel the rasp of his stubble.

What a dumbass I was.

I stepped back as Tommy cleared his throat.

"It's not about the shirt. Not exactly. My uncle Blue met his husband at a family wedding weekend in kind of a similar situation." Tommy waved a hand dismissively. "Anyway, it doesn't matter. I'm sorry about all of this. About, well, all of... everything."

Everything? Meeting me? Talking with me? Kissing me?

I told myself it didn't matter.

I hardened my heart and my gaze. "I'm sure. Especially

since you almost got caught." I folded my arms over my chest. "Maybe next time you cheat on that beautiful lady out there, you should clue in the guy you're kissing so he can help you keep it on the down-low."

Tommy's face flushed beet red. "That's not... I didn't... There won't *be* a next time. I—"

"There sure as fuck won't be with me," I gritted out. "But if you want, I can give you Matthew's number. Took me ages to figure out he'd been hooking up with my deputy behind my back, and I'm sure he'd be happy to meet up with you and give you some pointers."

His eyes flashed to mine. No twinkle in the hazel now, I thought with vicious satisfaction. Just anger and confusion and hurt.

Well, join the fucking club.

"I don't cheat," Tommy said in a low, tense voice. "I've never cheated. But you kissed me, and—"

"Oh, *I* kissed *you*?" I shot back, incredulous. "So it was all me, then? I just imagined your tongue in my mouth, kissing me back?"

His hands clenched into fists. "That's not what I—"

"Tell me this," I cut in. "Have you told your bride about what happened?"

"No. But I will," he added quickly. "I told you in my note—"

I shook my head. I'd heard everything I needed to hear.

I'd come on this vacation looking for a no-strings hookup, but somewhere along the way, I'd bought into Daisy Sunshine's bullshit about kismet and The One.

And it turned out she was right: the worst part was, I never saw it coming.

"Take care, Tommy. Congratulations, I guess." I turned to move past him, to leave him to his nosy family and awkward explanation about why a stranger was wearing his shirt, when he stopped me with a hand to my chest.

"Wait. Please, Foster."

The warmth of his palm through the cotton went straight to my dick. I looked down at his hand before meeting his eyes.

His expression nearly brought me to my knees. Regret. Confusion. Exhaustion. I wanted to think there was even a little bit of hope there, but I knew that was ridiculous wishful thinking.

One thing I knew for sure was that whatever Tommy Marian's future held, it had nothing to do with mine.

I reached for the hand on my chest and removed it. "Good luck to your bride, Dr. Marian. She's gonna need it."

4

TOMMY

WHEN FOSTER WALKED out of the conference room, I wanted to both vomit and sob. The feeling reminded me of one of those long shifts in the ER where absolutely everything went wrong, where lives seemed to slip away at every turn, no matter what I did.

The ghost of Foster's hand on my wrist burned like a brand as I made my way back to the lobby. My family and friends were still standing around chatting, happily unaware that my world had just been tossed into a blender and set to Max Crush.

"There you are," Kari said, a divot of concern between her eyebrows. "I was about to send a search party after you, but Tilly said you ran into a friend. Was it anyone I know?"

"No," I said, trying to force a smile. "A guy I met on the plane yesterday. He, uh, lost his luggage, so I helped him out. Listen... can we go somewhere and talk?"

The following conversation—in the same empty meeting

room where Foster had walked away from me with pain and contempt in his eyes—was one of the worst of my life.

In the end, I didn't tell Kari the truth about kissing someone else. It might have made *me* feel better to confess but would have only hurt her further. Kari deserved better than to be hurt more than she already was.

Instead, I told her another truth. That I was confused about what I wanted, that I needed time to reassess... and that I was so very sorry.

Kari crossed her arms in front of her chest, drawing attention to the sashes her best friend had thrown over our heads in the lobby earlier. "We've been together for a decade, Tommy. How much more time do you need?" she demanded. "Is this about the anesthesia thing? Because this is an incredibly immature way of handling it. My mother will be disappointed if you back out on her mentorship, but she'll get over it."

I blinked at her. "You think I'm calling off the wedding to get out of pursuing an anesthesia specialty?"

"What other reason could there be?" She lifted her hands and let them flop back down to her sides. "Everything else has been lining up perfectly, just the way we planned, and now this." With the kind of disappointed grimace you might give a tantrum-throwing toddler, she added, "It's not like you, Tommy. You usually have your shit together."

Kari didn't look hurt. She looked annoyed. Frustrated.

"This isn't about my career," I argued. "Or not *just* that. I feel like I've been on this carefully planned trajectory for a long time. College, med school, residency... find a nice partner and settle down. Start a family. I've had such a perfect image in my head of what I *should* do, I didn't stop to consider what I *wanted* to do. I don't want to get married until I figure that out."

"Don't be ridiculous." She waved a hand. "You want to have a successful medical career and a wife who understands and supports that career. I want to be that wife. And I'm prepared to give you a family, too. That's the dream."

The memory of stubble scraping my chin, bourbon-tinged lips pressing against mine, and the strong grip of thick fingers on my thigh made my head swim.

"It was," I said, recognizing immediately how right it was to say that in the past tense. "It *was*."

An image flashed through my head—a scene in which Kari's and my future children, dressed in matching outfits and with perfectly combed hair, stood by the fireplace at her parents' country club for family portraits. I imagined them being told to sit quietly and use their manners. To be mature and not "ridiculous."

And then I remembered a scene from my own childhood. When I was just learning to read, I'd confessed to Uncle Teddy —my most fun uncle—that I couldn't remember the sound *th* made. Teddy had pulled a Sharpie pen from his camera bag and drawn a "cheat sheet" on my forearm of the letters *T* and *H* next to drawings of a feather, a mouth with a tooth, and a thumbs-up. I'd refused to wash it off before our family's Christmas party, so our family photos that year had featured a tow-headed boy with Sharpie drawings down his arms and hands... and a giant grin on his face as he held up his very own copy of *The Thing That Went Thump*.

That picture was far from perfect. But the life it captured—a supportive family, a mom who cared more about my happiness than my appearance—*that* was perfection.

"I want to live a life that's genuine," I admitted to Kari. "I want to deviate from the plan sometimes. Even if it's messy."

"Which is fine, but not on *my* wedding weekend," she snapped. "C'mon, Tommy. Ten years together without so much as a fight over a toothpaste cap being left off, and now this? I don't understand."

Kari was right. We never fought. I'd thought it was a sign of how strong our marriage might be.

But what if it meant something else entirely? The realization that my parents had fought plenty over their forty-year, rock-solid marriage only left me more confused.

The trick, I realized in that moment, was that in order to fight for something, you had to care about it. Truly care. Care enough to make yourself uncomfortable and vulnerable. Care enough to make yourself known.

I could see now that I hadn't done that with Kari. So maybe it shouldn't have been a surprise that even after ten years, she didn't understand me well at all.

"Tell me right now, Tommy." She folded her slender arms in front of her chest, the Bride sash crinkling and shedding glitter onto her skin. "Is this cold feet, and we need to talk it through? Or are we done? Because if you're calling off the wedding and we leave Hawaii without getting married... we're over."

Sweat broke out on my skin despite the cool bite of the air-conditioning. My stomach felt like it was filled with battery acid. My respiration rate was elevated, and my heart thundered. Was this what my panic attack patients felt in the ER?

Meanwhile, Kari didn't have a hair out of place. Her carefully applied eye makeup hadn't smudged. She was still perfectly put together when I felt like I was spinning apart.

Her cool confidence made me doubt myself for a second. *Was* this just pre-wedding jitters?

But the warm press of Foster's hand still lingering on mine told me it was much more. I squeezed my fingers into a fist.

I didn't believe in love at first sight, no matter what my uncles said, and I knew Foster would rightly never want anything to do with me, even if we ever happened to cross paths again. But kissing him had felt so fucking good, being with him had felt so freeing, I couldn't simply go back to the life I'd been leading. I would not be rushed into a life-long commitment I was suddenly and very clearly sure I wasn't ready for.

"I'm sorry," I said again. I licked my suddenly dry lips and swallowed. "I don't know what I want, but it's not this. Not right now. I'll catch a flight home today and be out of the apartment by the time you get back."

Kari's jaw tightened. "Fine. I need to tell my parents. Take care, Tommy." She nodded once... and then the only serious relationship I'd ever had walked out the door.

I blew out a breath and made my way down the resort's hallway to my room, avoiding the lobby, where my family was hanging out. If I knew the Marian clan, they'd be banging down my door momentarily, asking questions, offering quiet support, and gently teasing. They'd understand my decision—hell, I suspected my parents had been biting their tongues about my relationship with Kari for a while, so they might even be relieved. But I still wasn't ready to face them yet.

I glanced out the window at the beach below. Palm trees swayed lazily in the breeze coming off the ocean. People on loungers read books, scrolled phones, or took sips of cold drinks while talking to friends or family. Everyone seemed happy. Content. Relaxed. All the things I'd expected to be when I'd arrived last night... before a chance encounter with a beautiful stranger had led me to question everything.

I really hoped Foster wouldn't hate me forever.

I looked away and began to pack my bags, considering how to rebuild the life I'd imploded. Even though it had been my decision, the idea of starting over from scratch without the relationship that had been the cornerstone of my adult life was seriously fucking overwhelming.

Fortunately, I still had my work to focus on—the ER was continually understaffed and slammed with patients, so they'd be happy to have me back early. And for the first time in a long time, I'd have space and time to figure out what the fuck I truly wanted.

Six Months Later

It turned out, what I truly wanted was to get the fuck out of New York City.

"Chest trauma, ETA five minutes," Marcy called from the nurses' station, her voice flat but loud enough to cut through the chaos. "Blunt force. Motorcycle versus SUV. Guess who lost."

"Of course," I muttered, aborting my attempt to reach the coffee machine and instead grabbing a fresh pair of gloves as I pivoted toward Trauma 2. "Memorial Day—the official start of dumbass season."

The irony wasn't lost on me. Six months ago, I would have been thrilled by a day like this—multiple traumas, complex cases, the adrenaline rush of high-stakes medicine. Now, it felt like being trapped in a hamster wheel, running faster and faster but never getting anywhere I actually wanted to be.

I barely finished intubating the last patient—a heatstroke victim pulled off the Coney Island boardwalk—and I still had a toddler seizing in Bay 3 waiting on a neuro consult. The monitors were chirping like demented birds, someone was yelling about pain meds in Bay 5, and my scrubs were soaked in a patient's blood... again.

"I need a damn clone," I said to no one in particular, pushing through a gaggle of med students huddled like scared ducklings near the supply closet.

"Dr. Marian, you're needed in Curtain 4—Code Gray. Combative psych hold."

"Seriously," I said, half laughing, half groaning. "It's a freaking circus today."

"Circus has better snacks," one of the residents said as he jogged past, waving an empty vending machine wrapper.

"And better hours," I muttered under my breath, though no one was close enough to hear.

I forced myself to breathe as the paramedics rolled in the biker, his shoulder a raw mess of blood and gravel. The sight should have triggered my usual surge of professional focus, but instead, I felt oddly detached, like I was watching someone else's life play out in front of me.

I made eye contact with Marcy so she could get someone else on the psych patient and followed the biker into Trauma 2.

"Vitals are tanking," the medic shouted over the controlled chaos. "Pressure's 80 over 40 and dropping. Lost consciousness twice en route."

I stepped up, forcing my mind to engage despite my bone-deep exhaustion. "Let's get two large-bore IVs and hang O-neg, now. Somebody page trauma surgery. And where the hell is radiology?" My hands moved automatically—checking pupils, palpating for injuries, calling out orders.

This was what I was good at, what I'd trained for years to perfect.

But even as I worked to save this man's life, part of me was thinking about Foster Blake's hands on my skin six months ago, about the way he'd tasted like mountain air when we'd kissed on that beach. It was a thought that had popped up *more* often, not less, as the months went by.

I caught my reflection in the stainless-steel cabinet—wild eyes, bloody gloves, stubble I hadn't had time to shave in two days over skin so pale I looked damned near anemic. When had I started looking like a ghost haunting my own life?

My uncle Teddy's teasing voice from a recent video call rang in my memory. *"Maybe you need to get outside and touch some grass, Nimrod,"* he'd said, his teasing tone and use of the old nickname he'd bestowed on me not hiding the worry in his gaze.

Six months ago, I would have agreed with him. Would have

made plans to head out of the city on my next day off and hike a bit of the Appalachian Trail up at Bear Mountain. But now? Now, I was lucky to get a day off once a month, let alone time to actually leave the city. All the free time I'd anticipated having to figure my shit out hadn't materialized. In fact, I'd barely had time to think.

Not long after the aborted trip to Hawaii, my boss had assigned me to a "patient flow taskforce committee," which demanded additional long hours and reporting duties that now took up almost every spare minute of my time. The assignment had been presented as an honor, recognition of my dedication and clinical skills.

It had taken me six weeks to learn that the assignment "recommendation" had come from above, from the hospital CMO, who just so happened to be in the same social club as Kari's mother, my former anesthesiology mentor.

The guilt had kept me from complaining initially, but it hadn't kept me from researching other job opportunities. It was time to get away from this toxic environment and onto the next stage in my life. Preferably somewhere closer to my family and farther away from Kari and hers.

"Pressure's stabilizing," I called out as the trauma surgeon finally arrived to take over. "Good peripheral pulses, pupils are reactive. He's got a chance."

I stripped off my gloves and gown, already mentally moving to the next crisis. That was the thing about emergency medicine—there was always a next crisis.

"Dibs on new guy," one of the female nurses whispered to Marcy as she hustled past. I looked up and noticed a new nurse standing nearby, checking out the board. He was tall and jacked and also clearly confused.

"Hey, you need help?" I called. "Marcy doesn't bite, I promise."

I glanced at Marcy, expecting a chuckle or eyeball, but all I saw was the ivory skin of her cheeks turn dark with a blush as she stared at the guy. I took another look at the new hire and back to Marcy, raising an eyebrow.

"Nah, man," the guy said. "I'm just waiting for Kendra to get back from the ladies room. I'm shadowing her today."

I nodded and turned back to Marcy before lowering my voice. "Do we like him, like *like* him, like him?" I teased.

She swatted at my arm. "You wouldn't understand. But that man is entirely beddable. Like, fifteen on a scale of one to Pedro Pascal beddable."

After a moment of trying to act cool, I glanced again. Yes, he was objectively attractive. But bed him? Meh. But then again, I wasn't into g...

Jesus.

I was, though. I was clearly into guys. Somehow, I'd made it thirty-two fucking years without knowing it, but for the past five months, I'd been pretty much only into guys.

Well, *guy*, singular.

I closed my eyes and tried to picture it with the new guy. Hot nurse holding the back of my head. Kissing me. Pressing me tightly against him with those biceps. Everything in me rejected the idea, not because he was a guy but because he wasn't *my* guy.

My eyes flew open as I shook my head. Not my guy, of course. I didn't have a guy. But *a* guy. A specific—

"Your sister's trying to get a hold of you," Marcy said, interrupting my strange, bi-sexual confusion. "Said to give her a call on your next break."

I faked a smile. "Did you tell her only lightweights need breaks?"

She grinned. "No, I told her I'd never heard that word before and wasn't sure what it meant."

I pulled out my phone and looked at my texts instead of asking Marcy which sister. Chances were, it wasn't actually one of my sisters but my cousin Ella, who'd somehow convinced half my family to use her as their intermediary when they were worried about me.

ELLA

Guess what? Trace has a job for you at SERA for the summer session!

And before you shake your head or roll your eyes, I also have inside info on a soon-to-be open position in the ER at Stanford. Call me.

I stared at the messages, my heart doing something complicated in my chest. SERA—Slingshot Emergency Rescue Academy in Legacy, Montana. Even if my family hadn't helped fund its establishment, and the owner, Trace Bishop, wasn't a close family friend, I would've heard about it. Everyone in wilderness medicine knew SERA. It was the kind of place I'd dreamed about during residency, back when I'd thought I might specialize in emergency medicine with a focus on wilderness and disaster response.

Before Kari had suggested anesthesiology would be more stable.

Before I'd convinced myself that stability was what I wanted.

Before Hawaii had reminded me maybe I had no idea what I actually wanted anymore.

Before I could click to call Ella back, Marcy's voice rang out again. "We've got a triple incoming—MVC on the BQE. Two pediatric, one ejected, one unconscious at the scene. ETA seven minutes!"

Six more hours passed in a blur of blood, adrenaline, and the controlled chaos that defined emergency medicine. By the time my shift ended, I was running on fumes and coffee, my hands shaking slightly from exhaustion and caffeine overload.

I finally managed to call Ella back when I began my walk home, dodging through pedestrian traffic as the summer heat brought out every smell in the city.

"Jesus, finally," she said by way of greeting. "I was starting to think you'd disappeared."

"Tell me about the SERA job," I said, cutting straight to the point.

"Trace needs a medical director for the summer session. It's eight weeks long, starts in a week—"

"A week?" I nearly knocked into a woman as I stopped abruptly.

"Yup. It's a last-minute opening since the previous guy left unexpectedly. Kismet, right?"

The word brought back memories, and I shook my head slowly, though she couldn't see me. "Ella, that's impossible. I can't just—"

"Can't what? Leave the job that's slowly killing you? Escape the city that's become a prison? Get the hell away from Kari's family and their petty revenge schemes?"

When she put it like that...

"Tommy." Her voice was gentle now, the teasing edge gone. "When's the last time you were happy? Really, genuinely happy?"

The question hit me like a physical blow. I knew the answer immediately, though I couldn't bring myself to say it out loud. Six months ago. On a beach in Hawaii, with Foster Blake's hands in my hair and his mouth on mine.

"It's complicated," I said finally, resuming my walk home.

"It doesn't have to be. Look, I'm not asking you to move out here permanently and give up your big career. I'm asking you to take a break that will help you fall in love with your work again... and spend the summer in Legacy near your very favorite cousin, while you're at it."

"I mean, it *would* be nice to see Alex again," I teased.

"Asshole," she said fondly. "Now say, 'Thank you, Ella, that's a brilliant idea,' and *maybe* I'll forgive you enough to tell you about the potential opening at Stanford."

I stared up at the buildings around me, all glass and steel and artificial light. Somewhere in the city, Kari was probably at another charity dinner, making connections and advancing her career. Her mother was probably at her club, having drinks with influential doctors and administrators while discussing ways to make my life more difficult.

And here I was, standing in the middle of the crowded sidewalk, seriously considering throwing away everything I'd worked for to spend eight weeks in Montana teaching wilderness medicine to a bunch of adrenaline junkies.

It should have been an easy decision. My career was here, in a big city with the world's best level one trauma centers, highly respected physicians, and the kind of recognition and upward mobility my high-achieving self demanded.

The smart decision was to stay, to weather the political storm, to keep building toward the kind of career that would make my parents proud and secure my financial future.

But smart decisions had led me to nearly marrying someone I didn't love. Smart decisions had led me to a job that was slowly crushing my spirit.

Maybe it was time to make a decision with my heart instead of my head.

"Thank you, Ella, that's a brilliant idea," I repeated obediently. "And if you can help me figure out how to get out of here in only a week without screwing up my career..." I took a deep breath of the fetid air around me and let it out. "I'll do it."

By the time I hung up, my hands had stopped shaking, and something that felt dangerously like hope was unfurling in my chest.

Six hours later, I handed in my resignation.

And six days after that, I boarded a plane to Montana.

5

FOSTER

I TOSSED another dart at the board across my office, smirking when it hit just to the left of the smiling doctor's face. The photo, snagged from a hospital website after weeks of obsessing about the stranger from Hawaii, didn't do Tommy Marian justice. It didn't capture the way his eyes crinkled when he laughed or how his face had flushed when I'd kissed him outside the pool bar.

It also didn't capture the way I'd felt after not only learning he was straight but then witnessing him with his arm around *his* fucking *fiancée* the following day.

I huffed out a noise of incredulity. Even now, six months later, I couldn't believe his audacity.

To send me a note thanking me for the conversation and the kiss... while on the eve of his very own wedding? Who did that?

Assholes, that's who.

He was no better than Matthew, who'd not only slept with

my best deputy but also convinced the guy to move to New York with him and get a job with the NYPD. The loss of the deputy had angered me more than the loss of a faithless lover.

I threw another dart, and this one stuck right between Dr. Marian's eyes.

Served him right.

I was angry at Tommy Marian. Angry at him for pinning me with those twinkly hazel eyes. For clearly wanting to have his cake and eat it, too. For luring me down the dangerous path of letting myself want someone again, when he was so epically unavailable.

I closed my eyes and silently cursed myself for thinking about him yet again.

The man was an asshole. A married asshole. And no matter how it had felt at the time, he would never be *mine*.

A bead of sweat rolled down my back as the ancient ceiling fan spun lazily overhead. Sometimes summer in Wyoming meant scorching days and warm nights, even here in Majestic, where the elevation usually kept things cooler. I'd stripped down to my undershirt hours ago, the uniform shirt hanging on the back of my door.

"You ever gonna tell me who that pretty doctor is on your dartboard?" My cousin and best friend, Waylon Fletcher, leaned against my doorframe, arms crossed over his chest. "Because if you got bad medical news and are keeping secrets from me..."

I plucked the darts from the board and returned to my desk. "Nope."

"Better not be." He eyed me skeptically. "Your mom called.

Said you bailed on dinner with Dr. Moore last night. Supposedly, that's the third setup you've ditched in two months."

I groaned. "Thought I was agreeing to have dinner with my mom. Instead, she bails and sticks me with the new dentist, who, by the way, wears enough cologne to choke a moose." I shuffled some papers, giving myself something to focus on besides Way's knowing look. "Soon as I saw him sitting there, I hightailed it home and told her to come clean to the guy that I had no interest in her setup schemes. How'd you find out about it anyway?" As our small town's mayor with the world's gossipiest assistant, I wasn't really surprised so much as annoyed.

"She cornered me at the grocery store." Way shook his head, amused. "Said, and I quote, 'That boy needs someone to warm his bed besides that ridiculous dog of his.'"

"Chick is not ridiculous," I defended, though I couldn't help the slight smile. My hound dog puppy, all floppy ears and oversized paws at six months old, perked her head up from her bed in the corner and wagged her tail. "She's just... enthusiastic."

Way moved over and squatted down to give her a head scratch. "She ate my hat last week. You'd better be glad it wasn't my favorite."

"She was teething."

He stood back up and crossed his arms as he leaned back against the door frame again. "Your mom's worried about you, Foster. We all are. You haven't been the same since you got back from Hawaii."

The mention of Hawaii wiped the smile from my face. I turned back to my computer. "I'm fine," I insisted, the lie bitter in my mouth. "Just busy."

Way didn't look convinced, but he knew better than to push. "Whatever you say. Speaking of busy, another hiker lost their way up near Dead River Canyon. Cole said to tell you the search team's assembling."

Relief washed over me. Action. Something I was good at. I stood up and grabbed my shirt, calling out for my dispatcher. "Cole, tell Hanson to meet me at the trailhead in twenty." I turned back to Way. "Sorry, duty calls."

Way paused before leaving. His forehead crinkled in concern. "You know, it wouldn't kill you to talk about whatever happened. You've been grumbling like a bear with a thorn in his paw for months. Whatever the story is behind Dr. Did-You-Wrong over there, consider it might be time to move on."

I kept my eyes on my shirt front as I finished fastening the buttons. As much as I usually shared with Way, this time, I was keeping my shit close to the vest. Way had gone to Vegas a couple of years back and struck the jackpot, bringing home a hot, rich husband as easily as playing the slots. The last thing I needed was relationship advice from a man who had it all.

"Nothing happened," I insisted.

Except, of course, something *had* happened. Something I couldn't forget, no matter how hard I tried.

I'd gone to Hawaii and fallen—instantly, ridiculously, and apparently *irre-fucking-versibly*—for a man I couldn't have and who didn't deserve me. Like getting struck with Cupid's dart when the tip had been soaked in poison.

Six months ago, I'd been sure I'd get over it. But now?

Jesus, now I felt like Tommy Marian with his stupid hazel eyes, his soft fucking smile, and his awful-wonderful way of really listening when I talked had weaseled his way under my skin and burrowed so deeply into the very core of me, even my white-hot anger at his betrayal couldn't burn him out.

And believe me, I'd tried.

The good news was there was plenty of work this summer to keep me distracted. Tourists like this one were bound and determined to get themselves in trouble on our watch. Lost hikers were as reliable in summer as hot dogs and hamburgers.

I made my way out of the office and hopped in my vehicle, thankful for the distraction.

MY PHONE BUZZED JUST as my deputy and I were finishing up the rescue of a middle-aged man from Virginia who'd wandered off-trail and twisted his ankle.

"Blake," I answered, tucking the phone against my shoulder so I could help load the guy into the ambulance. My uniform shirt was plastered to my back with sweat, and I couldn't wait to get back to the station for a shower.

"Sheriff," a woman's voice said. "This is Captain Reynolds with Wyoming Search and Rescue."

"Ma'am," I said, instantly alert.

Usually, when the state SAR director called, it was to coordinate a response to a larger operation, which meant things were about to get real complicated, real fast. So I was surprised when she continued, "How would you feel about a special assignment?"

I signaled to my deputy that I was stepping away before

trudging through the dusty parking area toward my truck. "What kind of assignment?"

"SERA up in Legacy, Montana, just lost their Search and Rescue director. They've requested you as a temporary instructor for this summer's cohort. It's an eight-week intensive starting this weekend."

SERA, Slingshot Emergency Rescue Academy, was one of the world's best wilderness emergency training programs. The academy offered courses in SAR, wilderness medicine, aerial insertion and extraction, wildfire management, swift-water rescue, along with any other kind of outdoor emergency response you could think of that wasn't ocean-based.

The man who ran the academy, Trace Bishop, was a legend in tracking, someone I'd once worked with on a complex search and rescue op in the Tetons.

Still, I hesitated. "What happened to Desi Warren? She's been running SAR at SERA since it started several years ago. She okay?"

The captain sighed. "I personally am not a fan of marriage, but apparently, she feels differently. Married another SERA instructor. The guy's family is in Chile, so she's got a job lined up in Patagonia, starting immediately," Reynolds continued. "Which left SERA down two instructors. They want you to fill her spot to give them time to find a permanent replacement."

My heart leapt a little at the chance to work with Trace again, even for a little while. He was the best SAR guy I knew, and his program was top-notch.

The chance to work at SERA was a dream come true, even if

it was temporary. Hell, *especially* because it was temporary since there was no way I could leave Majestic permanently.

"I'd have to find someone to run the sheriff's office during our busy season," I said, allowing reality to deflate the dream for a moment.

She scoffed. "If only you had contacts in Wyoming law enforcement. Jesus, Sheriff. Do you want it or not? I told Trace I'd help him find someone, and you were his first choice, but I've got fifteen people begging me for a shot at this if you're not interested."

I debated quickly. Two months away from Majestic meant eight weeks of my mother unable to set me up with every available man in the county. Eight weeks of new challenges and exciting work instead of writing up speeding tickets for all the vehicles coming out of Yellowstone and brooding over a stranger I'd spent a few hours with six months ago. There wasn't much to debate.

"Count me in," I said before I could overthink it. "Send me the details."

When I got back to the office, my lead deputy was already there, filling out the rescue paperwork. I settled in across from Hanson and grabbed my half of the forms.

"Reynolds called," I said. "They need me up at SERA for the summer."

Hanson looked up, eyebrows raised. "SERA? No shit? That program's amazing. Maybe this is what you need. Get out of town for a bit, stop throwing darts at Doctor Dreamboat."

I ignored him. "You're in charge while I'm gone. I'll get you some more help, but try not to let the town burn down."

"No promises." He grinned. "When do you leave?"

"Friday." I glanced at the calendar. Two days to get ready.

"Taking the pup?" he asked, nodding down at the lanky dog currently sprawled out on her back with her paws curled in the air. The hiker we'd rescued had school-age boys who'd run her around at the trailhead, resulting in a rare moment of napping hound right now.

I sighed. "Yeah, good practice for her." And good company for me, even though I knew she'd be a handful.

That night at my cabin, I went through my usual routine—dinner alone, training with Chick in the yard, a beer while finishing up a few reports. The evening was warm enough that we stayed outside longer than usual, with Chickie chasing fireflies in the growing twilight.

"Come on, goofball," I finally called. "Time to go in."

Chickie bounded up the porch steps, all gangly legs and wagging tail, then stopped to shake vigorously, sending dirt and grass flying everywhere.

"Thanks for that," I muttered but couldn't help smiling as I ruffled her ears. For all her chaos, she was alright. I'd gotten her as a puppy despite knowing better, and she was just as all over the place as I'd imagined. It was going to take forever to train her up right.

Yet another thing to blame Tommy Marian for.

Inside, I opened the fridge to grab a beer and frowned at the meager contents. Maybe SERA's dining hall would offer me a chance to escape my usual slim pickings.

When I went to grab a clean shirt for tomorrow, my hands froze over the dresser.

I'd started calling the second drawer from the top the "T-shirt Drawer of Shame" in my head because it held the one thing I should have thrown away months ago—the T-shirt Tommy had given me that night in Hawaii.

I stood there, fingers twitching, knowing I should just shut the drawer and go to bed. Instead, I pulled it out, ran my thumb over the soft, worn fabric.

The memories hit me like physical blows. Tommy's smile as he'd handed it to me. Waking up to his note and the bourbon he'd sent to my room. Finding him in the hotel lobby with a fucking fiancée and a hundred pairs of eyes staring at me. The regret and confusion on his face when I'd walked out of his life for good. My desperate rush to leave Hawaii immediately so I could start to forget everything about Dr. Thomas Marian. And all the nights since, whether in the shower or sprawled naked on my bed with my cock in my hand, when remembering Tommy was the only fucking thing that brought me any relief.

I shoved the shirt back in the drawer and slammed it shut. Chickie whined from her bed in the corner, sensing my mood shift.

"It's okay, girl," I said, crossing the room to kneel beside her. She licked my face, her warm weight against me comforting. "We're going on an adventure soon. Just you and me."

Friday morning came with clear skies and a forecast of another scorching day. I loaded my gear and Chick into my truck and pointed us north toward Montana, windows down to catch whatever breeze we could find.

The drive gave me too much time to think. About my mom's worried face when I'd told her I was leaving for the summer.

About Way's not-so-subtle suggestion that this trip might "clear my head." About the way I'd been holding everyone at arm's length since Hawaii.

Maybe they were right. Maybe a summer in Legacy was exactly what I needed. Maybe there'd be hot firefighters and pilots at SERA who could help me forget about the last man I'd kissed.

"What do you think, Chick?" I glanced over at my co-pilot, who had her head out the window, ears flapping in the wind. "Ready for an adventure?"

She barked enthusiastically as I reached for the knob on the radio and turned up the music.

The landscape changed gradually as we crossed into Montana—the land a little wilder, the forests denser. The temperature dropped as we gained a little elevation, a welcome relief from the heat wave we'd been experiencing in Majestic.

Legacy itself was a charming town with rustic character, nestled at the bottom of Slingshot Mountain with a river running through its center. Local legend said it was named by a gold miner who'd struck it rich and declared the town would be his legacy to his children. The gold had run out eventually, but the town had persisted, reinventing itself as a quirky little place with similar but less robust outdoor tourism than Majestic and a burgeoning art and eatery scene. With only two slopes, it would never compete with the ski traffic at Vail or Jackson, but it had enough visitors in summer to justify an eclectic collection of shops and restaurants that had, themselves, become a draw for tourists year-round.

Now, in peak summer, the main street was bustling with

sporty tourists in hiking boots and artsy types in flowy hemp pants and cropped tank tops. Outdoor gear shops and artisan cafés lined the road, along with a few bars that looked like they'd been there since the mining days.

After driving through and then out of the town center for several more miles, I pulled up to SERA headquarters—a sprawling lodge with several outbuildings and small cabins, nestled against the base of the mountain. The parking lot was packed with vehicles sporting license plates from half a dozen states.

Chick and I were late. I'd stopped to help a family change a flat on the side of the road, and by the time we made it into the main building, instructor orientation was already underway. I slipped into the back of the room, Chickie at my heels, and scanned the setup, which included about a dozen people, equipment displays along the walls, and detailed maps of the surrounding wilderness.

My attention shifted to the front of the room, where a man with an award-winning ass was speaking, his back to me as he pointed at a topographical map.

"—conditions are particularly challenging this season. Which is a good opportunity for us to teach the importance of improvisation in wilderness emergency response."

His voice hit me like a physical blow, and I froze.

Tommy?

It couldn't be.

He turned then, and our eyes locked across the crowded room. I blinked in shock.

Tommy fucking Marian was standing at the front of the

room, looking just as stunned as I felt. For a moment, he faltered, the words dying on his lips as he stared at me.

My heart hammered against my ribs. Six months. Six months of trying to forget, and now this. The one man I never thought I'd see again. Didn't *want* to see again.

Asshole.

Tommy recovered first, breaking eye contact to address the other people in the room again with a small clearing of his throat. "But it also means we need to be ready for the unexpected, which I'm sure you already know."

The rest of his words faded to background noise as I tried to process what was happening. What were the odds? What was he even doing here? He was supposed to be a hotshot ER doctor on the verge of selling out to anesthesia. He was supposed to be in *New York*, playing happy family with his poor, unsuspecting bride.

I felt a tug on the leash and looked down to see Chick sitting alertly, head tilted as she studied Tommy with great interest.

Great. Even my dog was captivated by him. The traitor.

When orientation ended, people began milling about, talking in groups, and I turned to go. Maybe I could use Chick as an excuse to get some fresh air.

A friendly woman with a clipboard and a name badge that said *Robyn* stopped me and introduced herself as one of the program coordinators.

"Sheriff, welcome to SERA. Trace will come find you as soon as he has a free minute. In the meantime, here's your room information and key, as well as a property map. Don't hesitate to let me know if you have any questions. We're so happy you could join us!"

"Thanks, sorry I was late. But, uh... can you tell me what Tommy Marian is doing here?"

Her face lit up. "Oh! He's the temporary medical director. His family helped Trace start SERA. In fact, the land we're on was originally part of the Marians' property. They donated it to the program. You'll love Dr. Marian. He's amazing."

I could tell she was the victim of a little hero worship, and part of me wanted to ruin her pretty image of the man by explaining he wasn't quite as amazing as she thought. Instead, I nodded and murmured my thanks.

As I made my way back out to my truck, Chickie trotting at my heels, I tore open the flap of the envelope and pulled out my room key, along with a couple of folded pages.

"The fuck?" I breathed, staring at the rooming assignment.

Cabin 8: Dr. Thomas Marian, Director of Emergency Medicine, and Foster Blake, Director of Search and Rescue.

I stared at the names to see if my brain or eyes could possibly be playing tricks on me. But no, the words were there.

The two of us were sharing a cabin.

I ran a hand through my hair and huffed out a humorless laugh. Seriously, what were the fucking chances?

Actually, probably pretty good if Desi had been shacking up with the previous medical guy. *Fuck.*

Chick looked up at me with those trusting brown eyes, completely unaware of the shit storm brewing. I took a deep breath and tried to get ahold of myself.

Maybe I should leave. Maybe this was a sign I should go

back to Majestic and focus on my own damned career instead of my SAR obsession.

I gritted my teeth and shook my head. I'd be damned if I'd let some selfish-as-fuck, *married* city boy take away my opportunity to teach and learn about one of my favorite topics.

No, I wouldn't be leaving. If Dr. Marian didn't want a reminder of his indiscretions, then he would have to be the one to leave.

"Come on, girl," I said, tugging gently on her leash.

I walked out of the main hall without looking back to see where the good doctor was, but there was no need. The image of Tommy Marian's beautiful fucking face had been seared into my memory six long months ago.

It was going to be an excruciating summer.

6

TOMMY

I was freaking the fuck out.

The moment Foster Blake walked out of orientation, my professional facade cracked. My hands shook as I gathered my papers, barely registering the confused looks from the other instructors as they filed out.

How was it possible this man was here right now? He was a sheriff in a completely different state—okay, fine, the state right next door, but sheriffs didn't have time to go off teaching wilderness courses, especially during peak tourist season. Did they?

And how had I known it was his peak tourist season? I might have googled Majestic, Wyoming. I might even have bookmarked the sheriff's office page and spent several hours going down rabbit holes until I found a gap-toothed photo of him holding up a silvery-scaled river trout: *"Local legend in the making! 14-year-old Foster Blake snagged 'Biggest Catch' at this year's Majestic River Round-Up."*

The universe had a sick sense of humor, throwing Foster back into my path just when I'd convinced myself our kiss in Hawaii had been a fever dream brought on by pre-wedding panic and too much bourbon.

Except I knew it hadn't been the alcohol. It had been him. All him. His laugh, his eyes, the way he'd pulled me against him like he'd wanted to climb inside my skin...

"Tommy? You good?"

I jumped, scattering papers across the floor. Trace, the program director and a good friend of our family, stood in the doorway with one eyebrow raised.

"Fine! Totally fine. Just..." I gestured vaguely at the mess. "Gravity, you know?"

"Uh-huh." Trace crossed his arms. "Want to tell me what that was about?"

"What what was about?"

"The tension thick enough to cut with a knife between you and my SAR guy? The way you both looked like you'd seen a ghost?"

Fuck. I should have known Trace would notice. The man tracked mountain lions for fun. Reading people was child's play by comparison.

"It's..." I swallowed hard. "I know him. From Hawaii."

Trace's eyes widened. "Hawaii, as in...?"

"Yeah. I, uh, met him on the plane when I was heading there for the wedding. And later, we had a drink—"

He cut me off. "Foster Blake is your *T-shirt guy*?"

My cheeks went hot. "How did you hear about that? You weren't there."

"Your Uncle Derek told me about what happened because he was worried about you, but he said no one really got the full story." Trace crossed his arms in front of his chest. "So what happened between the two of you?"

"Nothing?"

"I see." Trace leaned against the doorframe, watching me intently. "This going to be a problem?"

"No." I tried to project nonchalance, even though I knew he wouldn't buy it. "I was just startled, that's all. We're both grown adults. Professionals. Besides, we'll be working on different aspects of the program."

"You'll be sharing a room," he said, lifting an eyebrow. "Medical and SAR are in the same cabin."

I groaned, slumping into a chair. "Maybe I should go stay with someone else." There were plenty of people to choose from, not to mention my grandparents' lodge only a few miles from here, but I'd hoped to stay on campus since I knew the program meant early mornings and long days.

"Don't be ridiculous. Living on-site is part of the deal. The program has a demanding schedule, you know that. Besides..." Trace's expression eased. "I'm hoping you're going to fall in love with SERA and decide to stay on permanently."

I huffed out a laugh. "Unlikely. My interview at Stanford is in a few weeks, remember? I'm a level one trauma specialist."

"Billings is only an hour and a half away, and they have *two* level one trauma centers." His eyes bored into me. "Besides, I seem to recall you had a thing for wilderness medicine at one point. It's why I wanted you here."

He was right. We both knew it. Part of the reason I'd said yes to his offer was to spend time in one of my favorite places, breathe mountain air for a little while, and practice the kind of medicine that felt more like an indulgence than a job.

But that didn't mean I was about to give up on all of my career plans.

"I appreciate the offer," I said. "But for right now, I should go make sure Foster doesn't set my shit on fire."

"Because that's a normal response when nothing happened?" Trace let out a breath. "Look, Tommy, we need both of you for this program. Figure it out, or I'll have to send him home. Don't want to do that, though. Foster's the best SAR guy around, and I know how much he wants to be here."

"I'll talk to him," I promised, though my heart was threatening to jackhammer its way out of my chest.

Instead of going to the cabin, I took a walk across the wide expanse of grassland toward the fence along the highway in hopes of getting better cell service.

Ella picked up on the second ring. "What's up? You in the mood for steak? Lennon's grilling. I haven't left the office yet, but—"

"Did you know he was going to be here?" I hissed, my voice barely above a whisper.

She paused. "Who is *he* in this scenario? Trace?"

"Foster Blake."

"Foster... Wait! *Wait.* Hawaii Guy is at SERA?"

"Yes! And we're *roommates*."

Her squeal was so loud I had to hold the phone away from my ear. "Tommy! I told you this was kismet. The universe is giving you a second chance!"

"Or punishing me for being an idiot." I pinched the bridge of my nose. It was clear she hadn't known about it, but the coincidence was hard to wrap my head around. "You should have seen his face, El. He looked at me like I was something he'd scraped off his boot."

"Well, you did kiss him senseless a couple days before you were supposed to be marrying someone else," she reminded me unhelpfully. "What did you expect?"

"I don't know. I just..." I lowered my voice. "What if I say something stupid?"

"Then he'll know you're human. Stop overthinking it and talk to the guy. Worked pretty damn well last time, right? So follow your gut."

That was laughable. My gut had caused me to throw away a prestigious position in New York and fuck off to Montana. I wasn't sure my gut was in any position to be making important decisions right now.

"What do I even say to him?"

"The truth," Ella said simply. "You hated that he didn't give you a chance to explain everything that morning in Hawaii, so now's your chance. Tell him that meeting him made you realize you were living someone else's life. That you called off your wedding because of him. That you're finally trying to figure out who you really are."

"And what if he doesn't care?"

"Then at least you'll know you tried. Jesus, it's not like you need to marry the guy. Just fuck him. Gotta go!"

My face ignited at the image of a naked Foster Blake moving hungrily against a naked... *me*. I was so distracted, it took me a long moment to realize she'd hung up.

By the time I approached Cabin 8, the sun was touching the mountaintop, painting the sky in shades of pink and gold. I stood outside the door for five minutes, rehearsing what I'd say, before I finally knocked.

From inside, I heard a deep voice—*his* voice—saying something about "not chewing shoes," followed by a dog's excited yip. The sound made me smile despite my nerves. He'd gotten the puppy after all.

The door swung open, and there he was. Foster Blake, even more devastatingly handsome than I remembered. His dark hair was slightly damp, like he'd just showered, and he wore a faded henley that clung to broad shoulders. For a split second, I caught something in his eyes—surprise, maybe even a flicker of the same heat from Hawaii—before his expression hardened.

"Dr. Marian," he said flatly.

"It's Tommy, actually," I said, my shoulders around my ears. If he acted like this, it was going to be a long summer.

His jaw tightened, and he growled, "Tommy."

My skin prickled. Before I could think of anything to say, the puppy crashed into my legs—all floppy ears and oversized paws, tail wagging so hard her entire body wiggled.

"Chickie, no!" Foster commanded, but the dog ignored him completely, standing on her hind legs to paw at my thighs.

I couldn't help but smile as I crouched down to pet her. "Hello there. Aren't you friendly?"

"Ignore her," Foster muttered. "She's a mess."

"I don't mind." I scratched behind Chickie's ears, grateful for the momentary distraction. "She's adorable."

"She's a menace," Foster said, but there was unmistakable affection in his voice. He stepped back, reluctantly making space for me to enter. "I took the bed on the right."

The cabin was small—two double beds, separated only by a double nightstand with a coffee maker on top, a tiny table with two chairs, and a small bathroom. It had seemed fine when I'd brought my stuff over from Ella's house this afternoon, but now there was barely enough room for two grown men to coexist without constantly brushing against each other. This was going to be torture.

I sat on the edge of the other bed and turned to face him. "Foster, I think we should talk about—"

"No need," he said curtly. "I'm good."

"I'd still like a chance to explain."

"What's there to explain? You were in Hawaii to get married," he said, voice clipped. "I figured that out when I saw you literally labeled 'Groom' standing next to a lovely woman labeled 'Bride.' Couldn't have been clearer, so thanks for that."

I swallowed hard, trying to figure out how to tell him I'd called off the wedding. That I was single now. That if he would ever want to—

"It's eight weeks, Tommy," he clipped. "We're here to work, so let's do that." Foster moved away from me, focusing on emptying his duffle into the nightstand drawers.

My body betrayed me with a strange numbness.

Work. Right. Message received.

Chickie sniffed at my hand before giving it a big lick. I squatted down to stroke her silky ears. "How old is she?"

"Too young. Should have gotten a properly trained dog. I'll be lucky if she can track anything by next summer." He didn't bother turning around. "She has the tracking instincts of that fish in that movie who can't remember shit."

I let out a snort. "You sound like those people from the plane who talked about that guy with the dog and the thing."

He turned just enough for me to see the edge of his lip quirk up. "To Wade," he murmured, glancing at me for a split second.

"To Wade," I said, remembering the cheers from the crowd.

It wasn't friendship, but at least it was a little further from homicide than we were a few minutes ago. That was a start.

Before I could ask how he'd ended up at SERA, we were interrupted by a knock and a cheerful voice calling through the screen door. "Hey, bunch of us are heading to Timber for pizza and beer. You guys want a ride?"

Robyn, SERA's program coordinator, glanced between us with a big smile. "Come on. It's always good for the instructors to bond before the students arrive."

"Yeah, sounds good. You coming?" I asked, turning to Foster.

But the scowl on his face made it clear he wasn't interested in bonding... at least not with me. "Nah. Told Trace I'd catch up on certification paperwork."

"Right." I sucked in a breath and nodded at Robyn. "Let's go."

Timber buzzed with activity—tourists with kids overflowed the outdoor seating while SERA instructors filled the right side with noisy laughter.

"Rosso Inferno," my cousin Alex said, shoving a glass of red wine into my hand. He'd left his parents' vineyard in Napa to take over Timber only two years ago, and being able to spend time with him in Legacy had been a side benefit of spending the summer here. "I dare you to call this one pedantic."

I blinked at him. "I've never called a glass of wine pedantic in my life."

Even though my mind was still back in the cabin with Foster, I made an attempt to listen as Alex vented about dealing with the overly picky local fire marshal who'd been harassing him for months over kitchen upgrades.

"'Ongoing infraction mitigation,' he says." Alex made finger quotes. "'It takes as long as it takes, Marian.' What I'd like to know is at what point I can sue Chief Stick-Up-His-Ass Kincaid for harassment."

"Ha." I studied the slanting sunlight hitting the surface of the wine.

"Tommy," Alex said. "You with me? What's up?"

I blinked. "Sorry. Head was in the clouds. Just thinking about job leads."

"Job leads here?" His eyes widened. "Fuck yeah. That would be amazing."

I shook my head. "San Francisco. I have an interview with Stanford, but UC Davis might be hiring, too."

Alex looked disappointed. "But Hazel's here. And Ella and the rest of us."

He wasn't wrong. I loved Legacy—had loved it since I was a kid arriving for my first visit with Gran and Gramps. My cousins and I had spent summers here for years, and several of us had fallen in love with the place enough to make it home.

"I do love it here," I reminded him. "You know I do. But the only place around here that would even come close to the kind of work I do is in Billings. And I don't want to live in Billings."

We both knew I was too ambitious for a career in Billings anyway. In New York, I'd been well respected, admired, rewarded with opportunities I'd never get outside a big city.

A woman with double braids and a black Timber apron speed walked over. "Boss, need you in the kitchen. Juni's threatening to leave over that new fire extinguisher placement."

Alex sighed and stood. "Maybe you'll at least agree to murder a fire marshal for me before you go. Doesn't pay well, but comes with free wine and pizza."

I rolled my eyes as he walked away. Nearby, a SERA helo instructor and swift-water instructor argued good-naturedly about white-water rafting shoes. I moved closer and tried to listen, though I hadn't been rafting since college.

By the time pizzas arrived, the wine had eased my mood's sharp edges. I was deep in conversation with a few of the other team members about creating a swift-water rescue exercise when I noticed Foster and his dog settle at the far end of our tables.

Trace clapped him on the back and moved a plate with a

pizza slice on it in front of him. Chickie's tail wagged so hard it banged against the metal chair leg.

"...operational coordination between rescue swimmers and medical personnel under time pressure, right?"

I blinked back at Robyn, who was looking at me expectantly. Trace had chosen her as program coordinator because of her ability to bring people together, to break the ice, and I felt like an ass for making her job difficult.

"Oh, er, yeah. Right." I flashed her a friendly smile. "It's rare to get this crossover training opportunity."

She grinned back, setting her loose, blonde ponytail swinging.

From his end of the table, Foster shot me a ferocious scowl that had my smile dropping away.

I tried to focus on the conversation despite my distractibility. Over the next hour, I realized Foster was friendly and easy with everyone except me. When he talked about search and rescue, his face lit up—the same engaging manner he'd had in Hawaii. He commanded attention, was charismatic and kind.

I selfishly wanted a piece of it. My jaw ached with the urge to force him to look at me, but he refused. Throughout the entire planning session, he did the bare minimum to engage with me, only asking and answering questions when necessary.

By the time the group broke up, I was exhausted and annoyed. If the stubborn asshole couldn't treat me like an equal part of the team, then fuck him.

I stood to follow Robyn back to her car when my sister Hazel walked up. "Hey!" I said in surprise.

Her face brightened. "Tommy, what are you doing here? Avery's working late. I could have met you for dinner."

Before I had a chance to explain about the staff dinner, Robyn realized I wasn't with her and turned back to see what had happened. "Oh hi, Hazel. We were just finishing up a staff dinner."

Hazel smiled at her. "Sounds fun. Hey, do you mind if I borrow my brother for a few? I can run him back to SERA when we're done."

Robyn hesitated before pressing her lips together in an understanding smile. "You bet. See you back there, Tommy."

Hazel watched her walk away before turning and rolling her eyes at me. "She's obviously into you. The signals are so much clearer for straight guys," she murmured. It wasn't the first time she'd made a similar comment, but this time, it annoyed me.

"You jealous that Robyn is more interested in me than you? Because your wife might have feelings about that."

She laughed. "Easy, tiger. I happen to be picking up pickle-topped pizza because my wife is having pregnancy cravings. I adore Avery and have no interest in bubbly blonde women half my age."

"Sorry." I felt like an ass and muttered my apologies. "Long day."

Just then, Foster walked by without a glance. Chickie, however, stopped and waggled her tail at me, sniffing my leg and nudging my hand. When the leash pulled at Foster's hand, he turned back to see what had distracted her.

"Who's this cutie?" Hazel asked, squatting to pet the pup.

What happened next proceeded in slow motion. She turned to see who owned the dog and recognized Foster. From Hawaii. I hadn't even remembered she'd seen him.

Her eyes went wide, lips parting in shock. I tried to smooth over the awkward moment.

"Uh, heh, um, H-hazel, this is Foster Blake. He's... he's the search and rescue instructor for SERA this summer. He's standing in for Desi until Trace can find a permanent replacement. Foster, this is my sister. Well, one of them. Hazel, I mean. My sister. Hazel. She has a twin. There are two of them. Chloe."

So much for smoothing over the awkward. My sister stared at me as I stumbled over my words. I was known for being cool under pressure, so it was highly unusual to see me off my game. In the history of my life, there seemed to have only been one person who could make me this stammery and weird.

"How did this happen?" she asked, waggling a finger between me and Foster. "Did you tell Trace to hire—"

Out of the corner of my eye, I saw Foster's eyebrows shoot up in surprise.

"No!" I said quickly. "No. I didn't know he was coming. I had no idea he... well, it doesn't matter. He's here, and I'm here, and... we're all here. For SERA. For the program. Which starts tomorrow. So we should probably head back. To bed. To sleep, I mean. To *get* sleep. In bed. Not together!"

My face seared with heat as I tried not to think of my bed only a few feet away from Foster's.

"There are two beds," I added lamely, as if more words about the sleeping arrangements would help.

Hazel tilted her head at me. The edges of her lips turned up as if this was suddenly incredibly funny. "I see."

I closed my eyes. "Jesus fucking Christ."

"Mmhm." Hazel glanced between me and Foster. "Well, someone's obviously fucking someone. Foster, it's nice to meet you. Would you mind driving Nimrod back to SERA for me? Thank you ever so much."

My face ignited with embarrassment, not only at the implication that Foster and I were sleeping together but also at the old nickname, one I'd gotten before I'd even been born. "Nimrod Nickelback" was only trotted out these days when my sisters or Uncle Teddy wanted to hammer home a moment of my stupidity.

Once Hazel had disappeared into the restaurant without even a glance of apology, I took a deep breath and considered shouting a very bad word at her back.

"Don't do it," Foster said softly, tilting his head at the families seated nearby. Several kids eyed Chickie with interest. "You'll regret it."

I glanced at him. "Doubt it."

"C'mon. Truck's over here," he said in a gruff voice.

"I can catch a ride with someone else," I insisted, not wanting him to do me favors. And definitely not wanting him to continue to bear witness to my humiliation.

"Don't be ridiculous. Let's go." He tossed Chickie's leash handle at me before striding off—a neat trick that forced me to follow rather than turn back to find another ride.

I silently fumed as I fell in line behind him, pulling the pup along. She trotted happily beside me, taking quick sniffs at interesting things. Every time she leaned down, her ears dragged the ground in a way too cute to ignore. It softened my mood's sharp edges so that when we reached Foster's Sheriff's vehicle, I wasn't quite as homicidal as I'd been after my sister's teasing.

Until Foster opened his mouth to speak.

7

FOSTER

I'D REGRETTED COMING to dinner the moment I'd arrived and seen Tommy Marian sitting at one end of the table, looking like angels themselves had laid the man gently on earth to tempt me.

The setting sun had brushed warm golden stripes across his hair and face, creating shadows that sharpened his jawline and defined the muscles under his shirt.

But then he'd looked up at me, and I'd caught the flash of hurt and confusion on his face before his eyes had skittered away again.

Tommy's expression made me both angry and guilty. Angry because *I* hadn't been the one to withhold critical information before kissing the man. And guilty because I *also* hadn't been the one who'd remained professional when realizing we were going to be working at SERA together.

But now, I was even angrier for an entirely different reason.

"What the fuck kind of sister calls her brother Nimrod?" I snapped as we approached the truck. "Your family is a bunch of assholes."

Tommy's eyes widened in surprise before his jaw clenched, and he shoved Chick's leash into my sternum, hard. The breath punched out of me as I caught the leash out of reflex.

"Fuck you." He turned on his heel to leave. I quickly reached out and grabbed his biceps.

"You running away again? Seems about right."

"Leaving isn't the same thing as running away." He turned and shoved me off him before backing me up against my vehicle with forefinger pokes to the chest. "You don't know shit about me, and you don't know shit about my family. So back the fuck off."

Tommy's entire body leaned toward mine. His face was close enough for me to make out warm amber striations in his irises. To smell the scent of red wine on his breath.

I carefully clasped my hand around the wrist of his poking hand and lowered my voice. "Your body isn't asking me to back off, Dr. Marian."

I'd meant it as a tease, to provoke him and remind him of his blatant lack of self-control in Hawaii, but it came out sounding sultry and intimate. It came out sounding like pure, unadulterated *want*. Desire that sounded way more real and intense than I'd wanted to reveal to him. Or even admit to myself.

Tommy's cheeks darkened. For a split second, he looked... tired. Exhausted, really. Like he'd been carrying the weight of several small planets on his shoulders.

I had a momentary flash fantasy of him stepping into my chest and simply resting there. Letting me wrap my arms around him and be a safe space for him while he gathered his strength—

But then I remembered this wasn't a fantasy. I wasn't heading back to SERA hand in hand with my happy boyfriend. I was facing off against my angry enemy slash reluctant obsession.

Even so, when his tongue came out to wet his bottom lip, I almost, *almost* leaned in to taste it. We'd done it before, after all. Hell, he'd even thanked me for it.

It was a good thing I didn't because he might have bit my tongue clean off.

"Just because my body wants to fuck yours," he said in a low growl, "doesn't mean I want to hear your ignorant opinions about my family."

The admission sent heat straight through me, swelling my dick and stealing my breath... but it was immediately followed by a cold wash of reality.

I might still want Tommy Marian, despite my better judgment. Despite his mixed-up sexuality. And despite the fact that he lived in New York...

But he was married to someone else, and no matter how much I wanted him, that was the ultimate dealbreaker.

The thought made my jaw clench.

"Forgive me for thinking you deserve better than a sister who calls you hurtful names," I hissed.

He let out a breath and seemed to deflate. "It's a term of affection."

I scoffed. "That's a shitty way to show someone affection."

Tommy's eyes met mine again. "Don't tell me Anna never calls you names."

My eyes flashed to his. *He remembered my sister's name?*

I didn't want to interpret it as anything meaningful, like him caring enough to remember. A man who'd succeeded at medical school probably had a crack-shot memory. That was all.

"She's been known to throw an *asshat* my way a time or two," I admitted before stepping back, if only to keep myself from forgetting what the word "dealbreaker" meant and doing something stupid. "But Anna would never have called me a derogatory name in public."

"I told you it's not like that," he snapped.

Once we were loaded up in my sheriff's vehicle and Chick was sniffing happily through the partial opening in the nearest window, I noticed Tommy clenching his hands together in his lap so hard his knuckles were white.

No ring, I noticed for the first time, but plenty of people who worked with their hands didn't wear them.

"Then what *is* it like?"

"It's an inside joke," he muttered. "You know what? Never mind. We don't need to talk. Let's just go back to SERA and let this day fucking end, okay?"

I glanced over at him as I shifted into gear. Once again, Tommy looked tired and stressed. I wanted to know why. Wanted to know what had happened in Hawaii after I left. But none of it was my business.

I cleared my throat. "So are you, like, taking a summer

sabbatical or something?" I asked, trying to be normal. To ask him the kind of question a professional peer might ask. "I'm surprised the hospital let you go."

Tommy kept his gaze focused away from me and out the passenger window as we moved slowly through the pedestrian traffic in town.

"They didn't have to. I quit."

The surprising words sat between us like a fishing hook with an irresistible lure dangling from it.

So I bit.

"You quit? St. Ignatius is the top trauma hospital in the Northeast. A dream job for a high achiever like you. Why the fuck would you leave?"

He turned to me, eyebrows dipping in confusion. "How did you know I was at St. Ignatius?"

Embarrassment prickled my skin. "You must have told me that night. Does it matter?"

"Well, no. I just—"

"Wait, you're at SERA permanently?" I blurted, suddenly wondering if he'd done it. If he'd made the big change from big-city trauma ER to practicing the medicine he seemed drawn to. My heart leapt at the idea he'd be so close, only a few hours' drive instead of a day's worth of airline travel—

"No. God, no. It's only temporary. I'm interviewing for positions back home." He cleared his throat. "In California."

I raked my bottom teeth over my upper lip and nodded. "Right. Sure. Of course."

Tommy looked like he wanted to say something more, explain or maybe even judge me for being less than enthusiastic. But he didn't. He faced out the window on the opposite side of the truck.

The tension was killing me. This man who'd lived inside my head as a living, breathing obsession was sitting eighteen inches away from me in my own damned truck.

And he seemed a million miles away.

I swallowed and focused on the road out of town. SERA was several miles away on a large plot of land at the base of Slingshot Mountain. The sun was already behind the peak, and shadows filled the valley around us.

"Thank you," he said softly without turning to look at me. "For caring. About what Hazel said. I promise she didn't mean anything by it, but I do appreciate you standing up for me. Especially after..." He shrugged.

"Why does she think we're fucking?" I blurted. Her comment had been itching under my skin since she'd said it. "Did you say something to her?"

He finally turned to face me. "No! I only told one person in my family that we... that we kissed, and she wouldn't have told anyone else."

"Kissed," I said with an unamused huff of laughter.

Jesus, what an anemic word for what had actually happened.

"Yes. Kissed." Pink heat bloomed on his cheeks as he lifted his chin. "Twice."

I glanced at him again, if only to drink in his adorable flush. "You counted."

"Kind of hard not to notice when a guy's kissing you," he muttered, looking away again.

I watched him closely. "You'd never kissed a guy before, I take it?"

"I told you I was straight," he reminded me. This time, he glanced at me, and I caught his eyes.

"Tommy, why did your sister think we were sleeping together if you're so straight?"

His cheeks were painfully crimson now. I wanted to reach over and feel the heat on my fingertips and lips.

"I don't know." Tommy turned back to the window again. "My family doesn't know anything happened between us. They know you were there, and they know I acted..." He gave a little snort. "Let's just say I acted very much not myself. They've come up with their own explanations for that, and us hooking up was an easy one since our situation was similar to how my uncles met, like I told you."

"And I was wearing your shirt," I suggested.

He nodded and looked away again. "And you were wearing my shirt."

I glanced at him, taking in the flush still painting his cheeks, the way his lips were slightly parted. The urge to pull over and kiss him senseless hit me like a freight train.

"Fuck," I muttered under my breath, gripping the steering wheel tighter.

Tommy caught the word. "What?"

"Nothing." But it wasn't nothing. It was the realization that sitting here, talking like this, pretending we could be friends or colleagues or whatever the hell this was, felt like the cruelest kind of torture. "Just... maybe we should focus on tomorrow. On work."

The temperature in the cab seemed to drop ten degrees.

The rest of the drive passed in charged silence. Every time Tommy shifted in his seat, I caught a whiff of his scent—a hint of expensive deodorant over masculine sweat—that made my palms itch. When he reached up to run his fingers through his hair, the movement drew my attention to the line of his throat, the way his shirt pulled slightly across his chest.

I forced myself to focus on the road.

"Foster—" Tommy started as we pulled into SERA's parking lot.

"Long day," I cut him off, throwing the truck into park with more force than necessary. "And an early start tomorrow."

I was out of the truck and grabbing Chickie and my gear before he could respond. The walk to Cabin 8 was too short. Tommy followed slightly behind, and whatever he'd been about to say in the truck remained unspoken.

The cabin felt even smaller than I remembered. With both of us inside, plus Chickie sniffing around excitedly, the space was suffocating. I reached for the duffle on my bed and immediately regretted the choice when Tommy moved to his own bed directly across from mine.

Three feet away. Maybe four if I was being generous.

"Look," Tommy said quietly, sitting down on the edge of his own bed. "I know this is awkward. But we're going to be working together for eight weeks. Maybe we could just—"

"Keep it professional," I finished, turning away to find my shower stuff and something to sleep in. "Yep. Agreed."

The tension in his silence made me glance back. He was sitting with his shoulders slightly slumped, and for a moment, he looked lost. Disappointed. It reminded me of the expression he'd worn in Hawaii when he'd pulled away from our kiss on the beach.

My chest tightened with that unwelcome urge to comfort him again. To tell him I didn't mean to be an ass, that I was just trying to protect myself from wanting something I couldn't have.

Instead, I turned away and started rifling through my bag.

"I'll take first shower," I said gruffly.

The bathroom was barely big enough for one person, let alone the broad shoulders I'd inherited from my father. I stripped quickly and stepped under the lukewarm spray, hoping the water would wash away the tension coiled in my muscles.

It didn't help. If anything, it made things worse. Because now I was naked, alone, and thinking about Tommy Marian less than twenty feet away, probably getting undressed himself.

Stop.

I scrubbed my hair aggressively, focusing on anything other than the mental image of Tommy pulling his shirt over his head, revealing that lean torso I'd felt in Hawaii. The way he'd reacted to my touch, urgent and desperate.

He's not staying. He's going to California for some fancy job, and you'll never see him again. His wife is probably waiting for him there.

The reminder should have helped. Instead, it just made the hollow ache in my chest worse.

I dressed quickly in sleep pants and a T-shirt, then opened the bathroom door to find Tommy sitting on his bed, scrolling through his phone. He looked up when I emerged, and his gaze swept over me before he quickly looked away.

"All yours," I murmured.

He stood, grabbing clothes from his bag, and we did an awkward dance as he moved toward the bathroom. The cabin was so narrow that he had to brush past me, his shoulder bumping mine, his scent washing over me again.

We both froze for a heartbeat, standing too close, facing each other. His lips were slightly parted, his breathing shallow. I could see the pulse beating at the base of his throat.

Kiss him.

Instead, I stepped back, putting precious distance between us and trying to reject the memory of our kisses. "Get some sleep. Long day tomorrow."

Tommy's expression shuttered. "Right. Of course."

The bathroom door closed with a soft click, and I sank onto my bed, dropping my head into my hands.

This push-pull between wanting Tommy Marian and remembering I couldn't have him was like climbing a steep rock face and then falling back down, over and over, on fucking repeat.

I'd just manage to pull myself up, to remind myself that I was a professional who could be distant and civil with my bunkmate for the next eight weeks, when suddenly, the feeling of wanting him would overwhelm me.

I'd lose my grip on reality, forget all the reasons I couldn't have him, and find myself tumbling, weightless, with no sense of up or down, the only thought in my head that I needed to be close to him, to find that beautiful, easy connection we'd shared that night in Hawaii.

And then I'd remember that he'd lied—or close enough—that night. I'd remember the woman in the Bride sash. I'd remember his big-city aspirations. I'd remember his presence in my life was temporary. And I'd hit the ground with a thud so hard and painful, it felt like my chest would shatter.

I was already exhausted and hurting, pissed at myself for still caring this much over what should have been *nothing*, should have meant *nothing*. And we still had eight goddamn weeks to go.

Chickie padded over and rested her chin on my knee, looking up at me with sympathetic brown eyes.

"Yeah, girl," I whispered, scratching behind her ears. "I'm fucked."

When Tommy emerged from the bathroom twenty minutes later, his hair was damp, and he wore thin sleep pants and a fitted T-shirt that clung to his chest. He moved quietly to his bed, clearly trying not to disturb me, but I was hyperaware of every sound—the rustle of sheets, the creak of the mattress as he settled.

I lay on my back, staring at the ceiling, listening to him breathe in the darkness. Every instinct I had was screaming at me to cross those three feet, to slide into his bed and let him experiment with a man all he wanted.

"Foster?" His voice was soft in the darkness.

"Yeah?"

"I'm sorry. For Hawaii. For not telling you about the wedding. You deserved better than that."

My throat tightened. So there had been a wedding after all. "Forget about it."

"I can't." The words emerged as a whisper, low and tortured. "That night... it meant something to me. More than I knew how to handle."

I closed my eyes, fighting the urge to tell him it had meant something to me, too. That it had given me hope there was still someone out there for me... and then just as quickly dashed it, reminding me yet again that love was a false promise. Trust was an elusive thing, and it damned well didn't grow on trees.

If someone as seemingly upright and good as Tommy Marian could kiss the fuck out of me one day and get married the next, there was no way to tell a trustworthy man from an untrustworthy one.

"Go to sleep, Tommy. It's over and done."

It wasn't, not really, but there was no way in hell I'd ever let him hear it from me.

The silence stretched between us, heavy with everything we weren't saying. Eventually, his breathing evened out, but I lay awake for hours, acutely aware of his presence just feet away, knowing that eight weeks of this was going to be the sweetest torture I'd ever endured.

8

TOMMY

THE FOURTH DAY of the program started at 6:00 a.m. with coffee that could strip paint and a breakfast briefing that would be quickly followed by the students' first exercise in the field.

Just like the previous four nights, I'd barely slept, hyper-aware of Foster's breathing in the bed across from me. Every time he'd shifted, my body had gone on high alert, remembering the weight of his hands on my skin in Hawaii... and his obvious lack of interest now that we were in Montana.

Because despite our heated exchange on the drive back from town that first night, Foster had retreated back into professional mode as promised. Every attempt I'd made to talk to him since then had been shut down by polite dismissal.

Over and over since January, I'd told myself to stop thinking about the man. That our interaction had probably been a blip on his radar—and not one he cared to remember, given the way we'd parted.

But experiencing it up close and personal? Seeing him act cool and distant where he'd once been so warm and engaged? Having him so fucking close but not at all in the way I wanted him? It was soul-crushing. I felt even more depleted and hollowed out than I'd felt in New York.

Thankfully, the first few days of the program had been busy and overwhelming enough to distract me. Our schedules were packed with orientations, education sessions, and hands-on preparation. Although we'd been paired up several times in the course of our work, Foster had made it very clear he wanted to keep things professional, so I gave him the respect he deserved and stayed in my own damned lane.

During the day, that had worked fine. At night, however, it had been almost impossible. Being that close to something you wanted more than anything else in the world and knowing you couldn't have it was excruciating.

By the time my alarm went off this morning, I felt like I'd run a marathon in my sleep.

Foster was already up, dressed in tactical pants and a dark SERA T-shirt that stretched across his shoulders in a way that should have been illegal. He'd taken Chickie out and returned with two cups of coffee, setting one on my nightstand without a word.

The gesture was so thoughtful it made my chest ache.

"Thanks," I'd mumbled, wrapping my hands around the warmth.

He'd nodded curtly and gone back to checking his gear, his hands moving with calm competence.

It turned out Professional Foster was somehow even more

devastating than the man who'd kissed me breathless under Hawaiian palms.

I got dressed as quickly as I could and made my way out into the lingering chill of the Montana morning, needing a Foster-less minute to get my brain engaged and my pulse under control.

Despite the early hour, the SERA campus was already buzzing with instructors and students moving with purpose—some heading to breakfast, others coming back from the gym, chatting with coffees outside their cabins, or practicing harnessing techniques on the helo pad before the day heated up.

On the far side of the facility was a neatly arranged grid of clean-lined, single-story buildings that housed the classrooms, offices, dining hall, equipment garages, and the main building. Beyond, hiking trails of varying difficulties led through the foothills onto Slingshot Mountain, where the snow-dusted mountain caps were pink-tinged in the morning light.

I sucked in a deep lungful of air and felt my shoulders sink down from my ears. There was something about the air here, or maybe the call of the birds, or the way the sky stretched out so big and vast, that was both comforting and inspiring. I felt settled… and also like anything was possible.

A much calmer Tommy Marian walked into the yard outside the main building an hour later and found thirty students gathered around Trace. As our leader explained today's mission—the first rescue drill—they buzzed with nervous energy, all of them eager to learn, to impress, and to get out on the mountain.

"Alright, listen up," Trace began. "Everyone should already know which team they've been assigned to and which instructor will be overseeing your team for this first rotation."

Thirty heads nodded.

I caught Foster's eye across the yard, and we shared an amused look at their eagerness before he remembered *looking* was unprofessional, or whatever the fuck, and resolutely looked away.

"You'll be searching for a missing kayaker," Trace continued, "who didn't make it to their pickup point. Thirty-two-year-old blonde female, last seen at Hellgate Narrows near the Blacktail Overlook. She's known to paddle a blue Pyranha Scorch with purple accents. That means this is possibly a swift-water rescue." He nodded to Tevita, the instructor who specialized in swift-water rescues. "Group Four will be taking point on this, with the other teams providing support. Understood? Good. Everyone, gear up. You have ten minutes for prep and loading before we head to the river."

My group immediately huddled together to discuss the best approach. "Okay, Group Two, what are we thinking for medical supplies?" I asked.

One of the group, a SAR drone operator from Maryland named Omar, frowned. "We've gotta port it all in, so do we wanna take a standard med kit? Or maybe pare it down a bit?"

Sierra Vaughn, an experienced EMT from Asheville, tugged open the flap of a large dry bag. "Opposite, I think. We don't know what shape the kayaker will be in, so we have to assume the worst—blunt trauma, hypothermia, maybe even spinal involvement. I say we load up a hypowrap kit, airway adjuncts, and at least two thermal blankets."

I nodded. "Sierra's exactly right. Don't count on routine when prepping for emergency response. The most important lesson in wilderness medicine: triple-check your supplies before leaving base. Once you're out there, what you have is what you have."

Cody, a high-mountain ranger from Rainier, nodded. "Been there. You gotta be resourceful."

Omar flushed. "Shit. I should've known that."

"Nah." I nudged him lightly with my elbow. "If you were already an expert on everything, you wouldn't be here. Wait until it's time to work with drones, and you'll find that some people on your team have the hand-eye coordination of a rhinoceros." I mimicked moving a joystick in quick, jerky movements.

"That'll be me." Sierra sighed grimly. "He's talking about me."

Everyone laughed, and Omar brightened.

While the team finished loading up our gear, I couldn't help glancing over at Foster and his team... because apparently, my eyes were magnets, and Foster Blake was one large, sexy, muscular metal filing. His students had jumped into action, too, pulling out radios and topo maps of the area and asking Foster for access to the person who'd reported the woman missing.

"Jasper Lloyd," Foster said, calling out a name from his roster. One of his students snapped his head up in surprise. "You're on point for nav once we hit the river. Just like we talked about yesterday, yeah?"

"Whoa, no." Jasper shook his head. "I'm an EMT who relies heavily on the apps, if I'm being honest. No sense of direction. Let Kofi do it. He's—"

"I asked you. And I trust you to do it." Foster gave the man the full weight of his attention, and even from this distance, it made me shiver, remembering how it felt to be the center of his focus. "You're here to learn SAR, right? You can't search if you're shit at nav, so let's go."

"Yeah." Jasper swallowed and nodded once. "Yeah, okay."

We loaded into the bus for our drive to the trailhead, and while the SAR teams worked their case from the front seats and the swift-water specialists conferred about possible rescue scenarios and water conditions, I reviewed medical protocols with my team. The energy was infectious—everyone excited for their first real drill.

"This'll be sick," Cody said, grinning. "You think they're doing tagline or tethered swimmer?"

Sierra shifted her backpack. "Don't get my hopes up. For all we know, she'll be unconscious on the bank after taking a pee break."

My team continued chatting excitedly after arriving at the trailhead parking lot and watching the other teams hurry up the trail. After several minutes, the radio operator for one of the SAR teams alerted us on the radio to a victim spotted in the water just southwest of Blacktail Overlook.

"Alright," Sierra said, grabbing her pack. "Let's do this."

We headed out after them, keeping a quick but steady pace over the rocky terrain. But just before we arrived at our rally point, Foster's own voice rang out over the radio, giving us new information.

"Blake to all units. Drill is canceled. We've got a real emergency. Climber down on the south face of Devil's Backbone. Serious fall, unknown condition. Students and non-lead staff are to remain ready to assist. I need medical here ASAP. Repeat: drill is canceled. We're live. Over."

Devil's Backbone was one of the steeper ridges of Slingshot Mountain, a jagged spine of rock with loose scree at the base, sheer drops, and terrain that punished hesitation. As we hustled to the new coordinates, I took the radio from Sierra, my heart rate spiking as I switched from training mode to actual emergency response.

"Marian to Blake, we copy. Medical en route. We're a minute out. Has someone contacted local dispatch?"

As my team and I entered the clearing at the base of the climb, Foster was instructing his crew: "Dr. Marian and I will make the climb for in-field triage and extraction."

I raced forward while barking instructions to Sierra to hand over the supply backpack.

The climber had taken a popular but advanced climbing route called Spiny Tooth that led up the steepest part of Devil's Backbone. Foster was already rigging anchor points, his movements efficient and confident. When he worked, there was no wasted motion, no hesitation. It was mesmerizing to watch—and I caught myself staring at the fluid way his muscles moved as he handled the ropes.

Focus, Tommy.

"What do we have?" I asked, giving Chickie a quick head

scratch as I stepped up to the student offering to help me into a harness. "Any idea of the injuries involved?"

Foster quickly took over from the student, squatting at my feet and reaching for the webbing straps. "Possible head injury with loss of consciousness, multiple contusions. No report of compound fracture or bleeding," he called without looking up at me. "Medical up first. I'll belay you."

He quickly began strapping the harness webbing around my waist and thighs, his muscles moving under the tanned skin of his forearms. Being this close to him, feeling his hands on me even through the clinical necessity of the harness, sent heat racing through my body.

Not the time. Not the place.

"You have climbing experience," he said, remembering the stories we'd shared in Hawaii.

"Yes. I've climbed this route before."

He must have caught the hesitation in my voice because he glanced up from where he was crouched at my feet, and his eyes met mine. "But?"

The harness felt strange after months in emergency rooms and hospital corridors. My hands shook slightly as I clipped in, muscle memory from my climbing days rusty from disuse.

"It's been a while," I admitted.

"Like riding a bike," Foster said, his voice softer than it had been all morning. "You'll be fine. I've got you."

I met his eyes and saw kind reassurance instead of judgment, the first crack in his professional facade. "Okay."

He nodded and began talking me through the route, his voice calm and reassuring. As I climbed, I could feel the tension in the rope, the steady presence of Foster belaying me from below. It was trust in its purest form—my life literally in his hands.

There wasn't a single doubt among anyone present as to who was in charge of this rescue. Foster commanded the scene from his position on belay, never once taking his eyes off me.

As soon as I found the fallen climber on a rocky landing partway up Spiny Tooth, I dropped into assessment mode, running through ABCs while calling down vital signs to Foster and the rest of the team.

"Pulse is thready, possible internal bleeding," I shouted. "I need him immobilized before we move him."

"Copy that," Foster called back. "Coming with the spine board. I need you to find an anchor up there and clip in."

The young man and woman who'd been climbing with the injured patient showed me where the anchor was and then explained what had happened while I transferred from the belay line to the anchor point. Tears ran down the woman's face while the man gripped her hand tightly.

"How the hell did you get here so fast?" the guy asked, almost hyperventilating.

"We were already nearby, running a drill. There are at least twenty first responders at the base of the climb ready to help," I told him.

"He... he slipped and swung on his rope, but like... Jesus. I don't even know what really happened. He hit his head, and... then he was gone." The man ran a hand over his head and pointed upward. "Over that outcrop."

"He's going to kick himself when he wakes up." The woman's face crumpled. "He... he *is* gonna wake up, right?"

I set a hand on her arm. "My name is Dr. Marian, and I'm a trauma doctor. I promise we'll do everything we can to help your friend. Right now, I need you to give us room and keep yourselves safe, okay? Stay hydrated and reapply sunscreen if you have it."

Foster's helmet appeared over the edge of the rock ledge. He met my eyes and nodded slightly, recognizing I'd given them a simple task to help keep them distracted.

The next hour was a carefully choreographed dance between medical treatment and technical rescue. I had to treat and package the patient while Foster coordinated the lowering system, both of us calling out constant updates. As the sun beat down on my head and shoulders, my heart pounded with adrenaline.

This was what I'd missed in the sterile environment of the ER—medicine that required improvisation, that forced you to adapt and overcome. Medicine that felt like an adventure. But also seemed like the difference between life and death in the field.

When we finally got the patient down the mountain and into the care of the EMT team waiting for him, Trace came over to shake our hands.

"Clean execution," he said loudly enough for all the gathered students to hear. "Medical assessment was thorough, rescue techniques were textbook. Great example of flawless teamwork."

As I opened my mouth to thank him, I heard the barest scoff

of disagreement from Foster. I turned to stare at him in disbelief, though no one else seemed to notice his reaction.

What the hell?

After the successful rescue, after what felt like perfect coordination between us, he was still finding fault? Professional distance was one thing, but undermining me in front of the students crossed a line.

Trace continued to review the situation with the gathered students and announced we would move our original missing kayaker drill to the afternoon. "Let's take our lunch break, and then we'll make another attempt at the drill, alright? Robyn brought sandwiches and fruit for everyone."

After stripping off my harness and stowing the remaining medical equipment with my team, I dragged myself toward a nearby bench. I was sweaty, filthy, and definitely dehydrated. Thankfully, Sierra and Kofi were both looking out for me, handing me ice-cold water bottles from the coolers.

"That was amazing," Sierra said.

I took a huge swig of water and enjoyed the cool slide down my dusty throat. "Thanks. If we get another injured climber this afternoon, I'm sending you up instead," I teased.

Trace tilted his chin up at Foster and then gestured for me to join them. "Listen, why don't the two of you head back to SERA and get cleaned up? I'll review this morning's case with the students and quiz everyone on it after lunch. It'll give you plenty of time to get back here for the drill." He handed Foster a set of car keys.

Foster nodded silently and handed Chickie's leash over to one of his students before heading toward a large black pickup truck with a SERA logo on the side. I fell in line behind him and climbed up into the passenger seat. Instead of speaking, I lowered the window and focused on drinking my water and inhaling the fresh mountain air as Foster drove out of the trailhead parking lot.

Long minutes passed in silence as tense as a long shift during a mass casualty event. The truck cab felt suffocating despite the open windows.

Screw this, I finally decided.

"What happened to being professional?" I snapped. "Trace says we worked well as a team, and you scoffed? What the fuck is wrong with you?"

"You were distracted on the way down."

I stared at him. "Distracted? I was trying to keep my patient alive while dangling from a fucking rope!"

"Can't have distractions when lives are on the line."

The words stung because they carried a grain of truth. I had been distracted—by the way his muscles flexed as he worked the ropes, by the memory of those same hands touching me in Hawaii, by the growing frustration of being treated like a stranger despite our obvious chemistry. But it hadn't been on the way down.

At every moment of our rescue, I had focused on the patient and doing the job to the utmost of my ability. How dare he call my professionalism into question.

"Name one thing I did wrong." My voice sounded low and accusatory.

He hesitated but persevered. "You were staring at my ass while I was rigging anchors."

Heat flooded my face because he wasn't wrong. "I was observing your technique as I approached the scene!"

"Bullshit." He stared at the road with nostrils flaring and his jaw clenching. "Look, I get it. You're having your little experiment, but some of us are here to work."

"Experiment?" The word came out strangled. "What the hell is that supposed to mean?"

"Married guys looking for some action on the side," he said without looking at me. "I'm not interested in being someone's dirty little secret."

I stared at him, my brain struggling to process what he'd just said. It snagged on one word. "*Married*?"

"Don't play dumb, Tommy. I was there, remember?" He pulled the truck into the lot by our cabin and shifted into Park before throwing the door open and striding toward our cabin.

I stumbled after him, legs shaky from the adrenaline crash and low blood sugar. "What?"

"Married, asshole!" The words exploded out of him as he yanked the cabin door open. "As in, you making *vows* to the woman who was wearing the Bride sash while standing next to you in that lobby. Ring a bell?"

My world tilted sideways. All this time, all the cold shoulders and professional distance—he thought I was married. He thought I'd kissed him while engaged to someone else... and then married her anyway.

"Foster," I said slowly, my voice barely above a whisper. "I didn't get married."

He went very still, shoulders rigid. "What?"

"I called off the wedding. That morning, after—" I swallowed hard, my throat suddenly dry. "Kari gave me an ultimatum—marry her that day, or we were done. I chose done. I thought you knew."

The silence stretched between us, broken only by the distant sounds of birds in the trees through the cabin's open windows. Foster's face went through a series of expressions—confusion, disbelief, and something that might have been hope before he seemed to catch himself.

His hands slowly unclenched. "You called it off."

"Yes."

Foster's breath came out in a rush. "Jesus, Tommy." He raked both hands through his hair, pacing to the window and back. "All this time, I thought—"

"I tried to tell you, but you wouldn't let me explain—"

"You tried to tell me?" His voice cracked. "When?"

I stepped closer. "The other night, in here. You kept cutting me off, saying we should keep it professional." Frustration bled through my words. "I wanted to explain everything, but you made it clear you didn't want to hear it."

Foster tossed the keys on the nightstand and scrubbed his hands over his face. "Fuck. I thought—Jesus, I thought you were married. I thought you were just looking for some guy to screw around with while your wife was back home."

"I would never do that," I said, surprised by how much his assumption hurt. "I'm not that kind of person."

His eyes met mine, something raw and vulnerable flickering there. "You're the kind of person who kisses someone else, on the eve of his fucking wedding."

Foster's accusation punched the breath out of me. I moved

to the edge of my bed and fell onto it, accidentally dropping my water bottle and watching it roll under Foster's bed.

The feeling of the blankets under me reminded me how tired I was. I wanted to crawl under the covers and sleep for twenty-four hours. But that wasn't an option. I was still on the clock.

"I'm going to take a shower," I said, forcing myself back up and over to the drawers to grab clean clothes. If I sat on the bed any longer, I'd pass out. And if I stayed here trying to defend myself to him anymore, I'd lose all self-respect.

When I reached for the bathroom doorknob, I felt Foster's big body step up behind me. "Tommy, wait."

I didn't turn around. "Wait for what, Foster? You obviously don't know me, and I get it. I'd probably think the same thing about me if I were you. But I'm not a cheater. Well, maybe it would be more accurate to say I'd never cheated on anyone until that night, and I thought I did a pretty damned good job of keeping myself from doing what I actually wanted to do with you."

"I thought you were married," he repeated, his voice softer now.

I turned to face him, noticing something desperate in his expression, like he was trying to rewrite six months of assumptions in real time.

The weight of our misunderstanding settled between us. All the walls Foster had built, all the professional distance—it had been based on a lie. On assumptions neither of us had bothered to correct.

"But I'm not."

"So you're... single," he said, like he was testing the words. His eyes searched mine.

"Very," I confirmed. "Have been since Hawaii."

"Because of me?"

The question hung in the air like a challenge. I could lie, make it about my career or cold feet or a dozen other safer explanations. But Foster Blake had changed my life that night in Hawaii. Changed it for the better. He deserved the truth.

"Yes," I said quietly. "Because of you. I knew I'd never see you again, but you gave me a glimpse of something amazing, and I couldn't go back to the life I'd planned."

Foster's chest rose and fell rapidly. I could practically see him recalibrating, adjusting his entire understanding of our situation.

I hesitated, then added, "It shouldn't have been because of you. There were obviously things wrong in my relationship I'd chosen not to see. But I can honestly say I would've gone right on ignoring them and married her that weekend if I hadn't met you." I took a step closer, my heart hammering. "That night made me realize what I'd been missing. Because kissing you felt more real than anything I'd experienced in ten years with her."

Foster's breath hitched. His eyes dropped to my mouth for just a second before meeting my gaze again. Something flickered across his face—want, hope, fear—and the air between us felt electric, charged with possibility. For a moment, I thought he might close the distance between us, might kiss me the way he had on that Hawaiian beach.

Instead, he stepped back, though I could see the effort it cost him. "But it wasn't real," he muttered.

I suddenly realized this man had the ability to cut me deeper than anyone else I knew. And what was worse? He did it quietly and without warning.

"And you think it's my family who has no right to hurt me," I murmured through lips that felt numb.

I turned back to the bathroom door.

"It doesn't matter anyway," he said, his deep voice unmistakably defensive and petulant. "You're leaving. Moving back to California."

"You're right, Foster." I turned to close the door and met his eyes before the door closed completely. "It doesn't matter."

When I stepped under the shower, I tried not to think about the look on his face as I'd closed the door.

Because if I allowed myself to believe there was even a single part of him that still wanted me, I would put myself in a position to let him hurt me again.

And being hurt by Foster Blake was a new kind of hell.

9

FOSTER

THE COLD WATER of the shower in the SERA gym did absolutely nothing to cool the fire burning under my skin.

Tommy's not married.

The words ricocheted around my skull like a pinball, bouncing off every assumption I'd built since leaving Hawaii. Knocking down every wall I'd constructed to protect myself from wanting something I couldn't have.

He called off his wedding. Because of me.

He'd actually flat-out said, "*...kissing you felt more real than anything I'd experienced in ten years with her.*"

And his face when he said it—so fucking vulnerable and hopeful and determined—had made me want to kiss him more than I'd ever wanted anything in my life.

Christ. What was I supposed to do now?

I braced my hands against the shower wall and let the spray hit the back of my neck.

I'd spent six fucking months trying to convince myself Tommy Marian was an asshole who'd used me for some pre-wedding experiment. Six months trying to hate him for making me want him when he belonged to someone else.

And *still*, despite believing I had every reason in the world to be pissed at him, the second I'd seen Tommy again, my whole chest had seized, my heart had fucking fluttered, and I'd very nearly thrown away my own self-respect by offering to fuck around with a man I'd thought was married.

So how the hell was I supposed to resist him now that I knew he was single? Now that I knew he'd been single *the whole goddamn time*? Now that I knew he was a man who'd chosen honesty over comfort, truth over security, and walked away from a ten-year relationship rather than go through with a marriage that felt wrong?

I had no clue. But one thing I knew for sure was that I *did* need to resist him.

I wasn't built for temporary relationships. I'd learned that lesson the hard way over the years as tourists and seasonal workers came and went from Majestic, as men like Matthew picked up stakes and moved on, brushing the dust of my small town from their boots. Guys had found me fun enough for a few weeks or a summer, promised to visit or call, and swore geography didn't matter... but when push had come to shove, their real lives were elsewhere, and I was just an interlude.

In most of those cases, it hadn't been a big loss. A sting, maybe. A little bruise to my heart. A few weeks of disappointment.

But with Tommy?

After a single evening with Tommy Marian—one conversation, a few drinks, two mind-melting kisses, eight hours or less —I'd caught a terminal case of feelings and spent the last half a year all up in my head over him.

So what would happen if I gave in and actually got to know him? If I spent the next seven and a half weeks trading smiles with him across a canteen table, seeing his hazel eyes twinkle, listening to how much he loved his family, watching him do his job with skill and compassion, and mapping the precise texture of his lips, his skin, and his dick with my tongue? What would happen if I let myself really, truly fall for him and pretend we had a future together?

Nothing good, that was what.

Because Tommy might have left his high-profile job in Manhattan, but I'd bet anything the California job he'd mentioned applying for was just as fancy. He still belonged in a world of hospital politics and medical conferences that was as foreign to me as Mars.

And I belonged in Majestic, Wyoming, where the air never smelled like car exhaust and the cows outnumbered the people two to one. Where I had family and community. Where my own career was as much a part of my identity as Tommy's career was of his.

It was hopeless, and therefore, I needed to keep my guard up. That was the smart thing to do.

I turned off the water and grabbed a towel, catching my reflection in the small mirror. My hair was dripping, my skin flushed from the heat, and my eyes were wild.

I looked like a man on the edge of making a very *stupid* decision.

I dressed quickly in clean tactical pants and a fresh SERA shirt, trying to ignore the way my hands shook as I pulled the fabric over my head. When I arrived at the truck, Tommy was waiting in the passenger seat, staring at his phone.

The drive back to the trailhead was torture of a completely different kind than the trip to SERA had been. Instead of anger and misunderstanding, the cab was filled with awareness so acute it made my skin burn. Every time Tommy shifted in his seat, every time he ran his fingers through his still-damp hair, I felt it like a physical touch.

By the time we pulled into the trailhead parking area, I felt like I was going to combust.

"You okay?" I asked stupidly.

"Peachy," he said before climbing out of the truck. "Despite what some of my fellow instructors think, I'm capable of remaining professional and ignoring distractions. Besides, there's nothing around to distract me anyway."

I stared after him as his cold words washed over me. He sounded pissed. He sounded hurt.

Good, I told myself. This was good. It was better this way. Nothing left to do but focus on the job.

I couldn't focus for *shit*.

The drill itself went off without a hitch. The "missing kayaker" was an instructor playing the role of a hypothermic victim with a dislocated shoulder—challenging enough to test the students' skills without being life-threatening.

But despite my earlier bitching at Tommy, this time, *I* was the one who was distracted as hell.

I kept finding my attention drawn to him as he worked with his medical team. His confidence as he gave instructions, the gentle manner he used with nervous students, the way his pants pulled tight across his ass when he bent to examine their "patient." The way he calmed a panicked student who was second-guessing his own decisions with a reassuring "You've got this. Trust your training" that reminded me so much of the voice that had whispered my name in Hawaii.

At one point, he caught me staring and raised an eyebrow in accusation. The slight flare of his nostrils sent heat straight to my groin...

Professional, I reminded myself. *Keep it professional.*

Easier said than done when every cell in my body was hyperaware of Tommy's presence.

"Sheriff Blake?" One of my students, a park ranger from Colorado named Marcus, was looking at me expectantly. "The lowering system?"

I blinked, realizing I'd completely zoned out while Marcus was asking about rope techniques. "Right. Sorry. Show me your anchor setup."

I forced myself to focus for the rest of the drill, but by the time we loaded back onto the bus, my nerves were stretched tight as piano wire. The students were chattering excitedly about the day's events, comparing notes and asking follow-up questions, but I barely heard them.

All I could think about was the coming evening, when Tommy and I would find ourselves alone again in the cabin.

Dinner in the dining hall had quickly become one of my favorite parts of the day at SERA—good food, easy conversation with fellow instructors and the students, and the satisfaction of a productive day. But tonight, it felt interminable. I sat at one end of the long table, picking at the grilled vegetables in front of me and trying not to stare at Tommy, who was deep in conversation with Robyn about the next day's activities.

He laughed at something she said, the sound warm and genuine, and my chest tightened with an emotion I didn't want to examine too closely.

"You planning to actually eat that or just move it around your plate?"

I looked up to find Trace studying me with knowing eyes. "What?"

"Your dinner. You've been pushing the same piece of carrot around for ten minutes." He leaned back in his chair, arms crossed. "I sensed some tension out there today between you and the doc."

"Don't know what you're talking about," I said automatically.

Trace lifted his eyebrows in surprise before tilting his head at me. "Right. I see." He glanced down the table at Tommy, then back at me. "Look, I don't care what you two do on your own time, but this tension is starting to affect the program. The students are picking up on it."

My jaw clenched. "We're handling it."

"Are you?" Trace's voice was quiet but firm. "Because from

where I'm sitting, it looks like you're both coiled tighter than a rattlesnake. I can't decide if you want to punch the guy or sleep with him. Figure your shit out, Foster, whichever one it is."

Before I could respond, he stood and moved to the other end of the table, leaving me alone with my untouched dinner and his blunt assessment.

Figure your shit out.

The problem was, I didn't know how.

I could hate Tommy Marian—okay, not really, but I could give a decent impression of it by acting cold and dickish.

I could fall for Tommy Marian in a heartbeat.

But one thing I didn't know how to do, had never known how to do, was to be indifferent to the man.

My brain couldn't comprehend the notion of liking him just a little. Of being friendly and casual with him like I was with the students and the other instructors. I didn't know how to pretend he hadn't rocked my world six months ago and left me reeling. That I didn't want him still.

As I watched him laugh with the other instructors, saw the way his eyes crinkled at the corners and the genuine warmth in his smile, I felt my resolve to stay on guard cracking.

These next few weeks were my only chance to be with him. Did I really want to give that up, just to save myself from the pain of letting go of him later?

Wasn't it going to hurt to walk away from him regardless?

Maybe it was worth the pain if it meant I got to touch him again, to feel that connection we'd shared in Hawaii.

Maybe I was losing my goddamn mind.

"Foster?" Tommy's voice cut through my spiraling thoughts.

I looked up to find him standing beside my chair, most of the other instructors already heading out. There was something careful in his expression, like he was trying to read my mood. "You want to head back?"

I glanced around the nearly empty dining room, surprised to find that dinner was over and I'd barely touched my food.

Trace caught my eye and lifted his brow.

I gave Tommy a half smile. "Er, yeah. Let's go."

The walk back to Cabin 8 felt like the longest quarter-mile of my life. Chickie trotted between us, blissfully unaware of the tension crackling in the air. By the time we reached our door, my hands were sweating, and my heart was hammering against my ribs.

When Tommy opened the door, Chickie bounded inside and immediately collapsed on her spot in the corner, exhausted from the day's excitement. Tommy stopped in the middle of the small space and turned to me until we faced each other like gunfighters at high noon.

"Listen," I said, running a hand through my hair. "I'm sorry about—"

He cut me off by holding up a hand. "I'm going to go stay at my sister's and leave you in peace. I'll be back in the morning for breakfast."

The coldness in his voice, the exhaustion in his eyes—it was undoing me piece by piece. "Tommy—" I began, wondering how to beg him to stay without acting like I gave a single shit.

"I cannot stay here with you like this," he continued, his voice low and intense. "I have wanted you for six fucking months, Foster. And I get that you don't want me back, okay?"

He stepped closer until I could see the flecks of gold in his hazel eyes. "But nothing good will come of me staying here. Believe me."

"Stay." The word came out rougher than I'd intended. His proximity was making my brain blink and fizz. I couldn't think when he was this close. And I wasn't sure I wanted to.

Tommy's eyes flashed. "Stay for what? Another evening of you pretending to be professionally indifferent?" He let out a humorless laugh. "Because I've gotta tell you—"

I grabbed the back of his neck and pulled him in for a kiss, the kiss I'd waited a hundred and sixty-two days to repeat. A small, shocked sound escaped him, followed by the softest whimper.

And then his hands reached up and grabbed handfuls of my shirt to pull me in closer. The kiss deepened, and my blood roared.

How was it possible for this to be so good again? I'd replayed our other kisses so many times, I'd convinced myself I'd overblown them in my memory.

But I was wrong.

The grip I had on the back of his neck loosened so I didn't hurt him, but the moment I eased up, he pulled me closer and made a frustrated sound in his throat. "Don't fucking stop," he urged against my lips.

My fingers slid through his hair as I pulled him into another kiss. This time, our tongues dueled, and I realized he didn't seem to have any hesitation about kissing another man.

Absolutely nothing was holding Tommy back.

They say a peacefulness follows any decision, even the

wrong one, and fuck was that true. Once my lips were on Tommy's, once my hands were molding the trim muscles of his body, it was impossible to regret it.

I kissed him with reckless wonder. With months' worth of pent-up frustration. With a consuming need to brand myself on him permanently the way he'd done to me. And with the knowledge, deep in my soul, that our parting was inevitable... so I was going to take everything he had to give. I'd soak in enough of his greedy fingers, his hot mouth, and his harsh moans of my name to last me a lifetime. I'd enjoy every fucking second of the ride for as long as it lasted.

Tommy moved one of his hands down my chest to my stomach and then my hard cock. I jerked back in surprise while simultaneously groaning at his touch.

"Please," he whispered, his breath warm against my lips. "I want you so fucking bad, I can't sleep at night."

"Tommy." His name came out like a sigh of surrender, a warning, a plea all rolled into one.

"If you don't want me, I'll let it go," he said. His forehead rolled against mine. "I promise. It will be the hardest fucking thing I've ever done, but I don't want to make you miserable. You have to tell me if you don't want this."

I closed my eyes. With his hands on my skin and his body so close I could feel his heat, I had no concept of self-preservation. So I told him the truth.

"I want this," I admitted, my voice barely audible. The confession felt like jumping off a cliff. "I've wanted you since that first night in Hawaii. Even when I thought you were married, even when I hated myself for it."

Something blazed in Tommy's eyes—triumph, relief, pure desire. "Fuck, Foster—"

"It can't be more than this," I added quickly, the words coming out harsh and desperate. "Sex. Hooking up. Whatever you want to call it. When SERA is over, you're gone. I know that. You'll be at your fancy job, and I'll be back in Majestic, dealing with lost hikers and small-town bullshit."

His hands moved back up my chest to my face. "Eight weeks."

"Seven and a half." I nodded once. "And then it's over. No long-distance bullshit. No promises we can't keep. You go to your city life, and I go home. Alone."

His thumb traced my cheekbone, and I saw something flicker in his eyes—hurt, maybe, or disappointment. But then he nodded. "What if we—?"

"No." The word came out harder than I meant it to. "I can't do maybes with you, Tommy. I can't do hope. I've been down that road before with guys who lived somewhere else, and it nearly broke me."

Tommy's face darkened. "Matthew."

He had no clue. Matthew leaving had been a paper cut. The brief flash of pain that came from ripping off a Band-Aid.

Losing Tommy—after a single fucking evening—was an aching wound that hadn't healed.

I swallowed hard. "This is all I can give you. Take it or leave it."

"I'll take it," he said, his voice rough with want. "I'll take it, Foster."

Tommy's thumb stroked across my cheekbone, his eyes were dark with promise, and I shuddered out a breath.

"This is such a fucking bad idea," I said, even as my hands came up to rest on his waist. My fingers immediately snuck under the hem of his shirt to touch the same warm, golden skin I'd dreamed about since Hawaii.

"Maybe." His smile widened, and for the first time since Hawaii, I saw the full force of Tommy's charm directed at me. "But I'm tired of good ideas. They got me engaged to the wrong person and working a job I hated."

Before I could voice any more doubts, Tommy rose up on his toes and kissed me again.

It was nothing like the desperate, hungry kisses we'd shared moments before. This was slow, deliberate, a question and an answer all at once. His lips were soft and warm, moving against mine with a confidence that made my knees weak.

I groaned and pulled him closer, my hands sliding up his back to tangle in his hair. He tasted like chocolate and mint but also like relief, like finally getting everything I'd been denying myself for the past six months.

When we finally broke apart, both breathing hard, Tommy rested his forehead against mine again.

"So," he said, his voice slightly unsteady. "Eight weeks."

"Seven and a half," I corrected again, reminding us both that the clock had already started ticking.

But as Tommy smiled and leaned in to kiss me again, I found I didn't care. Temporary *was* better than nothing. And, as my mom used to say, it would be a learning opportunity.

Maybe I'd learn Tommy wasn't as special as I'd thought.

That I'd been suffering the lingering effects of a terrible, tropical *love fever* that wouldn't survive a month and a half in close proximity during a Montana summer. That I could scratch this itch and get Tommy out from under my skin.

Or maybe I was about to learn that some kinds of wanting only got stronger when you fed them.

Maybe I was about to discover just how much a heart could break when it had everything it wanted and then had to let it go.

10

TOMMY

WASN'T sure my dick had ever been this hard. Part of me wondered why the hell now? Why Foster Blake? What had happened after all these years to suddenly attract me to a guy?

Had I taken surreptitious looks at other guys in the gym? Fuck yeah, I had. Didn't everyone?

Had it made my dick hard and my respiration rate spike? Never. Not like this. Not even close.

I was obsessed with Foster. Not a night—or day for that matter—had gone by in six months that I hadn't fantasized about being with him like this. Hadn't wanted his hands on my body and his laser focus on me.

"Fuck." The word was an embarrassing whimper. As soon as Foster's hand came down to press against my cock, I arched into it. It was hot but also a lot like relief. Relief to finally be touched where I wanted but also to finally move past this wall between us.

Foster's voice was rough when he spoke against the hot skin of my cheek. "I trust you to stop me if—"

"Shut the fuck up," I said, arching into him again. "If we have to talk about this anymore, I'm going to fucking explode."

The low rumble of his laugh made me grin against his temple as I inhaled the intoxicating scent of him. My hands moved under his shirt, exploring ridges of hard, broad muscles across his back and shoulders.

"That's how I felt when you said you were going to your sister's," he grumbled. "Thought I might have to tie you to the goddamned bed."

The words shot liquid fire through my veins. "Shoulda held my ground," I said on a gasp as his deft fingers moved to the button on my fly and flicked it open. "Sounds intriguing."

I realized belatedly there was a whole lot more of this man than the chaste skin of his back and quickly moved my hands down to explore further.

"Yeah? You kinky, Dr. Marian? Want me to—*oh fuckkk.*"

My hand gripped his long shaft as we both groaned.

He was fucking huge.

I almost wanted to laugh, remembering how startled I'd been that first night in Hawaii, to realize that I was noticing Foster not in the clinical way of a doctor assessing a patient but as a seriously aroused man thinking about a guy he wanted to fuck. It didn't seem startling at all anymore. I couldn't imagine how anyone could see Foster Blake and *not* want him.

"Not gonna lie," I admitted in an embarrassingly breathy voice. "This is a little intimidating."

"Yeah?" The edge of Foster's lip curled up. "You in over your head, Doc?"

My knees wobbled as his cock jerked in my hand. *I did that. I made him feel good.*

It was heady power, the ability to make this big, strong guy lose control a little. I wanted more of it.

We unzipped each other's pants, shoving at the material with no finesse until we were both bare to our thighs. Foster grabbed my shaft and held it together with his, pulling up with his firm grip. The press of our cocks together was something I'd obviously never experienced before, and I felt a moment of regret for all the lost opportunities because this felt fucking amazing.

My heart thundered, and my breathing came fast. "Foster, fuck."

"You feel so good," he murmured roughly. "Fuck, I want to suck your cock. Pull your balls into my mouth and hear those noises you make."

Oh, god. Hearing him talk like that, in the deep voice that had transfixed me since the plane ride to Hawaii, nearly made me come—my release was *right there*—but I didn't want this to be over. I reached down to cup his balls, tugging slightly and exploring his taint with my fingers.

He hissed in a breath that was a groan in reverse. "Shit, Tommy."

I licked along the stubbled bump of his Adam's apple. The difference between this and everything I'd ever done with a woman was striking. This was rough and aggressive, raw and... *powerful*. It was strength matched and mirrored. Unfiltered and unpretentious. I didn't even know how to describe it, but I knew I wanted—*needed*—more.

Foster's guttural voice vibrated through my lips. "Gonna make me come."

"You're the one doing it," I said, suddenly feeling giddy.

"Driving me crazy, swear to fuck." He tightened his grip and changed the rhythm.

I gasped and leaned into him, grasping the fabric of his shirt to keep from falling.

"Need you to come, sweetheart."

That was all it took. The tender command spoken in his broken voice. My release hit hot and hard. The entire thing had lasted seconds, mere moments of frantic desperation, but the orgasm that ripped through me solidified the line between Then and Now. Between who I was before and who I wanted to be.

The real me. A man not afraid to take what he wanted, to feel pleasure without apology. To let someone take care of me, command me, and show me how good it could be.

Foster grunted before his hot release joined mine on my stomach. The sound of his release in the otherwise quiet room caused Chickie to lift her head up, jingling the tags on her collar.

"'S'okay, girl," I said with a laugh, breath heaving and sweat curling along my spine. "Go back to sleep."

"Fuck," Foster mumbled. He turned his face and pressed his lips against my hot cheek. "Fuck."

I turned my face until our lips met. This time, the kiss was slow and indulgent, lingering and sweet. In all the times I'd fantasized about kissing Foster, never had I imagined it would be this good, this… patient and gentle.

Eventually, the cooling jizz on my skin began to itch, and I pulled away. "Any chance you'd let me clean up before letting me get you dirty again? I'm going to need to gather more data before making any scientific conclusions about men versus women and all that."

I tried for an easy, flirty smile, but inside, I felt like I could barely breathe, waiting for his response. I needed him to say yes, to agree this wasn't just a onetime thing. He'd made it sound like he was willing to give me eight weeks.

And I was ready to take advantage of every single hour of them if he'd let me.

His eyes pinned me, even though his grin was easy. "Mmm. Maybe we should shower together instead. For the sake of the environment."

I blew out a breath and grinned back.

Thank fuck.

THE FIRST THING I noticed when consciousness crept back in the next morning was the weight of Foster's arm across my chest, heavy and warm and *real* in a way that made my heart skip.

The second was the steady rhythm of his breath against my neck—the slow and even respiration of deep sleep—and how each exhale sent goose bumps racing down my spine.

And the third was that I was terrified to move.

We'd fallen asleep tangled together after... *Christ*. After I'd had my soap-slicked hand wrapped around Foster Blake's cock, watching his face transform as he came apart under my touch. After he'd whispered my name like a prayer and pulled me against him like he never wanted to let go.

Now, in the pale dawn light filtering through the cabin's thin curtains, I was cataloging every point of contact between our bodies. His thigh thrown over mine. His fingers still loosely curled around my hip. The warm press of his chest against my shoulder.

Eight—no, seven and a half—*weeks*. That was all he could give me.

The memory of his hands on my skin, the way he'd responded to my touch, the broken sound he'd made when I'd brought him over the edge—it played on repeat in my mind. I'd never been with a man before, but touching Foster had felt as natural as breathing. The weight of him in my palm, the way his breath had hitched when I'd found the rhythm he needed, the vulnerable expression on his face in those final moments.

I was in so much trouble.

"It can't be more than this," he'd said, his voice rough with want and something that sounded dangerously close to fear. *"When SERA is over, you're gone."*

I'd agreed because what choice did I have? A summer with Foster was better than a lifetime of wondering what if.

But lying here now, listening to his steady breathing and his thumping heart, I wondered if I was setting myself up for the kind of heartbreak I'd never recover from.

Touching him, being with him like this—it hadn't felt temporary. It had felt like coming home.

Now, I kept my eyes closed and lay as still as possible, afraid that the slightest movement would shatter whatever spell had settled over us. That Foster would wake up, remember all the reasons he'd said this was a terrible idea, and retreat behind his walls again.

He shifted slightly, a soft sound escaping his throat, and I held my breath. His arm tightened around me for just a moment before he seemed to surface from sleep.

"Mmph," he mumbled, burrowing his head into his pillow, voice rough with sleep. "Fuck."

I stayed perfectly still, wondering if I should pretend to be asleep, too. Give him space to process. But then he turned his head slightly, and I felt his lips brush the shell of my ear.

"Damn it," he muttered, so quietly I almost missed it. "Now you've ruined me for morning wood."

Heat flooded my face. This unguarded honesty, this admission that what we'd done had affected him as much as it had me, was only because he thought I was still sleeping.

"I heard that," I whispered back, opening my eyes.

Foster went completely still. "Shit."

"Your ears are turning red," I added, unable to keep the smile out of my voice.

"Christ, Tommy." He started to pull away, but I caught his wrist.

"Don't," I said softly. "Please. Not yet."

For a moment, we lay there as the morning light grew stronger around us. Then, Foster's thumb traced a small circle on my hip bone as he arched his hard cock against my hip. I had to bite back a groan.

"We should probably get up," he said but made no move to do so.

"Smart thinking."

"Breakfast starts in an hour."

"Sure does."

Foster's thumb continued its lazy pattern. "People will notice if we're late."

"An observant group for sure."

I felt rather than saw his smile against my shoulder. "You're not helping."

"Wasn't trying to."

Finally, inevitably, Foster did pull away, sitting up and running both hands through his sleep-messed hair. The sight of him—bare-chested, dark hair sticking up at odd angles, a faint red mark on his collarbone that I barely remembered making—sent a fresh wave of want through me.

"Coffee," he said, like it was a magic word that would solve all our problems.

"Good plan."

What followed was the most erotically charged coffee preparation in the history of caffeine.

The cabin, which had seemed merely small before, now felt like a dollhouse. Every movement required negotiating around each other, every task an exercise in spatial awareness that had nothing to do with efficiency and everything to do with the way Foster's sleep pants hung low on his hips, the thin fabric high-lighting the outline of his full cock.

I'd never spent so much time thinking about another man's dick before, and suddenly I was obsessed.

Focus.

"Can you—" I started, reaching for the coffee filters.

"If you just—" Foster moved at the same time, moving toward the pot next to the supply caddy.

"Move your—" We both stopped, me pressed against the tiny table with Foster's chest nearly touching my back as he reached around me for the pot.

We froze like that, his arm bracketing me against the table, his breath warm on the back of my neck. The heat radiating off his skin seared through me and the lingering scent of sleep mixed with a faded hit of masculine deodorant did more to wake me up than coffee ever could.

"Tommy," he said quietly, and there was a warning in his voice.

"Foster," I replied, intentionally matching his tone.

His free hand came to rest on my hip, thumb finding that same spot that had driven me crazy moments before. "We're going to be late."

"Are we?" I leaned back slightly, just enough to feel the solid warmth of his chest. "Oooh. Your pulse just spiked, Sheriff Blake."

"Stop that."

"Stop what? Making medical observations?"

"You know what." But his thumb didn't stop its movement, and he didn't step away.

"Ah, am I being a professional distraction again? I seem to have a habit of that." I turned in the circle of his arms, suddenly feeling braver than I had any right to. "You keep looking at me like you're annoyed, but your ears turn red every time I stretch."

Foster's eyes darkened. "You want to keep poking, Doc? Go ahead and find out what happens."

The challenge in his voice sent heat straight through me. "Yeah, I do. I've heard that poking a bear results in a physical and aggressive response."

For a heartbeat, I thought I'd pushed too far. That I'd brought our secret nighttime activities into the morning and across some unspoken boundary of his. Foster's jaw clenched, his eyes flashing with something that might have been frustration or desire or both. Then he stepped closer, until my ass was pushed against the table, and then further, forcing me to lean back and brace myself on one arm. His big hands bracketed me on either side, closing me in.

"Mm. I believe this is called agonistic display," I said softly, even as my heart hammered against my ribs. "When wild animals try to intimidate their prey."

"That right?" His voice was barely above a whisper. "Do you find me intimidating, Dr. Marian?"

"Maybe a little. And clearly I'm here for it," I said, letting my gaze drop meaningfully to where our hard cocks were now pressed together before meeting his eyes again.

Something shifted in his expression then, the last of his morning restraint cracking. "Fuck it," he muttered, and then his mouth was on mine.

This kiss was different from the desperate hunger of the night before. It was slow, thorough, like he had all the time in the world to explore. His tongue traced my lower lip before deepening the kiss, and I made a sound that should have been embarrassing but only seemed to encourage him.

My hands found the waistband of his sleep pants, fingers dancing along the edge, and he groaned against my mouth.

"Tommy," he said, but it sounded more like surrender than protest.

"Fuck, I like when you get all growly," I murmured against his lips, then nipped gently at his jaw. "New kink unlocked."

His response was to lift me onto the table, stepping between my legs and kissing me harder. The new angle let me wrap my arms around his neck and pull him closer, and suddenly, we were grinding against each other like teenagers.

"Christ," Foster panted, his forehead resting against mine. "We have jobs to do."

"Do we?" I was having trouble remembering why that mattered when his hands were sliding under my t-shirt, mapping the skin of my back with calloused fingers.

"The students—"

"Can wait five more minutes."

Foster's laugh was breathless. "Five minutes? That's optimistic."

"Fine. Two minutes." I kissed the corner of his mouth. "One minute."

"You're going to be the death of me," he said, but he was smiling as he said it.

I was about to respond when Chickie chose that moment to bark at the door, the sound jolting us both back to reality. Foster stepped back, running a hand through his hair again, and I reluctantly hopped down from the table.

"Right," he said, his voice rough. "Coffee. Breakfast. *Responsibilities.*"

"Very adult of us," I agreed, though my voice wasn't much steadier.

We managed to get through the rest of our morning routine with only minimal additional contact, though I caught Foster staring when I pulled my SERA shirt on.

"See something you like, Sheriff?" I asked, unable to resist teasing him.

Instead of answering, Foster crossed the small space between us and reached for my collar, ostensibly to fix where it had gotten twisted. But his hands lingered, smoothing the fabric over my shoulders, his thumbs brushing the base of my throat.

"You missed a spot shaving," he said quietly, his thumb tracing a patch of stubble along my jaw.

"Did I?" My voice came out embarrassingly breathy.

"Mmm." His touch was featherlight, almost reverent. "Right here."

I leaned into the touch without thinking, and he made a sound in his throat. For a moment, we just stood there, him touching my face like it was something precious, me trying not to melt under the tenderness of it.

Then I leaned up and whispered in his ear, letting my lips brush the sensitive skin just below. "Tonight, I want to find out what you taste like when you come in my mouth."

Foster's whole body went rigid. "Jesus fucking Christ, Tommy."

"Too much?" I asked, pulling back to gauge his reaction.

His eyes were blown wide, pupils dilated, and he was breathing like he'd just run a mile. "We're going to be late," he said, but it sounded more like he was reminding himself than me.

"Save it for later?" I suggested.

"Yeah," he said roughly. "Fuck, yeah. Definitely saving it for later."

I grinned and headed for the door, grabbing my backpack from its spot by the door. "See you at breakfast, Sheriff."

"Tommy," he called after me, and I turned back. He was standing in the middle of our tiny cabin, hair still messed up, shirt rucked up, looking like sin and temptation and everything I'd never known I wanted.

"Yeah?"

He opened his mouth like he was going to say something, then seemed to think better of it. "Nothing. Just... be careful today."

"Always am."

"Yeah, right. Your eyes on my ass during technical rescues says something different."

I laughed, feeling lighter than I had in months. "It's called situational awareness, Foster. First rule of wilderness survival is you gotta keep an eye out for predators." I waggled my eyebrows.

Foster's answering smile was small but genuine. "Get out of here before I teach you what predators do when you get too close," he growled.

I grinned. "Always eager to learn." Then I shot him a wink and hurried out of the cabin before he could make good on his growl. I practically floated to the dining hall, whistling under my breath like an idiot.

Behind me, I heard Foster mutter something to Chickie that sounded a lot like, "Don't judge me! You've been practically humping the man since you met him," and I had to bite my lip to keep from laughing out loud.

For the next seven and a half weeks, I was going to enjoy every minute of this wild thing we'd started.

And I wouldn't let myself think about what came next.

11

FOSTER

THE ALARM WENT off at five thirty, but I was already awake, staring at the cabin ceiling and listening to Tommy's steady breathing from the bed three feet away.

It felt like Christmas morning. Today was another big SAR drill, one I'd spent the past two evenings meticulously planning for this week's SAR cohort.

I fucking loved this job. Being able to spend every single day teaching search and rescue was a dream come true. Watching the students' eyes light up as they suddenly grasped a concept, or answering smart questions that showed just how much they cared about their jobs, was addictive.

As I ran through everything I needed to do to prepare for the day, I felt that familiar calm settling over me, the one that always came when I knew I was exactly where I belonged.

Chickie must have sensed my movement because she lifted her head from her spot in the corner, tail already starting its morning helicopter routine. At six months old, she was still more enthusiasm than skill, but something about today felt different. Like maybe we were both ready to prove ourselves.

"Morning, girl," I whispered, swinging my legs out of bed. "You ready to show these kids how it's done?"

She bounded over, pressing her cold nose against my palm and doing that full-body wiggle that meant she was ready for anything.

Across from me, Tommy stirred but didn't wake. I tried to remind myself it was a good thing. The only reason we'd slept in separate beds was so that both of us could catch up on sleep before the big day.

For the past several nights, we'd stayed up way too late fucking around. Then, after falling asleep together, one of us would inevitably wake up to take a piss and wake the other, starting the fuck-around-and-fall-asleep cycle all over again. I hadn't had this many frotting and hand-job sessions since the law enforcement academy when I discovered two guys in my rookie class and I all shared something in common.

Tommy had talked a big talk about sucking me off, but inevitably, neither one of us took the time to do more than reach for each other and get off as quickly and desperately as possible. And I, for one, wasn't complaining. As long as my orgasm happened at Tommy Marian's hands, I didn't give a shit how it came about.

I dressed quietly in the pre-dawn darkness—tactical pants, base layer, boots that had seen more miles than most people's cars. As I packed my gear, Chickie danced around my feet, somehow managing to anticipate every piece of equipment I reached for.

GPS unit. Extra batteries. Emergency beacon. First aid kit. Hydration pack...

The familiar ritual steadied me, each item in its designated spot on my person or in my pack.

The real test today wouldn't just be for my students. Chickie had been working scent articles for weeks now, but this would be her first complex search with multiple distractors and challenging terrain. If she could hold focus today, actually track instead of just following her nose toward whoever had the best treats...

"Ignore Tommy out there," I murmured softly to her as she sat perfectly, watching me with those intelligent brown eyes. "He is not today's victim, understand? I promise you can find him all you want after the drill."

Her tail wagged in double time at the mention of his name, thumping on the bare wood floor with every pass.

Before I headed out to plant the clues and target dummy, I leaned over Tommy and blew hot air behind his ear before pressing my lips in the same spot and murmuring, "Wake up, Doc. Big day today. It wouldn't do to oversleep. I have it on good authority someone is going to need a complex medical response from your team later."

His hand snuck out of the sheet and into my hair as he held my face close. "Get your clothes off and get into this bed," he mumbled sleepily. "Doctor's orders."

"No can do. I need to get out and back before breakfast at

seven. Can you bring Chickie to the dining room? I don't want her cheating the drill by coming with me to plant the target."

"Mmhm. Chick, come." He took his hand out of my hair and patted the bed. Two seconds later, he was covered in hound.

By the time I slipped out of the cabin, the sky was starting to lighten behind the mountains, painting everything in shades of gray and gold. The morning air bit at my skin—crisp enough to keep me alert, but not cold enough to need special gear.

Perfect SAR weather, actually. It was forecast to be the kind of day that drew tourists to this region every summer. Giant blue sky, comic-book clouds, and clean, pine-scented air.

I fucking loved living in the Rocky Mountains, and this was one of the many reasons why.

The trail was almost deserted this time of morning, with the exception of one pair of older hikers, talking softly between sips of coffee from insulated aluminum mugs.

"Morning," I said, moving past them at a quick clip. As I made my way further down the trail, I thought back to the past several days. During the day, Tommy and I were—*mostly*—professional. Colleagues. Co-instructors intent on ensuring our groups were cross-trained on all aspects of wilderness emergency response. People who took our jobs and our mission seriously.

At night, however, we were like dogs in heat. As soon as the cabin door closed behind us and we were finally alone, we were grappling to get each other's clothes off, to get hands on bare skin and lips wherever we could.

There'd been no holding back for Tommy, no moment of awkwardness about hooking up with another man. In fact, he seemed to thrive on the physicality of it—being able to wrestle and command, pin each other, and even relish a little pain. Hair pulled a little too much, throat clasped firmly, wrists restrained in a strong grip.

Maybe he'd begun to see that he might have been missing something with women, something he needed and even craved.

And, if so, I tried my best to give it to him.

But strength wasn't the only thing Tommy Marian seemed to crave. He also melted under tenderness and kind consideration. I'd noticed his surprise when I'd offered to take care of him after a particularly messy hand job, when I'd washed him up with a warm cloth or kissed tender bruises I'd accidentally left on his wrist.

His eyes would flare wide and turn molten, and his chest would expand with a sucked-in breath. Every damned time.

And every time, I'd remember this was supposed to be casual and that I was blurring my own fucking lines. But it was impossible not to want to take care of him.

The radio squawked, scaring the fuck out of me and almost causing me to lose my footing.

"Base to Blake. Status check."

I shook my head and refocused on work before thumbing the radio. "Blake to base. ETA ten minutes."

THE TRAILHEAD BUZZED with nervous energy as the summer SAR cohort gathered under impossibly sunny skies. The group was a good mix of about thirty park rangers and deputies,

EMTs, a couple of adventure guides, and one guy who'd flown in from Switzerland just for this program.

"Alright, listen up," I called, spreading the terrain map across the hood of my truck. "We've got a missing hiker, twenty-six-year-old male, last seen on the Ridgeline Trail around fourteen hundred yesterday. He was supposed to meet friends at the parking area by eighteen hundred but never showed."

One of the students leaned in closer to study the map. "Any idea about his experience level?"

"Moderate. He's done this trail before, but weather moved in faster than predicted last night. Possible injury, possible exposure, possible he just got turned around in the fog."

I watched their faces as they processed the information. Good. No panic, but I could see the wheels turning.

"Weather's going to be a factor today, too," I continued, glancing up at the crystal clear sky. "You can't see it right now, but we've got a fictional weather system moving in quickly. Anticipate the unexpected. If visibility drops to shit, we'll have to pull everyone off the mountain. That's always a possibility in wilderness search and rescue, which means time is precious. Efficiency matters. The longer it takes to find our target, the more likely medical intervention becomes."

My students glanced over at Tommy's team about fifteen yards away. Even from here, I could see him moving through their equipment check with the same methodical efficiency I'd grown to admire. No wasted motion, no uncertainty. Just quiet competence that made everyone around him better.

Focus, Blake.

"Terrain's going to challenge you," I said, turning back to my students. "Dense undergrowth for the first two miles, then rocky scrambles with plenty of places to fall. The trail splits three times, and there are at least a dozen game paths that look legitimate if you're not paying attention."

I pointed to different areas on the map as I spoke, watching to make sure everyone was following along. "Jasper, you're team lead today. Sarah, you're backup. I want radio check-ins every thirty minutes, and I want you calling out everything you see— every piece of trash, every broken branch, every scuff mark that doesn't belong."

Jasper straightened his shoulders and glanced at me in surprise. "Me? You sure?"

I nodded.

He took a deep breath and swallowed hard but didn't disagree.

Jasper was one of the quieter students, and he got along well with both students and staff. I liked him a lot, on a personal level. But it frustrated me that he always tended to defer to other students in the group. If he wanted to be effective in an emergency situation, he needed to start thinking for himself and take some initiative.

When I'd said as much to Tommy the other night, though, those hazel eyes had twinkled at me, and he'd shaken his head. *"Sometimes it takes people a minute to find their footing in a new situation,"* he'd reminded me gently. *"Why don't you talk to him and find out what his deal really is? Or, at the very least, give him a fair shake and a chance to prove himself?"*

This made sense, so I'd decided to see what Jasper was capable of.

"Any questions?" I asked the group.

"What about the dog?" asked Jenna, a guide from Utah who'd been skeptical of Chickie from day one. "She's still pretty young. Can we rely on her?"

I glanced down at Chickie, who was sitting at perfect attention despite the chaos around us. "Consider her a student, just like yourself. She'll rise to the challenge today, or she won't. Since this is a learning experience for everyone, there's no failure here, only opportunity for more learning."

As the teams finished their gear checks, I caught sight of Tommy in my peripheral vision. He was crouched next to his medical kit, walking one of his students through proper medication dosing for altitude sickness. Even from this far away, I could hear the patience in his voice, the way he turned a complex calculation into something his student could actually understand and remember.

The guy was a natural teacher. Hell, he was a natural at most things he tried, which should have been annoying but somehow just made me want to watch him work.

Or take him back to the cabin and watch him being a natural at other new things—

"Foster?" Sarah's voice snapped me back to attention. "We ready to move out?"

Right. Yes. *Focus.*

"Yeah. Gear up," I called. "Let's move before our storm comes in."

The first hour on the trail was exactly what I'd expected—controlled chaos as my team tried to remember everything they'd learned while navigating terrain that seemed designed to trip them up. Gradually, though, they found their rhythm.

Jasper proved he had the backbone for leadership, making decisive calls about witness interviews and search patterns while keeping everyone focused on the task at hand. Sarah backed him up without trying to take over, and even Jenna started working with Chickie instead of around her.

"Hold up. Our twelve o'clock, about forty yards," Jasper called out, pointing a finger. His voice carried easily across the rocky terrain. "Marcus on scope, see anything?"

Marcus pulled up his binoculars, scanning the tree line. "Nothing yet. Wait—is that fabric caught on that pine branch?"

"Good eye, Jasper," Tommy called, adjusting his medical pack as his group picked their way up the slope to join mine. "Foster, remind me again why you couldn't have hidden our victim somewhere with less elevation change? My quads are filing a formal complaint."

"Lightweight city boy," I muttered, shooting him a wink. "Forty-five minutes of hiking and you're already whining. What happened to all that residency stamina?"

"That was *standing* stamina. For twelve-hour shifts in climate-controlled buildings with vending machines every fifty feet." Tommy paused, making a show of pressing his hand to his chest. "This is cruel and unusual punishment."

"Marcus," I called to one of the students, giving Tommy a chance to catch his breath. "What's your next move?"

"Assess the evidence quickly but carefully," Marcus replied promptly. "And maybe leave Dr. Marian here to recover?"

"Hey!" Tommy protested with a breathy laugh. "I'll have you know I was an excellent rock climber in college."

"*Was* being the operative word," I teased, steadying Tommy's elbow as he nearly slipped on loose rock. "When were you in college again? When the Beatles were hot?"

"How about Imagine Dragons? I'm only thirty-two, you ass. Two years younger than you, I might add."

Chickie bounded ahead of the group, nose to the ground, tail wagging frantically. She'd definitely caught something.

"At least someone's doing their job properly," I observed, watching Chickie work. "Unlike certain medical professionals who are too busy complaining to notice we've got visual contact with our target."

Tommy glanced at the "injured hiker"—actually Robyn in a torn shirt and dramatic fake blood—waving weakly from behind a boulder about twenty yards ahead. "I'm here in a supervisory role, Sheriff. My team can handle the medical assessment. I run a tight ship."

He dropped his pack and stretched. "Where are those endorphins I learned about in medical school?" he asked with a grin.

"I thought you were one of those good-boy types. Didn't Matthew say you two went to the same gym?"

He grinned. "Working out in a New York gym is different. Surprisingly low altitude variance, for one thing. And much thicker air."

My cohort stood nearby and chuckled at Tommy's teasing. Jasper asked, "Wishing we'd had this drill in Brooklyn instead?"

Tommy shrugged and pulled one knee up in an exaggerated glute stretch. "Nah. I've always loved this mountain. There's nothing I miss about New York—except I wouldn't mind if someone would set up some food trucks out by the trailhead."

I couldn't help but laugh, the sound echoing off the rocks and trees around us. "Not likely, Doc. But how about we take these guys out for pizza and beer tonight?"

"If you're talking about Timber, you've got a deal."

We were standing closer now, the familiar rhythm of our banter pulling us into our own little bubble despite the crowd around us. Tommy's eyes were bright with laughter, and I caught myself staring at the way the light caught the gold flecks in his irises.

Dangerous territory. We were supposed to be professional out here.

Thankfully, Omar, one of the med cohort students assessing the "victim," asked Tommy a question, causing him to move closer to Robyn for the response.

My SAR group and I huddled together to determine the best way to extract her back to the trailhead safely.

Forty minutes later, when we'd finished rigging up the ropes and harness and successfully sent Robyn off in a fictional ambulance, we began our walk back to SERA from the trailhead.

Tommy and I ended up at the back of the pack, watching the students chatting excitedly ahead of us, proud of a job well done.

This—this day, this rhythm, this partnership between our teams—was what happiness could look like. Two people who were good at their jobs, good together, building something that mattered.

Tommy glanced over at me. "This kind of medicine… it's exactly what I went to medical school for. The improvisation, the teamwork, working with limited resources…"

He trailed off, but I caught the wistful note in his voice. The longing.

Then stay, I wanted to say. *Stay here and do this kind of work. Stay close to me.*

Instead, I deflected. "Better than standing in some fluorescent-lit ER all day, right?"

Tommy glanced at me for a beat before plastering on a smile. "In summer, maybe. In winter, the ER seems downright cozy compared to dangling off a rock face in the ice and wind."

I thought back to that exact same scenario I'd been in only six months before.

"Been there," I muttered, making him laugh.

"No shit?"

I nodded and met his eyes. "The day I met you, actually."

Before I could tell him the story, Robyn appeared. "Great work today, you two," she said. "Tommy, can I grab you for a quick debrief before lunch?"

He smiled at her, an expression that seemed more genuine than the one he'd given me. The sharp bite of jealousy surprised me. I knew Robyn was interested in Tommy, if her flirty smiles and the way she swished her ponytail were any indication, but I hadn't sensed any particular interest on his part.

You're being ridiculous, I warned myself. *And besides, it doesn't matter. This is a summer fling. Physical only, remember?*

I knew better than to want more than that.

Didn't I?

As the teams dispersed and headed for lunch, I found myself standing alone at the trailhead with Chickie, watching Tommy disappear down the path. Even from here, I could see him falling into easy conversation with Robyn and the students around them, his natural charisma drawing everyone to him like a magnet.

Chickie whined softly and pressed against my leg, as if she could sense my mood shifting. I reached down to scratch her ears, grateful for her uncomplicated affection.

"Come on, girl," I said, shouldering my pack. "Let's go get something to eat."

But as we walked toward the dining hall, I couldn't shake the image of Tommy's face when he'd talked about this kind of medicine. The way his whole expression had lit up, like he was remembering who he used to be before hospital politics and city life wore him down.

And I couldn't stop wondering what would have happened if I'd been brave enough to say what I was really thinking.

Stay. Please. Just stay.

Let's figure it out together.

12

TOMMY

THE ADRENALINE from the morning's drill was still humming through my veins as I watched my team head to the dining room, their faces flushed with the kind of satisfaction that only came from nailing something difficult. Sierra was practically glowing as she recounted her triage decisions to the others. And even Omar, who'd initially been skeptical about SERA's requirement that all students participate in a medical training rotation since he was eager to get to practice "real SAR stuff," was asking thoughtful questions about medication protocols in wilderness settings.

"Dr. Marian," Cody said as he stopped by the door to the dining hall and held it open for me to pass, "that was fucking awesome. I have first aid training and some field experience, but this was next-level. How do I get more training like this after SERA?"

Familiar warmth spread through my chest—the same

feeling I used to get during my wilderness medicine rotation in residency, before staffing nightmares and endless paperwork had slowly leached the joy out of practicing medicine.

"There are other programs, including the advanced level one here at SERA," I said. "But honestly? The best training is exactly what you're doing now. Get out here, make mistakes, learn from them. Medicine in the field isn't about having the perfect equipment or the latest protocols. It's about adapting and trusting your instincts."

As I said it, I realized how true it felt. How *right* it felt to be standing here in pine-scented air, my hands still steady from the morning's challenges, surrounded by students who were hungry to learn not just the mechanics of emergency medicine but the art of it.

When was the last time I'd felt this energized after a shift? When was the last time I'd looked forward to the next challenge instead of dreading another twelve hours of controlled chaos and electronic medical records?

"You look happy," Robyn observed, falling into step beside me as we headed through the dining room toward her office.

"Just thinking," I said. "About how different this feels from hospital work."

"Good different or bad different?"

"Good different," I said. "Very good."

"Excellent!" Robyn said with cheerleader-like enthusiasm. "That's wonderful to hear."

As we entered her office, she turned to face me. The fake blood from the training exercise was smeared on her torn shirt, making a funny contrast with her signature friendly smile.

"On that topic, I wanted to let you know your medical licensing came in." She rocked back and forth on her boots. "You're licensed to practice in the state of Montana. Isn't that great?"

I blinked at her. This was good news, but hardly a surprise. "Uh, yeah. Great."

"This means you can practice here!"

"I... yeah, I got that. Trace wanted me to get licensed if I could, and reciprocal licensing was pretty quick and straightforward."

She propped her hip on her desk. "I think he was hoping to convince you to stay on permanently."

I laughed. "He mentioned that. But he also knows I'm interviewing for a position in California, near my family. Besides," I said, trying to keep it light, "he can't afford me."

She smiled up at me, eyes bright. "Just think about it, okay? I'm sure he'd make as strong of an offer as possible."

"I appreciate that, Robyn. I really do. But I'm an ER doc. I can't turn down the opportunity to work at a world-renowned teaching hospital."

Her smile faltered, but she nodded. "I understand. Worth a shot."

I reached out and squeezed her shoulder. "I really appreciate it. It's nice to know I'm doing well enough for you not to want to boot me out."

She laughed and gave me a quick hug. "We just think the world of you, Tommy."

I pulled away awkwardly with a mumbled *thanks* and turned to head back to the dining room. Foster had just passed the office on his way to the men's room, so I followed him there instead.

As soon as the door closed behind me, I glanced under the stalls to make sure we were the only ones in there.

"You get what you need in there?" Foster asked, keeping his eye on the urinal as he reached for his fly.

I kicked a nearby rubber wedge under the door so no one could open it, and then I walked up behind him and crowded him against the urinal. "Not one single bit," I said in a low voice.

"Mpfh. Looked plenty friendly to me," he grumbled. "Back off. I can't do this with you watching."

I eased off but pressed my forehead to the center of his back, just above his shoulder blades. "Good drill this morning."

"Yep."

"Is it wrong to wish the workday came with a sex break?" I asked softly, just in case someone was near enough to hear me.

He finished up and moved to the sink, gently dislodging me by rolling his shoulder. "I could go for it. Maybe we should form a union and make some demands."

I met his eye in the mirror and was happy to see his eyes sparkling with humor. I took his place at the urinal and opened my pants, trying to hurry now in case someone else needed to use the bathroom.

Foster yanked out a couple of paper towels and turned to face me as he dried his hands. I tried to stay relaxed.

"What did Rainbow Brite want with you?"

Was it my imagination, or was there a tinge of jealousy coming from the big guy?

"Hmm. Take a guess." I finished and refastened my pants

before moving to the sink. This time, Foster crowded up against my back, his arms snaking around my front and his hot lips landing on my neck.

"I'm thinking she wants to join your union," he grumbled. The sound was low near my ear, enough to make the hairs stand on end all over my arms and legs.

I shuddered. "No. Just wanted to tell me my licensure came through. Now maybe I won't get arrested for playing doctor."

His big hand moved down over my fly and pressed my cock. "Mmm, arresting someone for playing doctor... I knew I became a sheriff for a reason."

I finished washing my hands and dried them as quickly as possible.

And if there were wet handprints on Foster Blake's clothes when we returned to the dining room, it was nobody's business where they came from.

AFTER LUNCH, Robyn appeared with a mischievous glint in her eye that usually meant "a super-fun activity" for someone. This time, apparently, that someone was all of us.

"Alright, listen up," she announced, clipboard in hand. "We're doing something a little different this afternoon. Since you'll all be moving to your new rotations tomorrow, Trace and I put together a friendly team-building competition. Winner gets first pick at tonight's s'mores supplies. I'll tell you more when we get to the trailhead."

Once we were there, she waved us over to a couple of

nearby picnic tables, where she placed a brown paper bag on the center table.

"We're dividing up into two teams, on the hunt for a missing person. The twist is that your instructors will be equal members of the team, if they're up for it. You can use them as resources however you want. Each team will get a fabricated patient history, recent medical records, a medication list, terrain maps, weather data, and witness statements. First team to locate and properly assess the victim without additional evidence wins."

Everyone chattered with excitement as she explained that the instructors had already been divided up, but the students would be drawing numbers to see who was on which team for the game.

I felt a competitive spark ignite in my chest. It had been years since I'd been a true member of a SAR team, so I relished the chance to play. Problem-solving under pressure, medical deduction, teamwork—all the things that had drawn me to emergency medicine in the first place.

"Dr. Marian," Cody said, grinning widely, "I got Yellow Team. Please tell me you're in."

"I am." I pulled on the yellow buff Robyn handed me and glanced across the field where Foster—in a blue buff—stood with his arms crossed, one eyebrow raised in what looked suspiciously like a challenge. When our eyes met, his mouth curved into that slow, devastating smile that made my pulse spike.

"Game on, Sheriff," I called, earning whoops of approval from my team.

Foster's answering grin was sharp as a blade. "Hope you're ready to lose, Doc."

The next hour unfolded like the world's most entertaining puzzle. Yellow Team—which comprised me, Tevita, Gus, and our students—huddled around a picnic table, mostly focusing on the fabricated medical records Robyn had provided. Our missing person was a fifty-three-year-old male with a history of diabetes, recent knee surgery, and a prescription for pain medication that could cause disorientation.

"Look at this," Sierra said, pointing to the medication list. "Oxycodone prescribed three days ago, but the bottle's nearly empty. Either he's not following dosing instructions, or..."

"Or he's having breakthrough pain that's affecting his judgment," I finished. "Good call. Someone in that much discomfort isn't going to be thinking clearly about navigation."

Meanwhile, I could see Foster's team poring over topographic maps, Marcus tracing elevation lines with his finger while Jenna studied weather pattern reports from the past twenty-four hours.

"The witness statement says he was headed for Miller's Point," Marcus was saying, voice carrying across the meadow. "But look at this terrain. If he was disoriented, he could have easily taken the wrong fork at Cascade Junction."

"And if he did," Foster added, "he'd end up in Willow Basin instead. Classic mistake for someone not thinking clearly."

I felt a thrill of professional appreciation watching him work. Foster's tactical mind was impressive—the way he could read terrain like a story, predict human behavior under stress, see patterns that others missed.

"Dr. Marian?" Sierra's voice pulled me back to our own strategizing. "Earth to Tommy?"

Heat crept up my neck. "Sorry. What were you saying?"

"I said, based on his medical history and current medications, where would you expect to find him?"

I forced myself to focus on the papers in front of me, but I remained acutely aware of Foster's presence across the field. The confident way he moved, the respect his students showed him, the occasional burst of laughter from his team that made me want to be part of their inner circle.

Concentrate, Marian.

"Okay," I said, studying the medication list again. "Diabetic, recently post-surgical, probably in pain, and possibly not thinking clearly. He's going to seek shelter somewhere comfortable—not necessarily the most logical hiding spot, but somewhere that feels safe."

"Like where?" Cody asked.

I thought about it, remembering my own experiences with post-surgical patients. "Somewhere enclosed but not claustrophobic. Somewhere he can sit or lie down comfortably. Maybe somewhere that reminds him of home."

Twenty minutes later, both teams converged on a small wooden shelter near the base of Miller's Point—Foster's team arriving thirty seconds ahead of us, but my team carrying a more comprehensive treatment plan for the "victim" we found inside.

"Only a doctor," Foster muttered as we debriefed later, "would win a rescue challenge by diagnosing a sprained ankle from a half-eaten Clif bar wrapper."

"Clinical deduction based on years of treating post-surgical patients with complications," I protested, grinning.

"Show-off," Foster said, but there was no heat in it. If anything, he looked impressed.

"Sore loser," I shot back.

"I'm not sore. My team got there first."

"But did your team correctly identify the secondary injury and implement proper pain management protocols?"

Foster's students were watching our exchange with barely concealed delight, like they were witnessing something entertaining unfold. Sierra elbowed me and grinned.

"You two are ridiculous," she said. "You bicker like my parents."

Foster's cheeks turned pink, but he didn't deny it. Instead, he turned to address both teams with exaggerated formality. "Excellent work today, everyone. Yellow Team wins on technical points—"

My team gave a deafening cheer.

"— but my Blue Team maintains our superior tracking abilities."

Blue Team chuckled and fist-bumped one another.

"Diplomatic," I said with a laugh.

Foster shrugged. "I'm a peacekeeper by nature."

"You're a competitive asshole by nature."

"Says the man who diagnosed a sprained ankle from trash!"

And just like that, we were bickering again, our students laughing around us like this was the best entertainment they'd had all week.

Maybe it was.

THE CAMPFIRE that night glowed like a beacon in the meadow behind the main building. Most of the students had drifted off early, exhausted from the day's competitions and anticipating tomorrow's early start, leaving just a handful of instructors scattered around the crackling flames.

I'd claimed a spot on one of the log benches, close enough to the fire to feel its warmth but far enough back to see the stars emerging overhead. The night air carried the scent of woodsmoke and pine, and somewhere in the distance, an owl called through the darkness.

Foster appeared at my elbow with a flask and two cups. "Bourbon, Dr. Marian?"

"God, yes."

He settled beside me, close enough that I could feel the warmth of his thigh against mine. The flask made its way around our small circle—Trace, Robyn, Monroe, Tevita, and a couple of others—but somehow, it kept coming back to rest between Foster and me.

"Alright," Trace said, poking at the fire with a long stick. "Time for ridiculous rescue stories. It's a SERA fireside tradition. I'll start."

He launched into a tale about a tourist who'd gotten "lost" just to meet the famous country singer who happened to be vacationing in the area, complete with staged ankle injury and a suspiciously well-stocked emergency kit.

I recognized the story since it was about my uncle, Jude, but

I enjoyed hearing Trace tell it with all the embellishments that had been added over the years.

The stories got progressively more absurd as the bourbon flowed. Robyn told us about a search and rescue operation that turned into an impromptu engagement when the lost hiker's boyfriend proposed at the rescue site. Another instructor shared the saga of a park ranger's pet iguana with a talent for opening first aid kits.

"Your turn, Tommy," Foster said, nudging my shoulder.

I took a sip of bourbon, feeling its warmth spread through my chest. "River rescue in North Carolina during my wilderness rotation. Got called out for a possible drowning, but when we got there, we found this guy with a broken arm, sitting on a rock in the middle of the river and raving about something at the top of his lungs. By the time we figured out he was upset about a fucking goat—which, by the way, sounds an awful lot like *fucking boat*—said goat had consumed half our medical supplies."

"A goat ate your med kit?" Robyn asked, incredulous.

Foster chuckled beside me. "Please tell me you at least got the guy off the rock."

I rolled my eyes. "Eventually. But not before the goat bit the laces off my boot, and I had to improvise with a vine just to get back to the trailhead."

His laughter was big and warm like the man himself. Magnetic. Addictive.

Our eyes met, and something passed between us—easy and comfortable and charged with possibility. This felt *right*. Sitting here, trading stories, the bourbon making everything hazy around the edges while the stars wheeled overhead.

Like kismet, Ella would have teased.

"Your turn, Sheriff," I said. "And it better be good."

Foster shifted, his shoulder brushing mine. "Search and rescue call last summer. Elderly tourist from Florida, supposedly lost on the Upper Maude switchback. We mobilized half the department, called in volunteers, spent six hours combing the wilderness..."

"Uh-oh," Tevita groaned.

"And?" Trace prompted, already grinning.

"Found him at the Love Muffin—our local cafe—browbeating the owner, who happens to be my mother, and asking detailed questions about my relationship status."

The laughter that erupted from our group was loud enough to echo off the surrounding trees. Even Robyn nearly fell off her log.

"He got lost on purpose?" I asked while silently thinking, *Can't blame the guy.*

"Oh, it gets better. Turns out he'd read an article about me in some tourism magazine—'Eligible Bachelor Sheriff Saves Lives and Hearts' or some shit like that. He figured a rescue scenario was the perfect meet-cute opportunity."

Trace hooted.

"Awww. Please tell me you let him down gently," Robyn said.

Foster grinned. "I introduced him to a local judge, who happened to be single and looking. He and Judge Whiteplume are on a monthlong motorcycle trip in Colorado right now."

"You hopeless romantic," I said, before I could stop myself.

Something shifted in Foster's expression, the easy humor replaced by something more serious. "Maybe."

The conversation continued around us, but I found myself increasingly aware of Foster's presence beside me. The way his fingers drummed against his thigh. The occasional brush of his arm against mine when he reached for the flask. The way the firelight caught the amber flecks in his hair.

Eventually, the other instructors began drifting away, murmuring about early mornings and evaluation reports. Soon, it was just Foster and me, the fire burning lower, the bourbon making everything feel soft and possible.

"You were kind of amazing today, you know," I said quietly, bumping his knee with mine.

Foster ducked his head, but he didn't pull away. "Experience."

"Maybe." I studied his profile in the firelight—the strong line of his jaw, the way his lashes cast shadows on his cheeks. "But the way you read that terrain, predicted exactly where someone in distress would go... that's not just training. That's instinct. And the way the students look at you—they don't just respect you, they trust you completely."

"It's a good group."

"It is. But you make them better."

Foster was quiet for a long moment, staring into the flames. When he finally spoke, his voice was barely above a whisper. "You're good at this, too, you know. Better than good. These students would follow you anywhere."

The compliment hit me squarely in the chest, warm and

unexpected. No one in New York had seen me like that, but here...

Here, I felt like myself again.

Spending the summer in Montana had definitely been the right choice.

I leaned back on my hands, tilting my head to study the stars scattered across the mountain sky. The Milky Way stretched overhead like a river of light, clearer than I'd ever seen it from the city.

"I forgot how beautiful it is out here," I said. "How quiet. How..." I searched for the word. "Clean everything feels."

Foster followed my gaze upward. "Living out here, under this sky... it gets in your blood after a while. Makes it hard to imagine being anywhere else."

Something in his tone made me look at him more closely. There was a wistfulness there, a longing that spoke to something deep in my chest.

"Foster," I started, then stopped. What was I going to say? That I wished I could stay? Give up everything I'd worked for on the off chance things might work between us?

It was crazy. It was impractical. It was exactly the kind of romantic notion that my rational, achievement-oriented brain should have dismissed immediately.

But sitting there in the firelight, the taste of bourbon on my tongue and the memory of today's perfect partnership still fresh in my mind, it didn't feel crazy at all.

It felt real. It felt *true*.

"Just... thanks," I said finally. "For today. For experiencing this with me."

Foster's smile was soft and genuine. "Thanks for making it interesting."

We sat in comfortable silence after that, watching the fire burn down to embers while the night settled around us. Eventually, the cold drove us back toward the cabins, but I found myself walking slowly, reluctant to break the spell of the evening.

For the first time in a long time, I didn't feel like I was running toward something or away from something else. I felt like I was currently, even if just for a short time, exactly where I was supposed to be.

And if I was honest with myself, that had everything to do with the man walking beside me, hands shoved deep in his pockets, looking like he belonged under these stars in ways I was only beginning to understand.

13

FOSTER

THE PAST TWO weeks had been a blur of stolen moments and sleepless nights. Of Tommy's hands on my skin, his mouth on mine, and him whispering my name against my throat when he thought I was asleep.

Strictly physical, I'd said.

Well, fuck knew, we had the physical part down.

The "strictly" part wasn't going quite as well for me. Not when my stomach somersaulted every time Tommy smiled at me from across the training yard, or a mountain trail, or a classroom. Not when I found myself holding him—fine, *cuddling* him—long after he fell asleep, just so I could spend a few more minutes inhaling the clean, citrus scent of his shampoo. Not when I'd had to stop myself multiple times from thinking, "Next summer, Tommy and I should..." as though another summer with him was a thing I might have.

But I wasn't the only one suffering from my distraction. Chickie's training had suffered, too.

And that stopped today.

"Come on, girl," I called, clipping on her leash as she bounded toward me with her usual enthusiasm. "Time to actually learn something useful."

I'd picked a secluded meadow at the outer edge of campus, far enough away that we wouldn't be disturbed but close enough people could find us if we were needed. The morning sun slanted through the pine trees, warming the grass and creating perfect conditions for scent work.

Tommy appeared from our cabin, looking unfairly good in tactical pants and a fitted SERA T-shirt. "You sure you want me for this? I don't know anything about dog training."

"You don't need to," I said, trying to ignore the way his shirt pulled across his chest. "You'll be the victim. Chickie needs to learn to track."

"I can do that," Tommy said, crouching down to let Chickie lick his face. "Hey there, girl. Ready to learn some new tricks?"

I rolled my eyes but couldn't help smiling. These past weeks had shown me a side of Tommy I hadn't expected—playful, curious, completely lacking in ego about learning new things. He'd asked a dozen questions about search and rescue techniques, had practiced rope knots until his fingers were sore, and never once acted like his medical degree made him too important for other wilderness skills.

It was endearing as hell. And dangerous for my peace of mind.

"Alright, first lesson," I said, pulling a plastic bag from my pack. "Scent articles. She needs to learn your specific scent, not just follow any human trail."

Tommy raised an eyebrow. "How exactly do we do that?"

"By giving her something that smells like you." I handed him the bag. "I stole the shirt you wore yesterday. Rub it on your hands, maybe your neck. The stronger the scent, the better."

I watched as Tommy worked the fabric between his palms, then dragged it along his throat. The simple motion shouldn't have been erotic, but the damned tease wanted to make an entire meal out of the thing.

"Like this?" he asked, batting his eyes with mock innocence.

I yanked it away from him and muttered, "I feel like I'm suddenly in a threesome with that shirt."

For the first fifteen minutes, everything went smoothly. I walked Tommy through the basics. How to lay a scent trail by walking normally but letting the shirt drag the ground slightly behind him. Where to hide so Chickie would have to work to find him but not get frustrated. How to reward her with praise and treats when she succeeded.

The problem was that every lesson required me to touch him. Guiding his hands to show him the right angle for dragging the shirt. Crouching behind him to demonstrate how to move quietly through the underbrush. Standing close enough to smell his shampoo—that fucking delicious shampoo—while I explained the theory behind scent dispersal.

"Alright," I said after Tommy had successfully laid his first practice trail. "Now, hide behind that fallen log, and let's see if she can find you."

Tommy jogged over to the designated spot while I held Chickie back, letting her get excited about the game. "Find Tommy," I told her, releasing her leash.

What happened next was not tracking. It was a missile launch.

Chickie took off like she'd been shot from a cannon, completely ignoring the careful, meandering scent trail Tommy had laid and heading straight for his hiding spot. She didn't pause to sniff or investigate—she just ran directly to him like she had GPS coordinates.

"Chickie, *no!*" I called, but it was too late.

She launched herself at Tommy, knocking him backward onto his ass and covering his face with enthusiastic licks before he could even attempt to make her sit and wait for her reward.

"Well, she found me," Tommy laughed as he tried to fend off her overexcited affections.

I jogged over and grabbed her collar, pulling her back. "That's not tracking. That's just... following her favorite person around. She's supposed to use her nose, not her emotional attachment."

"Well, isn't scent sometimes tied to emotional attachment?" he asked, grinning as he wiped dog slobber off his cheek.

I ran a hand through my hair and huffed out a laugh, thinking about my new fascination with citrus shampoo. "Christ, I hope not."

"What?"

"Nothing. Let's try again."

We tried again, but with the same result. Chickie ignored the scent trail entirely and went straight to Tommy like she was playing fetch with a person instead of a ball. She was clearly not learning to track. No matter how far into the trees he zigzagged and hid, she hotfooted it right to his location as fast as canine-ly possible.

"This isn't working," I muttered after the fifth failed attempt. "She's too excited about you to focus on actual tracking work."

Tommy sat up, brushing grass off his shirt. "So what do we do?"

"We switch," I decided, handing him Chickie's leash. "You handle her, I'll be the victim. She needs to learn to work with someone who isn't her obsession."

"Are you sure? I don't know the first thing about handling a tracking dog."

"You'll learn," I said, yanking off my T-shirt and rubbing it under my arms before handing it over. "Besides, it'll be good practice for both of you."

Tommy's eyes blinked a few times in rapid succession as he stared at my bare chest before glancing up at my eyes with a dazed look on his face. "Practice makes perfect."

For the next thirty minutes, I coached Tommy through handling techniques while I laid trails with volunteer scent articles from other students while hiding others. This worked much better—Chickie actually had to use her nose to find the target, and Tommy learned how to read her body language, when to encourage her, and how to reward success.

"You're good at this," I called from behind him as Tommy guided Chickie through a particularly tricky section of trail. "She's actually working now instead of just running to her favorite person."

"She's incredible," Tommy called back, and I could hear the genuine pride in his voice as Chickie successfully navigated around a fallen tree to continue following the scent. "Look at her go!"

When Chickie finally found the target, she sat and waited for her reward like she was supposed to, tail wagging but focused on Tommy for direction.

"Good girl!" Tommy praised, giving her a treat and lots of pets. "You did such a good job!"

The sight of them working together, Tommy's patient encouragement and Chickie's growing confidence, did something dangerous to my chest, and I had to admit that exactly what I'd been afraid of had come to pass. It wasn't just physical attraction that made me crave him the way I did, but this. The way he fit into my world like he'd always belonged here. The way he looked at Chickie like she was his dog, too.

The way he looked at me like I was something more than... well, something *more*.

"You try being the victim again," I said, trying to keep my voice steady. "And this time, make the trail more challenging."

We'd just started the next round—thankfully with my shirt back on—when I heard voices approaching through the trees. I turned to see Robyn striding toward our meadow, her blonde ponytail swinging as she walked.

"There you are!" she called out cheerfully. "I've been looking everywhere for you two."

My jaw clenched automatically. "We're training."

"I can see that," she said, her attention immediately focusing on Tommy as he emerged from behind a boulder with

Chickie trotting proudly at his heels. "Tommy, you're so good with her! You have such a natural way with animals."

I watched as Robyn stepped closer to Tommy, her hand briefly touching his arm as she praised his technique. The casual contact set my teeth on edge.

"It's all Foster," Tommy said, completely missing the way Robyn was looking at him. "He's an incredible trainer."

"I'm sure," she said, but her eyes never left Tommy's face. "Actually, that's why I was looking for you. We're planning the evening campfire program, and I thought you might want to help. You'd be perfect for it."

"Oh." Tommy glanced at me, then back at Robyn. "It's nice of you to ask, but—"

"It'll be fun," Robyn continued, stepping even closer. "We could use someone with your people skills. And your..." She grinned up at him. "Your way of explaining things."

I felt something hot and possessive flare in my chest. *Mine.* The thought came unbidden and unwelcome, but I couldn't shake it. Tommy was mine, at least for now, and watching Robyn flirt with him like I wasn't even there made me want to mark my territory in the most primitive way possible. Like the predator he'd once jokingly accused me of being.

That was impossible for several reasons, of course.

First, he wasn't actually mine. At no point had we made a commitment to anything other than hooking up. We'd never said we'd remain exclusive, not even for the summer.

And then there was the fact he wasn't out. Or... whatever. It wasn't my business to even act in a way that might imply Tommy was less than the straight man he appeared to be.

"Foster and I have training to finish," Tommy said politely.

"I can send a student to take your place," Robyn said, tilting her head at me. "Maybe one of your *search* and rescue students?"

"No need," I said, my voice flat. "Come on, Chickie. Let's take a walk."

I turned and started walking toward the trees, Chickie's leash tight in my hand. Behind me, I heard Tommy say something apologetic to Robyn, then the sound of footsteps following me.

"Foster, wait up."

I kept walking, my jaw clenched so tight it ached. This was exactly what I'd been afraid of—that I'd start thinking of Tommy as mine when he wasn't. When he never could be.

"Foster." Tommy's hand caught my arm, spinning me around. "What the hell was that about?"

"Nothing." I glanced over his shoulder toward the meadow before realizing we were too deep in the trees to still catch sight of Robyn. "You should go help with the campfire program. Sounds important."

Tommy stepped closer, his eyes narrowing. "Are you... jealous?"

"Don't be ridiculous."

"You are," he said, and I could hear the amazement in his voice. "You're actually jealous of Robyn."

"Why would I be jealous?" The words came out sharper than I intended. "You can flirt with whoever you want. It's not like we're—"

Tommy backed me against the nearest tree before I could

finish the sentence, his hands braced on either side of my head. "Not like we're what?"

His body was pressed against mine, warm and solid and completely focused on me. I could smell his scent mixed with pine needles and fresh air, could see the challenge in his eyes.

"Together," I finished weakly.

"No?" Tommy's voice was low, dangerous. "Then what do you call what we've been doing every night for the past week?"

"*Two* weeks," I corrected. My face heated, and my brain scrambled for an answer that didn't make me sound like a complete asshole. "And I call it... temporary."

Something flashed in Tommy's eyes—hurt, maybe, or anger. But then his mouth was on mine, hard and demanding, and all rational thought fled.

This wasn't the gentle exploration we'd been doing in our cabin. This was possession, claiming, a reminder of exactly who I belonged to, whether I cared to admit it or not. Tommy's tongue swept into my mouth as his hands fisted in my shirt, pulling me closer.

I groaned and kissed him back just as desperately, my hands sliding down to grip his ass and pull him flush against me. He made a sound low in his throat that went straight to my cock.

"Just temporary, huh?" he asked against my lips.

Before I could answer, he was kissing me again, one hand sliding up to tangle in my hair while the other worked its way under my shirt. His fingers found the sensitive spot just below my ribs, and I had to bite back a moan.

"Tommy," I managed, though I wasn't sure if it was a warning or a plea.

"Tell me you don't want this," he said, his mouth moving to my throat. "Tell me you don't think about this every second of every day."

I couldn't. Because I *did* think about him constantly. Had since Hawaii. Every breath, every heartbeat, every quiet moment—he was there.

"I can't," I admitted, the words torn from somewhere deep in my chest.

Tommy pulled back to look at me, his eyes dark with want and something softer. "Then stop pretending this doesn't mean anything."

Instead of answering, I spun us around, pressing him back against the tree. His eyes widened in surprise, then heated as I dropped to my knees in front of him.

"What are you—oh, fuck." His words dissolved into a groan as I worked open his belt, then the button of his pants.

"Can this conversation be over?" I asked, looking up at him through my lashes. "Because I can think of something I'd like on my tongue way more than fucking feelings right now."

Tommy's head fell back against the bark, his breathing already ragged. "Christ, please."

I pulled his cock free, already hard and leaking, and wrapped my lips around the head. Tommy's hips jerked forward involuntarily, and his hands flew to my hair.

"Foster, *fuck*—"

I took him deeper, hollowing my cheeks as I worked my way down his length. The taste of him, salt and musk, was just as exciting as I'd known it would be.

For weeks, I'd been trying to hold back with Tommy. To

keep from rushing him when I guessed this was all new to him. To keep from rushing myself, when I knew how close I was to swan diving into love with him. But now I couldn't hold back.

Seeing how much he wanted me made my own cock throb against my zipper. His fingers tightened in my hair, not pushing but holding, like he needed the anchor.

"Jesus, your mouth," he gasped, trying to keep his voice down. "I can't—oh god, just like that."

I pulled back to tongue at his slit, gathering the precum there before taking him deep again. His thighs were trembling against my shoulders, and when I looked up at him through my lashes, his head was thrown back against the bark, mouth open as he fought to stay quiet.

"Foster, I'm not going to last," he warned, his voice strained.

Good. I wanted him desperate, wanted him to remember this every time he looked at me for the rest of the summer, no matter who was standing beside him. Wanted him to remember long after the summer was over, too, the sight of me on my knees for him, making him shake and moan and beg.

I redoubled my efforts, using my hand to work what my mouth couldn't reach while I sucked harder.

"Shit, shit, I'm—" Tommy's warning cut off in a strangled moan as he came, his release hitting the back of my throat in hot pulses. I swallowed it all, working him through it until he was boneless against the tree.

When I finally pulled off and sat back on my heels, Tommy was staring down at me with something close to awe.

"That was..." he started, then seemed to lose the words.

"Good?" I asked, wiping my mouth with the back of my hand.

"Devastating," he said roughly. Then he reached down to pull me up for a kiss that tasted like both of us.

Afterward, we ended up in a clearing of soft pine needles, Chickie happily napping in a patch of sunlight nearby. Tommy sprawled next to me, still catching his breath, his hair full of pine needles and his lips swollen from my kisses.

"So," he said eventually, turning his head to look at me. "Still jealous?"

I couldn't help but smile. "Maybe a little."

"Good." He reached over and laced our fingers together. "Because I'm not interested in anyone else."

The simple words shouldn't have meant as much as they did. This was supposed to be temporary, just a few weeks of scratching an itch. But lying here with Tommy's hand in mine, watching him smile at me like I was something precious, I had to admit the careful distance I'd been trying to maintain had crumbled... or had maybe been a figment of my imagination since the beginning.

My chest ached to tell him, but I knew better. No point in confessing feelings I couldn't afford to claim.

"I should probably get back," Tommy said after a while, though he made no move to let go of my hand. "I did tell Robyn I'd help with the campfire thing."

"Plenty of other people around to help," I grumbled, then caught myself. "I mean, do whatever you want."

Tommy's smile was knowing. "Jealous again?"

"Protective," I corrected. "She's obviously interested in more than your campfire skills."

"And?"

"And you're…" I stopped, the words getting tangled on my tongue.

What was he? Mine? Temporary? Something I couldn't define?

"Busy," I finished lamely. "With training. And… other things."

Tommy laughed, the sound warm and genuine. "Other things, huh?"

"Important things," I said, pulling him closer. "Very time-consuming, important things."

"Such as?"

"Well, Chickie still needs work on her sit-stay command."

"True."

"And we need to work on your training, too." I brushed my thumb across his lower lip.

"My training?"

"Mmm. Seeing how well you focus even while distracted. Maintaining your… situational awareness, I think you called it?… in case there are wild predators in the area."

Tommy's breath hitched. "That could take a while."

"The rest of the summer," I agreed, then immediately regretted the words. Because summer would end, and Tommy would leave, and I'd be right back where I started.

In fact, I'd be worse off than before. The Foster I'd been two and a half weeks ago had only *imagined* what it would be like to have Tommy Marian in his bed, in his life. Now, I knew.

"Speaking of summer," Tommy said casually, sitting up to brush grass off his shirt. "I'm flying out day after tomorrow for my Stanford interview. Just overnight—I'll be back for the weekend exercises."

The words hit me like a physical blow. I'd known about the interview, of course, but hearing him say it so casually—like it was just another item on his calendar—reminded me exactly what I was to him.

A summer distraction before he went back to his real life.

"Right," I said, my voice carefully neutral. "Stanford. Big opportunity."

"The biggest," Tommy agreed, and I caught the excitement he was trying to hide. "Emergency medicine position, research opportunities, possibly even teaching at the medical school. It's everything I've worked toward my whole life."

Everything he'd worked toward. Not here, with me, but in California. In a world where I didn't exist, where I'd never feel at home.

"You'll get it," I said, because it was true. Tommy was brilliant, dedicated, exactly the kind of doctor a place like Stanford would want.

"Maybe." He was quiet for a moment, then looked at me with an expression I couldn't read. "You ever think about leaving Wyoming? Doing something different?"

The question caught me off guard. "Like what?"

"I don't know. SERA's expanding—Trace mentioned they're looking for a permanent SAR director. Or there are programs in Colorado, California. Places where your skills could make a real difference."

I stared at him, trying to figure out where this was coming from. "I do make a real difference. As sheriff of Majestic and a member of Wyoming SAR." I'd told him so, that first night in Hawaii.

"You're right. I'm sorry. I didn't mean it like that. I just meant..." He hesitated. "Don't you want to do SAR full-time? Be outside instead of chained to a desk half the time?" He gestured around us at the peaceful stillness. The warm shafts of summer sun breaking lazily through green pines and the deepest blue sky visible beyond. The soft buzz of bumblebees and the periodic skitter of small animals under the deadfall.

There was something in Tommy's voice—hope, maybe, or testing—that made my breathing uneven. Like he was asking for a reason that had nothing to do with career advice.

"There is no full-time SAR job where I live, and Majestic is my home," I said carefully. "My family's there. My life."

"Right." Tommy looked away, and I caught a flicker of disappointment before he hid it. "Of course."

We straightened up and brushed the pine needles off in silence after that, the easy intimacy of moments before replaced by something more complicated.

As we walked back toward SERA with Chickie trotting between us, I found myself wondering what the hell I was doing. Not just with Tommy, but with everything. Was I really happy mediating the same neighbor disputes and tourist mishaps year after year? Watching my good friends and family move forward in their lives, toward the direction of their dreams, while I stayed in the same old place, comfortable and safe and increasingly alone?

Was I just scared? Scared of taking risks, of wanting more, of admitting that maybe a small-town sheriff's department wasn't enough anymore.

Scared that when Tommy left for Stanford, he'd be taking the best part of me with him.

"Foster," Tommy said quietly as we reached the main campus.

"Yeah?"

"Whatever happens with Stanford..." He stopped walking and turned to face me fully. "I need you to know... I never wanted this to be just temporary."

Before I could respond—before I knew *how* I wanted to respond—he was walking toward the main building, leaving me standing there with Chickie and a chest full of feelings I had no idea what to do with.

Because if this wasn't temporary for him, if he was starting to feel the same terrifying pull I was fighting every day, we were both in a lot more trouble than either of us had bargained for.

There was no world in which he'd be happy playing small-town doctor or where I'd be happy as a big-city beat cop.

As far as I was concerned, temporary was less about what either of us wanted...

And more about the only option we had.

14

TOMMY

Morning brought awkward coffee and stolen glances across the breakfast table in the cafeteria. Foster looked as tired as I felt, dark circles under his eyes and a tension in his shoulders that hadn't been there yesterday. He avoided my gaze, focusing intently on his eggs and bacon while Chickie begged shamelessly at his feet.

I'd made a point of staying at the bonfire until long after Foster had turned in. His nonresponse to my comment about not wanting our relationship to be temporary had been a cold dose of reality. This thing between us wasn't just about what *I* wanted, and I was embarrassed, hurt, and guilty that I'd put him in a position where he had to hold his boundary with me.

He'd done a masterful job at avoiding me all evening, and by the time I'd slunk back to the cabin, he'd at least pretended to be dead asleep.

Now, I was stuck in the position of trying to act like nothing was wrong... while all I could think about was figuring out a way to smooth things over between us. We'd had a good thing going—even if it was only physical and only temporary—and I'd ruined it.

"Sleep well?" Robyn asked cheerfully, sliding into the seat next to me with her clipboard and eternal optimism.

"Like a baby," I lied, forcing a smile while hyperaware of Foster's presence two seats away.

The students were chattering excitedly about today's exercise—a complex multi-team operation that would test everything they'd learned so far. I tried to focus on their questions about medical protocols and emergency triage, but my attention kept drifting to Foster as he explained rappelling techniques to his group.

"Dr. Marian?" Lorelai, one of the students on my team in this third week of rotations, called down the table. "Could you repeat the hypothermia protocols you mentioned yesterday?"

I blinked, realizing I'd completely zoned out while staring at the way Foster's tactical pants hugged his thighs. "Er. Yes. Hypothermia." I cleared my throat and tried to project professionalism while my brain was entirely occupied with memories of those same thighs pressed against mine. "Always assume severe until proven otherwise in wilderness settings."

Twenty minutes later, we were loaded onto the bus heading into the backcountry for today's exercise. The weather had been iffy all morning—thick clouds building over the mountains and an oppressive humidity that made everyone's clothes stick to their skin.

I found myself sitting across the aisle from Foster, close enough to smell his soap and see the way his jaw clenched every time our eyes met. The memory of his hands in my hair, the desperate sound he'd made yesterday when I'd whispered his name—it was driving me crazy.

"Focus," I muttered under my breath.

"What was that?" Foster asked, glancing over.

"Nothing." Heat crept up my neck. "Just thinking through medical scenarios."

Something flickered in his eyes—heat, awareness, maybe even concern. "Mm."

I shifted in my seat, grateful for the noise of the bus engine covering our conversation. "Can we…"

He lowered his eyebrows and leaned a little closer, lowering his voice. "What do you need?"

His kindness and concern washed over me. For a split second, I wondered what it would have been like if Kari had asked me the same question in Hawaii when I'd expressed my confusion and anxiety over the wedding. I got the feeling Foster would help me in any way I needed.

Any way, that is, except giving me a real chance at something more than a summer fling.

"To go back to the way things were," I said, almost silently. "I'm sorry I fucked it up."

Foster leaned back and met my eyes. "Not sure that's what you really want."

"It is," I said quickly before inhaling a deep breath and letting it out slowly. "It's not. But it's our only option."

That was a lie, of course. I believed if two people wanted it badly enough, they could find a way to make it happen. I'd heard many stories of my uncles doing it when they'd found someone worth fighting for.

But I also knew Foster and I had only been... whatever it was... for a couple of weeks. Expecting him to even consider changing his life for me—or mine for him—was absurd.

He studied me for a moment. "You sure?"

I took a breath and forced a grin. "Yes, please."

He rolled his eyes and nodded before turning back to answer a student's question, but I caught the way his gaze lingered on my mouth for just a second too long in the process.

We were so fucked.

The training exercise was supposed to be straightforward— a multi-team rescue scenario involving a hiker who'd fallen down a soft shoulder into rocks and trees, sustaining multiple injuries. SAR would locate and access the victim, medical would provide treatment and stabilization, and swift-water would handle extraction across a creek that had been swollen by recent rains.

What we hadn't counted on was just how much more challenging Mother Nature would make it for our students.

The first rumble of thunder came just as Foster's team had established a route up the embankment for the patient. I glanced up at the sky, noting the way the clouds had darkened from gray to an ominous green-black.

"How long do we have?" I called to Trace, who was monitoring weather reports on his radio. Had these been untrained amateurs in a beginner course, we would have aborted the drill at the first sign of bad weather, but in this case, with advanced students, drilling in real-world weather challenges was a gift we couldn't have asked for.

"Maybe twenty minutes before it hits," he replied, frowning at the device. "Lightning risk is high. Foster's team needs to—"

The SAR lead on Foster's team opened her mouth when Foster shouted, "I'm calling a halt for all nonessential personnel. Take emergency cover now!"

His words were punctuated by a flash of lightning that seemed to split the sky in half, followed immediately by a crack of thunder so loud it made everyone duck.

"Shelter!" Trace bellowed. "Everyone to the overhang, and I mean everyone!"

The next few minutes were controlled chaos as thirty-plus people scrambled toward a stone ledge jutting out of the mountain about a hundred yards away and the small cave nestled beneath it. The first fat raindrops were already spattering the ground as we reached the designated shelter—a cramped space meant to hold maybe fifteen people in an emergency.

"This is cozy," Cody muttered as we all pressed inside.

He wasn't wrong. The cave had a reinforced entrance, which was why the SAR team had selected it as our emergency shelter. Unfortunately, with our entire group crammed inside, there was barely room to breathe. I found myself wedged against the far wall with Foster pressed against my side, his warmth seeping through my shirt.

"Everyone accounted for?" Foster called, doing a quick headcount across the stack of various backpacks and equipment scattered on the floor in the middle of the circle.

"All here," Foster's team lead called from near the cave entrance. "Weather's expected to clear in sixty to ninety."

An hour or two. In a space the size of a walk-in closet. With Foster's thigh pressed against mine and the scent of pine, sweat, and whatever soap he used fogging up my brain.

This was either going to be the best hour of my life or the longest slow burn of all time.

Lightning cracked overhead, followed instantly by a boom so loud the cave floor trembled beneath us. A few of the younger students flinched, and I saw Foster shift into calming mode without missing a beat.

"It's just noise," he said gently to a woman from Oregon who'd gone pale. "Stone and earth are your best friends in a storm. This cave's solid. We're safe."

She gave a shaky laugh. "Easy for you to say. You probably grew up in caves like this."

"Wyoming," Foster said, nodding. "We've got blizzards, bears, and worse... matchmaking mamas. But I'll take a thunderstorm over a whiteout any day."

"Says the guy who probably skis to work," I said, trying not to think about the nice, small-town guys his mom wanted to set him up with. Probably a buff rancher in a cowboy hat or the local insurance salesman.

Foster caught my eye, and his mouth curved. "Only when Chickie pulls the sled too slow."

That earned a few chuckles from the group, but Sierra raised her eyebrows. "Please tell me you don't actually own a dog sled. Chickie would unionize after the first mile."

"No sled," Foster admitted. "Though I've thought about getting a fat-tire bike for winter patrol."

"Oh god," I groaned. "You're one of those."

"What kind?"

"The kind who thinks forty below is 'invigorating' and wears crampons to brunch."

Foster grinned, slow and wicked. "Forty below builds character. Separates the tourists from the locals."

"I'm from San Francisco," I said. "Winter there is sixty degrees and passive-aggressive fog."

He leaned in slightly, his breath warm against my ear. "Explains a lot. *Lightweight.*"

"Ass," I muttered, but I was smiling as I said it.

"How did the two of you meet?" asked Marcus. "You had to have known each other before this, but I thought Dr. Marian was from New York?"

Foster and I looked away from each other, both suddenly aware of how easily we'd fallen into this rhythm. How natural it felt to tease him, to see his eyes light up when he fired back.

"He is," Trace said without looking up, scraping a hunk of mud off his boot with a multi-tool. "You're looking at a recipient of Manhattan's Nightingale Valor award during his first year of residency. He won it for his extraordinary valor and lifesaving leadership on-scene during a mass casualty event."

Marcus leaned around Foster to gawp at me. "What happened?"

"Train derailment," I said brusquely, shooting daggers at Trace.

He winked at me. "He doesn't like talking about it," he explained. "Which makes it all the more fun to trot out from time to time. Remember the subway explosion that caused two trains to collide and one to derail? It was all over the news a few years back."

I felt Foster's eyes heat the side of my face. "You were the guy who did a *field amputation*?"

I winced. "To be fair, the train did most of the heavy lifting on that one."

Sierra's jaw had dropped. She finally closed it long enough to form words. "That was you? For real? Holy fuck. I thought that guy was a med student."

"The Subway Surgeon," someone murmured in disbelief.

I shook my head. "First-year resident. And definitely not a surgeon. More like a scared idiot who only muddled through it because he happened to have had the best first responders from FDNY and a top-rated field surgeon on speed dial." The attention was making me squirm. "Hey, so, Foster and I met on an airplane. Someone asked how we met. That's how. He was sitting in front of me, and his seatmate was drunk off her ass. Kept slurring her words and spilling vodka cran all over the guy."

Sierra shook her head as if still having a hard time believing she was this close to someone who'd been in a horrific medical emergency. "What I wouldn't give to respond to a mass casualty incident," she said wistfully.

Foster's voice was dry when he responded. "That's the spirit, Sierra."

Trace must have felt guilty for putting me on the spot

because he took Foster's lead and ran with it. "By a show of hands, how many of you have actually been through MCI training? Because tomorrow's scenario is going to test whether you can think on your feet when everything goes sideways."

I tried to focus on his words, but most of my attention was focused on Foster.

Once the attention was truly off me and completely focused on tomorrow's exercise, I leaned over and whispered, "Thanks."

"How about 'You owe me one, Doc'?"

Whenever his voice was that low and soft, it was like a hot breath on my inner thigh, all promise but not quite there yet.

I sucked in a breath and looked around before mouthing, "Promise?"

The conversation shifted to equipment maintenance and weather protocols. I tried to follow along, but the cramped space and Foster's proximity were making it hard to concentrate. When thunder crashed overhead again, I noticed a few students checking their phones.

We'd been getting spotty cell service all day, so when the storm had sent us into the cave, I'd powered mine down to preserve battery.

When I powered it back on, the notifications came pouring in. Seven missed calls from Ella. Three from my cousin Alex. Two from my mom. And a string of increasingly urgent text messages. All seemingly sent within the last ten minutes.

My blood went cold as I read the latest one.

ELLA

> CALL ME NOW. Hazel and Avery have
> been in an accident. They can't get
> Hazel out of the car.

My hands started shaking as I scrolled through the other messages, trying to piece together what had happened. The words "multi-vehicle" and "hydroplane" and "blood loss" jumped out at me like physical blows.

"Oh god," I whispered.

15

FOSTER

"Tommy?" I watched the color drain from his face as he stared at his phone. "What is it?"

The change in him was instant and devastating. One moment, he'd been laughing with the other instructors about our impromptu cave adventure, and the next, he looked like someone had punched him in the gut. His hands were shaking as he thrust the phone at me.

I read the messages, my stomach dropping with each line. Hydroplane. Hazel trapped. Blood loss. The words painted a picture that had my own pulse spiking in sympathy.

"I have to go," Tommy said, already moving toward the cave entrance despite the rain still pounding outside. "My sister. Her wife. The baby. There's been a multi-vehicle crash on Highway 170 south of town, and they can't get Hazel out of the car. I have to—"

"Tommy." I caught his arm, feeling the tremor running through his entire body. Around us, conversations had stopped. Everyone was watching as the composed doctor they'd known all week came apart at the seams. "Breathe. We'll get you there. Let's wait for a break in the lightning."

"Everyone, get out your med kits and bring them here." Jasper didn't add a *right now*, but his firm tone had everyone complying instantly anyway. "If there are multiple injured, responders might need more supplies than they've got, but Dr. Marian can bring ours to the scene. Pull anything trauma-related. I'm talking pressure dressings, tourniquets, burn dressings. If you've got extra gloves or thermal blankets, pull those, too."

As the group scrambled, Jasper moved with measured efficiency, sorting gear like he'd done it a hundred times—which, I guessed, he probably *had* as an EMT.

I'd spent nearly three weeks judging the guy harshly because he couldn't seem to think on his own. Now, it was clear he was more than capable. I just didn't get why he'd hung back before.

Just as Jasper finished prepping the supplies, Tommy turned from where he'd been scanning the weather from the mouth of the cave.

"The storm—" he began.

"We got the break we need," I said, understanding what he meant and already mentally calculating routes. "Trace, I need your truck keys."

Within minutes, Tommy and I were racing through the

storm-darkened afternoon to the vehicle. The rain was lighter now but still treacherous, turning the mountain roads into a maze of potential hazards.

"Fucking fuck," Tommy said, his voice tight with controlled panic as he tried to get his phone to cooperate. "I need to reach someone at the scene."

I kept my eyes on the road, navigating the slick asphalt while Tommy's fear filled the cab like a living thing. Every few seconds, he'd curse under his breath as another call failed to connect, the storm playing havoc with cell towers.

"We need to stop at SERA," I said, taking a turn faster than I should have. "Get my truck."

"We don't have time—"

"It has lights and sirens," I explained, seeing understanding dawn in his eyes. "We can make better time, and people will get out of our way."

The brief stop at SERA felt like an eternity, but the transfer was worth it. My sheriff's vehicle cut through traffic like a knife, emergency lights lighting up the gray afternoon as we flew toward Legacy's main highway.

This was what emergency response looked like when it got personal—when the victim wasn't a stranger but someone you loved. I'd seen it before, the way training could both help and hinder when your emotions were involved. Tommy was fighting between his medical expertise and his terror, and I could practically feel him vibrating with the need to do something, anything, to help his sister.

"Come on, come on," he whispered, holding his phone

toward the window. The blue glow of the screen reflected off his face, highlighting the tight lines around his eyes.

Finally, the call connected.

"Avery, honey, it's Tommy," he said, his voice still tight with barely controlled fear. "How are you and the baby?" His free hand tightened into a fist, knuckles white.

"Good, good—no, I know. I'm on my way. What's her status?"

All I could hear was a panicked woman's voice on the other end, but I watched Tommy's face change as he listened. The transformation was subtle at first—a straightening of his shoulders, a steadying of his breathing. The terrified brother was still there, but something else was emerging now that he had a task to focus on.

"Okay. Okay, that's good. Conscious is good." His jaw tightened as he reached into the center console for a pen. "Can you hand the phone to the nearest EMT?"

After introducing himself and asking about Hazel, he began scribbling notes on his palm. "Open femur fracture, possible head trauma. How long until the firefighters get her out? No, don't move her until they've got C-spine stabilized. I don't care —if her neck isn't cleared, they wait."

The authority in his voice was absolute, and something shifted in my chest. This was Dr. Thomas Marian, trauma specialist, taking control of a situation even though he wasn't there.

"We're not too far," he continued, glancing at me and pointing to the general location of the crash site on the dashboard's GPS screen. "Forty minutes, hopefully less. Tell Avery

I'm on my way. And DJ? Make sure someone's documenting everything for when I get there. I'll ride with her to Billings if I get there in time."

He hung up and immediately started typing on his phone. "They're working on getting her out and trying to keep her stable through a gap in the frame. Head injury, open femur fracture, but she's conscious and talking." His fingers flew over the screen. "I'm texting an ER doc I know in Billings so they know she's coming, but it sounds like it's going to take a while to get her out, especially in this weather. There are other accidents in the area, which is spreading emergency response thin."

The confidence in his voice sent something warm through my chest. I'd seen him work at SERA, had witnessed his competence during our rescue earlier today. But this was different. This was Tommy fighting for someone he loved, and the focused intensity of it was mesmerizing.

I glanced at the GPS. "ETA thirty-four minutes."

The headlights cut through the darkness ahead of us, reflecting off wet pavement and guardrails. Beside me, Tommy continued to field texts and calls, and I watched as the last traces of panic disappeared completely, replaced by something laser focused and unshakeable.

"No, listen to me," he said, his voice sharp with authority. "I don't care if that's protocol. I'm telling you what needs to happen. I've already reached out to the ER in Billings to have a trauma surgeon ready. It's your job to get her out of that car and onto a bus in one piece."

I found myself stealing glances at him as he worked, simultaneously awed and unsettled by this side of him. In the time we'd been at SERA, I'd seen plenty of instances of his natural leadership, but it had always been with a side of good-natured camaraderie. Leading by example and by consensus, encouraging his students to take charge. This was different. This wasn't a teacher or a teammate but a man making hard calls, fast. It was even more impressive under the high-pressure situation of responding to a critically injured loved one.

"Her pressure's dropping," he told me between calls. "They need to get her out now, but if they move wrong..." He didn't finish the sentence, but I could see the calculation running behind his eyes. Time versus risk. The impossible choices that defined his profession.

"How much farther?" he asked.

I glanced at the speedometer. We were doing ninety on a highway rated for sixty-five, and I was pushing it as hard as I dared in these conditions. "Thirteen minutes."

"Thirteen minutes," he repeated into the phone. "You can keep her stable for thirteen more minutes. I'm walking you through this."

The next several miles passed in a blur of emergency lights and Tommy's voice, controlled and commanding, talking people through procedures I couldn't even pronounce. I watched him guide what sounded like a nervous EMT through blood pressure management, coach someone through pain medication dosing, and somehow keep his pregnant sister-in-law calm while coordinating her wife's extraction.

Watching him remain steady under pressure was incredible. And with each mile that passed, something in my chest grew tighter, warmer, more dangerous.

This wasn't just competence. This was devotion in action. This was a man who could reach across miles of rain-soaked highway and save someone's life with nothing but his voice, his knowledge, and his absolute refusal to give up.

We were almost there, when we came around a bend in the road and saw bumper-to-bumper traffic backed up for the final two miles.

"Oh fuck," Tommy said, and for a moment, the fear crept back into his voice.

I quickly hit the "whoop" button and moved to the shoulder, pulling the radio and calling into local law enforcement to let them know we were coming down the shoulder with lights and sirens.

"Dispatch, this is Sheriff Foster Blake, Majestic County, en route to the MVA on Highway 170 at mile marker 82. Be advised, I'm running Code 3 down the eastbound shoulder of Highway 170, currently at mile marker 80. Requesting clearance and traffic advisories. Over."

The response was nearly immediate but harried. "Copy that, Sheriff. We appreciate the assist. Units on scene have been advised. You're clear to proceed Code 3 on the shoulder. Let us know when you're on-site."

We arrived within moments at an accident scene that looked like a war zone. Emergency vehicles lined both sides of the highway, their lights painting the rain and smoke in shifting reds and blues. Steam rose from the wreckage of what had been a sedan, now upside down and accordioned against the concrete barrier. There were three other vehicles turned at bad angles and dented, doors hanging open but with now empty seats.

My throat tightened when I realized how bad it was. Tommy went very still beside me, and I saw his hands clench in his lap.

"Jesus," he whispered, staring at the wreckage. For a moment, the professional mask slipped, and I saw the terrified brother again. "That's Hazel's car."

I pulled up behind the fire truck and immediately noticed what was missing—no law enforcement vehicles. The scene was being managed entirely by fire and EMS, which explained the slightly chaotic feel to the whole operation.

"Tommy, stop," I said before he could race out of the truck. "Disposable poncho in your gear bag. Put it on."

He nodded and shot me a look of gratitude that made my chest ache. "Thanks, Foster." As he raced away, I saw him pull out the poncho and yank it on.

"Sheriff Blake, Majestic County," I called out to the guy who seemed to be in charge as I approached the scene, my badge now hanging over a rain slicker. "How can I help?"

"Chief Judd Kincaid, Legacy FD. Unfortunately, lightning strikes have caused all kinds of shit today. We've almost got an opening to get her out, but we've got our hands full trying to manage extraction and crowd control. The lookie-loos are going to get themselves killed, and we don't have enough first responders for that."

As I shook hands with him, I watched Tommy move past us toward a very young EMT. "Are you DJ?" he called out over the noise of engines and radios. "I'm Dr. Tommy Marian."

The guy sagged in relief. "You made it."

Tommy nodded, and I watched something settle over him like armor. "Who's the most critical patient on scene?"

The EMT's eyebrows shot up so quickly it was almost comical. "Definitely your sister, sir. She's stable for now, but we're still having trouble with the extraction. The angle's all wrong, and—"

"Show me."

Before they reached the vehicle, Tommy noticed a young woman with auburn hair and tearstained cheeks sitting in the back of an ambulance with an EMT taking her vitals.

"Avery!" Tommy hustled over and pulled her into a hug. "You still okay?"

The relief on her face was heartbreaking. "Hazel's been asking for you. They won't let me—"

"Just worry about you and the baby. Let these folks take care of you, okay? I'm going to get her out, I promise." He gave her one last squeeze of reassurance, and I saw his hands shake slightly as he pulled away. Then he took a deep breath, squared his shoulders, and moved quickly toward the wreckage.

With each minute that passed, he seemed to grow more focused, more certain. This Dr. Marian was completely in charge and fearless—not the uncertain man from the cave, not even the ultra-capable instructor from SERA. This was someone who belonged in crisis, who thrived under pressure that would flatten most people.

When a news van tried to pull onto the shoulder for a better view, I intercepted them before they could get close enough to interfere.

"This is an active emergency scene," I told the reporter firmly. "You need to stay back at least two hundred yards."

"But we have a right to—"

"You have a right to report the news from a safe distance that doesn't interfere with lifesaving operations," I cut him off. "Move your vehicle, or I'll have it towed."

The authority in my voice brooked no argument. Several of my friends back in Majestic were famous or obscenely wealthy. I had more than enough experience keeping the media away from people who deserved privacy.

The van retreated, and I turned my attention back to Tommy, who was now coordinating with what looked like every emergency responder on scene, none of whom looked old enough to vote.

"Jesus Christ," I heard one of the local EMTs mutter to his partner next to one of the other ambulances where they were treating other victims. "Who does that guy think he is?"

Something hot and protective flared in my chest. "He's a top-tier trauma doc. If you can claim the same, I'm sure he'd appreciate an assist. Otherwise, get back to your patient."

Both men turned to stare at me, then back at Tommy, who was now crouched beside the wreckage, talking to someone I couldn't see.

"Where'd you guys even come from?" the other EMT asked.

"SERA," I said simply. Everyone knew the program had a stellar reputation for training emergency responders, and chances were, these guys would never have the privilege of being part of it.

Tommy's reassuring voice as he spoke to Hazel carried over

to us. "Hey, beautiful. I know it hurts, but we're going to get you out of here. Avery's fine—she's worried about you, but she and the baby are doing just fine."

A weak voice responded from inside the car, and I saw Tommy's shoulders relax slightly.

"I know, I know. But you're going to be fine, too. Better than fine. You're going to be terrorizing me again within a week."

His voice caught slightly on the words—the first crack I'd seen in his professional facade since we'd arrived.

For the next twenty minutes, I found myself divided between managing the scene and watching Tommy work. He knelt at Hazel's side, blood on his hands and muddy gravel on his clothes, issuing clipped instructions to the other EMTs while holding pressure on his sister's wound himself. When any of the first responders hesitated, Tommy didn't shout—he explained, voice steady, gaze unflinching, until they moved like a unit.

And through it all, he never let go of his sister's hand.

I'd seen competence before. I'd worked with plenty of skilled professionals in my years as sheriff. But this was something different. This was watching someone operate at the absolute peak of their abilities, doing exactly what they were meant to do.

The realization hit me like a physical blow: Tommy wasn't just good at this. He was extraordinary. This was who he was supposed to be—not stuck next to a sedated patient in an operating room, but here, in the moment of greatest challenge, making impossible decisions and saving lives when everything was falling apart.

"Careful with that leg," he called out as they maneuvered the stretcher. "The fracture's unstable. If it shifts..."

I saw him go still for just a moment as Hazel cried out during the transfer, and that crack in his professional armor widened just enough for me to see the terrified brother underneath again. Without thinking, I moved closer and put my hand on his shoulder.

"She's okay," I said quietly. "You've got this. *She's* got this."

"Right. Yeah." He took a deep breath, and I felt some of the tension leave his body under my palm. For just a second, he leaned into the contact, and the weight of him settled into my bones like gravity.

I couldn't imagine anything I wanted more than a life where Tommy Marian chose me to lean on.

The moment passed, and he was back in control, climbing into the ambulance and barking instructions to the driver about which route to take and how fast was safe, given Hazel's condition.

Avery had already insisted Tommy ride with Hazel instead of her, and I'd offered to bring her to the hospital myself. Not only did I want to help him—help *them*—but I also wasn't ready to leave him, to go back to Cabin 8 alone while he was worried about his sister.

"You sure?" Tommy asked before the rear doors closed, glancing over at me with an expression I couldn't quite read— gratitude, maybe, or something deeper.

"We'll be right behind you," I promised. "Call me if you need me, okay?"

Tommy looked back at me, his face exhausted but grateful. "I don't have your number."

"I'll fix that at the hospital," I said, and something passed between us... a promise, an acknowledgment of something neither of us was ready to name.

The ambulance pulled away, taking him with it, and I turned to help his very pregnant sister-in-law back to my truck.

"It's going to be okay," I said, opening the passenger door. "She's in good hands. The best."

As we made our way through the traffic behind the ambulance, I couldn't stop replaying what I'd just witnessed. The way Tommy had moved with absolute confidence, the way everyone had deferred to his expertise without question. The gentle authority in his voice when he'd spoken to Hazel, the fierce protectiveness when he'd fought for the best care for her.

He wasn't made for stillness, or small-town routines, or the quiet, predictable life I'd carved out for myself in Majestic. He was built for *this*—for running headfirst into other people's emergencies, for making impossible decisions under pressure, for saving lives when no one else could.

The drive to the hospital passed in a blur of dark mountain roads and the steady *taptaptap* of Avery texting. But all I could think about was Tommy's hands, steady and sure as he'd worked to save his sister. The way he'd looked at me in that final moment before the ambulance doors closed. And the terrifying realization that what I felt for him wasn't going away in a few weeks. If anything, after tonight, it was only going to get stronger.

Avery dropped her phone on top of her rounded belly and

blew out a breath. "I didn't even ask, how do you know Tommy? You two work together at SERA?"

I glanced over at her, the memory of Hazel's reaction still fresh in my memory from that first night at Timber.

"I'm the guy in the Made Marian T-shirt. The one from Hawaii."

And for the first time since that night six long months ago, claiming it made me a little bit proud.

16

TOMMY

THE FLUORESCENT LIGHTS in the hospital waiting room buzzed overhead like angry wasps, casting everything in a sickly pale glow that made the beige walls look gray. I sat in the same hard plastic chair I'd claimed six hours ago, staring at my hands.

They'd finally stopped shaking.

The blood under my fingernails had dried to a rusty brown, and somewhere in the back of my mind, the doctor part of me noted that I should wash them properly.

But I was a brother, too, and to that part of me, moving seemed impossible. Every time I tried to stand, my legs felt like they were made of water.

I thought of the thousands of family members I'd talked to in the ER over the years. People whose shoes I'd never truly been in. Until now.

I was one of the fortunate ones. Hazel was stable. The surgeon had been optimistic about her recovery. The femur fracture would heal cleanly with the titanium rod they'd inserted, and the head trauma was thankfully minor—mostly swelling that was already responding to treatment. She'd been lucky. We'd all been so damned lucky.

So why did I still feel like I was going to throw up?

"Tommy." Foster's voice cut through the fog in my head. He was standing beside my chair holding two cups of coffee, though I couldn't remember him leaving to get them. "How are you holding up?"

I looked up at him and tried to form words, but they felt stuck somewhere in my throat. Foster's face creased with concern, and I realized that, like me, he was still wearing the same clothes from our emergency response—tactical pants and a SERA shirt, now rumpled and stiff with dried sweat and rain.

He'd stayed. Through the entire surgery, through hours of waiting, through me being completely useless. He'd stayed so long his wet clothes had dried to his body. He'd just... stayed.

I let out a shuddering breath. "She's okay," I managed finally, my voice coming out hoarse. "The surgeon said—"

"I know." Foster sat down in the chair next to mine, close enough that our knees almost touched. "I heard the update. That's not what I asked."

I stared at the coffee cup he pressed into my hands, watching steam curl up from the surface. When had I become so cold? "I'm okay. I'm fine."

"Bullshit." The word was gentle but firm. "When's the last time you ate something?"

I tried to remember and gave up with a shrug. Breakfast felt like a lifetime ago. "I don't know."

Foster's jaw tightened, and he pulled out his phone. "Ella and Alex agree I should take you home."

"Oh?" I blinked around, half expecting my cousins to still be in the waiting room with me. "Where'd they go?"

"They're trying to convince Avery to get some sleep." He studied my face with those observant hazel eyes. "Tommy, you need to do the same. Hazel's going to be fine, but she's going to need you at full strength when she wakes up."

Before I could respond, I heard Alex's familiar voice as he and Ella walked up. "Listen to the sheriff, Tommy. You've done your part. Now it's our turn."

"I'm okay," I repeated automatically, even though we both knew it was a lie.

Alex and Ella pulled me up for a big group hug, creating a brief cocoon of family warmth that made my chest ache. "How's Avery?" I asked

"She and the baby are great, with the exception of a little seat belt bruising. You already know this. She won't leave, so they're setting up a bed in Hazel's room for her."

Ella stepped back and really looked at me for the first time, taking in my muddy, bloodstained clothes and whatever my face was doing. "Jesus, Tommy, you stink."

"Gee, thanks."

"I'm serious. You need to get out of here and let us take over for the night shift." She turned to Foster, who was watching our family reunion with careful attention. "You might need to hog-tie him."

"I've got cuffs in the truck," Foster said dryly. Then he

turned to meet my eyes and bounced his eyebrows suggestively where no one else could see him.

I was too tired to do more than huff out a breath of laughter.

"I'm taking you back to SERA whether you come willingly or not," he warned in a voice that was no longer teasing.

Now, that... *that* did something to me, even if his mention of the cuffs hadn't. I swayed a little closer to him without thinking.

"You're dead on your feet," Ella scolded, using the tone she'd perfected when we were kids and she was trying to talk me out of staying up all night studying. "Hazel's going to murder you if you collapse from exhaustion and steal her thunder."

"Besides, she's stable," Alex added, opening one of the containers he'd brought and releasing the smell of something that made my stomach growl loudly. "The hard part's over. She just needs to rest and heal now."

Ella gently pushed me back into my chair, then perched in the chair beside me. She put her hand on my arm. "Okay, I need to say this, so just hear me out."

Alex muttered under his breath while I shot a glare at Ella. I was pretty sure I already knew what she was going to say, but I let her continue anyway, mostly because I was too tired to argue.

"You leave for your interview tomorrow—"

I began shaking my head after the second word. "No way. I'll tell them what happened. They'll understand and reschedule—"

Her hand tightened a little on my arm until I met her eyes. "Tommy. Summer is when people go on vacation, which means rescheduling it anytime soon with the hiring committee will be nearly impossible."

"Ella, I'm not fucking going. What you're suggesting is—"

Alex cut me off. "Smart. And because we knew you were going to refuse, the whole damned family is turning up here at first light to make sure Hazel is covered. The only reason they're not already here is because of the storm, but now that the weather is clearing, I wouldn't be surprised if Jude's plane is already in the air."

I felt the weight of Foster's silence on my other side. The deliberate choice to stay out of a "family matter."

The lack of his input—arguing either side—struck me as annoying and wrong, which made no sense at all. He wasn't part of my family. Or my future.

I glanced at him anyway. Because silly wishes were like that, and I was too tired to pretend.

He was looking down at his phone. It took me a moment to register that the screen was blank.

Ella continued her argument. "You know there are level one trauma docs here. People who know how to care for broken legs and post-surgical patients. This is not a rare medical disorder for which Thomas Marian is the only prodigy with the skills to care for this patient." She lifted her chin at Foster. "You're going to let this guy take you back to SERA for the night. Then you're going to go to California. After you get back from your interview, you can visit Hazel at home."

Ella was right. I was scheduled to fly out in the morning, meet with the department chair for dinner, and then spend the following day touring the hospital, meeting the other stakeholders, and finishing out the panel interviews. Chances were high Hazel would be back home recovering by the time I returned, and there was nothing to indicate she was high-risk for complications.

She was also right when she said rescheduling the interviews would be an inconvenience for quite a lot of people.

But this was my sister. And I was a doctor.

Foster stood up, and something in his posture shifted—from neutral bystander to someone taking charge. "Let's go."

I looked between them—Ella with her determined expression, Alex pretending patience while most likely waiting for more fireworks between me and Ella, and Foster standing guard by my chair, radiating that same measured strength he'd shown all day.

"You need to get some sleep, Doc. Let's start with that."

Something in his voice—a promise, maybe, or just the absolute certainty that he knew what the next right step was—made the last of my resistance crumble.

"Okay," I whispered.

Ella's face flooded with relief. "Thank god. I was about to start mixing sedatives into your coffee."

Foster's hand appeared on my shoulder, warm and steadying. "Come on. Let's get you home."

Home. The word hit me strangely. When had Cabin 8 become home?

The drive back to SERA passed in a blur of dark mountain roads and the steady rhythm of windshield wipers against light rain. I sat in the passenger seat of Foster's truck, clutching the cooling coffee Foster had given me, and tried to process everything that had happened.

The accident. The surgery. Foster staying with me through all of it, never once suggesting he had somewhere else he needed to be. The way he'd taken control of the scene, the way he'd protected Hazel's privacy from reporters, the way he'd simply... been there.

"Thank you," I said finally, my voice barely audible over the engine.

"For what?"

"For driving me through the storm. For being right about needing lights and sirens. For *staying*. For—" I gestured vaguely, unable to find words for everything he'd done. "All of it."

Foster glanced over at me, something soft and unreadable in his expression. "You don't have to thank me for that."

"Yes, I do. You didn't have to—"

"Tommy." He reached over and briefly covered my hand with his. "Yes, I did."

The easy assurance in his voice made my chest tight with something I wasn't ready to name. Something I was sure *Foster* wasn't ready for me to name.

By the time we reached the cabin, I felt like I was moving through thick water. Everything seemed muffled and distant, including my own thoughts. Foster unlocked the door, and Chickie bounded toward us, tail wagging frantically, but even her enthusiastic greeting felt like it was happening to someone else.

"Shower," Foster instructed, guiding me toward the bathroom. "You'll feel better once you're clean."

I stood in the middle of the small space, staring at the shower controls like they were written in a foreign language. The simple act of turning on water seemed impossibly complex. Behind me, I heard Foster moving around, the soft sounds of him gathering towels and testing the water temperature.

"Arms up," he said gently.

I blinked at him. "What?"

"Your shirt. It's covered in blood and mud, and you're..." He studied my face with those careful eyes. "You're not really here right now, are you?"

I looked down at myself and saw what he meant. My clothes were filthy, stiff with dried blood and dirt from kneeling on the wet pavement beside Hazel's car. I couldn't remember the last time I'd been this completely wrung out. Not even on my worst ER shift.

I realized distantly that though I'd been through similar situations a million times—the adrenaline rush of a high-stress situation, followed by the overwhelming fatigue of an adrenaline crash—it really did hit differently when the crisis was happening to you. When it was someone you loved in danger. The emotional component made it harder to think reasonably and follow protocol in the moment and harder to overcome when the crisis was over.

"I don't think I can," I admitted, the words coming out smaller than I'd intended.

Foster's expression gentled. "Okay. That's okay."

His hands were careful as he helped me out of my ruined clothes, his touch clinical but infinitely tender. There was nothing sexual about it—just one person taking care of another who couldn't quite manage it himself.

When he started pulling off his own shirt, I found enough brain function to be confused. "What are you doing?"

"Making sure you don't fall down in there," he said simply, stepping out of his pants. "Come on."

The shower was barely big enough for one person, let alone two, but Foster guided me under the warm spray, and I immediately understood why he'd insisted. My legs felt like they might give out at any moment, and the steady pressure of his hands on my shoulder and hip was the only thing keeping me upright.

"Just relax," he murmured, reaching for the shampoo. "Let me take care of this."

I closed my eyes and let him wash my hair, his fingers working gently through the strands, massaging my scalp with a tenderness that made my throat tight.

When was the last time anyone had tried to take care of me like this?

When was the last time I had let them?

The warm water sluiced over my skin, carrying away the grime and tension of the day. Foster's hands moved with unshakable efficiency—washing the dried blood from my forearms, the mud from my knees, the salt tracks from tears I didn't remember crying.

"Hazel's really okay," I said, my voice barely audible over the water.

"She's really okay," Foster confirmed, his hands still moving in slow, soothing circles across my back. "You saved her life,

Tommy. You know that, right? If those young EMTs hadn't kept the leg properly stabilized during the extraction..."

Something cracked open in my chest—relief, maybe, or just the delayed shock finally hitting. The fear I'd been holding back since we got to the scene of the accident rushed through me like a dam breaking, and suddenly, I was shaking again, harder this time.

"Hey." Foster turned me around so I was facing him, his hands coming up to frame my face. "Hey, it's okay. She's safe. You got her out."

"I almost lost her," I whispered, the words torn from somewhere deep inside. "If you hadn't been there, if we'd been any later—"

"But we weren't. And you didn't." His thumbs brushed across my cheekbones, and I realized I was crying. "You did everything right, Tommy. Everything."

The sob that escaped me sounded like it came from someone else entirely. Foster pulled me against his chest, and I buried my face in the curve of his neck, breathing in the scent of his skin as everything I'd been holding back poured out of me.

He didn't try to shush me or tell me it was over. He just held me under the warm water, one hand stroking my hair, the other rubbing slow circles between my shoulder blades, while I finally let myself feel how terrified I'd been.

"I've got you," he murmured against my ear. "I've got you."

And for the first time in longer than I could remember, I actually believed someone did.

By the time my breathing steadied, the water was starting to run cold. Foster reached around me to turn off the taps, then wrapped me in the largest towel he could find, rubbing briskly to chase away the chill.

"Better?" he asked.

I nodded, not trusting my voice. Better didn't begin to cover it. Something fundamental had shifted during those minutes under the water—not just the physical relief of being clean but something deeper. The feeling of being truly cared for. Of letting someone else be strong when I couldn't be.

That wasn't a feeling I'd ever had with Kari. I'd tried to be the strong one, the protector. How surprising to realize now that I'd been missing something this vital and reassuring.

Foster handed me clean boxers and a soft T-shirt, then pulled on his own sleep clothes while I struggled with the basic mechanics of getting dressed. My hands were still shaky, and the simple act of pulling a shirt over my head felt monumental.

"Here." Foster's hands covered mine, helping guide the fabric down. "Almost done."

When I was finally dressed, he led me to my bed and pulled back the covers. "Get some sleep. I'll wake you if anything changes. Ella has my number, too."

I crawled under the blankets, suddenly exhausted beyond belief. But as Foster moved toward his own bed, something close to panic fluttered in my chest.

"Foster?"

He turned back immediately. "Yeah?"

"Will you..." I swallowed hard, feeling ridiculous and needy and not caring. "I feel like I can't get warm. Will you lie down with me? Just until I warm up?"

Something soft and unguarded crossed his face. "Of course."

He settled under the covers beside me, and I turned onto my side, facing him. In the dim light filtering through the cabin windows, I could see the tired lines around his eyes, the way his hair was still damp from our shower.

"Thank you," I whispered again.

"Tommy." His voice was gentle but firm. "You don't have to keep thanking me."

"Yes, I do." I reached for his hand, lacing our fingers together. "I don't know what I would have done today without you."

His thumb stroked across my knuckles. "You would have figured it out. You always do."

"Maybe. But I'm glad I didn't have to."

We lay there in comfortable silence, and I found myself studying his face in the low light. The strong line of his jaw, the way his lashes cast shadows on his cheeks, the small scar near the left edge of his lip that I'd never noticed before.

This wasn't the man I'd met in Hawaii six months ago—charming and flirtatious and slightly overwhelming. This wasn't even the professional, competent instructor I'd been working with at SERA. This was someone deeper, someone who showed up when it mattered, who stayed when things got difficult, who took care of people without expecting anything in return.

And that terrified me.

Because lying there with his hand in mine and his quiet breathing gradually matching my own felt dangerously close to everything I'd never known I wanted. It felt like home in a way that had nothing to do with geography and everything to do with the man beside me.

"Foster?"

"Mmm?"

I almost said it then—the words that were sitting heavy on my tongue, threatening to spill out into the darkness between us. But something held me back. Maybe it was the exhaustion, or maybe it was the sudden, crystal clear understanding of how completely fucked I was.

Because this wasn't supposed to happen. This tender intimacy, this feeling of rightness, this overwhelming urge to stay right here forever—none of it was part of the plan.

"Should I..." I started, then stopped, not sure how to finish the sentence. *Go to California? Stick to our agreement that this is just a fling? Stop falling for you before it's too late?*

Foster seemed to understand what I wasn't saying. His hand tightened around mine for just a moment before he carefully pulled away, putting inches of space between us that felt like miles.

"Yeah," he said quietly. "You should."

The words hung in the air like a door closing. I could see something shuttering in his expression, the careful walls going back up.

"The interview," I said, hating how the words tasted in my mouth.

"Stanford." Foster's voice was carefully neutral. "It's a big opportunity."

"It is."

"An unmissable one." Foster shifted and sat up. "So you need better sleep than you'll get with the two of us sharing this postage stamp."

The silence that fell between us was different now—heavier, more deliberate. We both knew what we were doing. Rebuilding the boundaries that had crumbled somewhere between the shower and this moment. Reminding ourselves that we had different lives waiting for us.

It was the smart thing to do...

So why did it feel like we were both making the biggest mistake of our lives?

"Foster—" I tried again.

"It's okay, Tommy." He paused at the edge of my bed, not quite looking at me. "Today was... a lot. For both of us. But you have plans. Important ones."

I wanted to argue, to tell him that my plans were just words on paper compared to this feeling blooming between us. But the rational part of my brain—the part that had gotten me through medical school and residency and a decade-long relationship I'd been too scared to leave—knew he was right.

Foster Blake had already prompted me to change my plans once, but I couldn't keep doing it. Who would I be if I couldn't achieve the goals I'd set for myself?

"Good night," I whispered.

"Good night."

Foster moved to his own bed, and I listened to the sounds of him settling under his covers. The cabin felt enormous suddenly, the three feet between our beds an insurmountable distance.

I lay there in the darkness, staring at the ceiling, and tried not to think about how right it had felt to have him take care of me. How safe I'd felt in his arms. How terrifyingly easy it would be to throw away everything I'd worked for just to stay in this moment.

Five weeks. We had just over five weeks left before I had to decide whether to chase the life I'd always planned or risk everything for something I'd never seen coming.

Five weeks to figure out whether what was happening between us was real or just the result of proximity and adrenaline and really good sex.

Five weeks to decide if love was worth changing the entire trajectory of my life.

As I finally drifted off to sleep, listening to Foster's steady breathing from across the room, I had the sinking feeling that I already knew the answer.

And that it was going to break both our hearts.

17

FOSTER

I SHOULDN'T HAVE COME to Timber alone.

The smart thing would have been to stay at SERA after the workday was over. Maybe take Chickie for a long walk, work on some training exercises… anything to keep my hands busy and my mind off the fact that Tommy had been gone for exactly ten hours and twenty-three minutes.

Not that I was counting.

But here I was, nursing a beer while Tommy's cousin Alex polished glasses behind the bar and shot me looks like he had a solid guess why I was drinking alone on a Tuesday night.

The inside bar area was mostly empty, with most people preferring the outside seating area to enjoy the beautiful summer night with friends and family. It should have been peaceful away from the crowd, from the chatter. Instead, every time the door opened, my head jerked up like a goddamn golden retriever waiting for its owner to come home.

Pathetic.

Even more pathetic than the sulking hound dog at my feet, who was currently missing her favorite person.

"It's funny," Alex said, setting down his towel and leaning against the bar. "Ella and I were sure you had a thing for our cousin, but since you know Tommy's not coming back until tomorrow night and you're still eyeing the door, maybe it's someone else."

I took a long pull of my beer. "It's not someone else."

Alex's eyebrows winged up.

I scrambled to correct myself. "Or him. Or anyone. I'm not waiting for anyone. Or him."

He did a shit job at hiding his smirk. "I see."

Before I could respond and most likely make the situation worse, the door chimed again, and this time, it was a tiny force of nature in outdoor-chic hiking pants, a designer puffer vest, and a cloud of expensive perfume.

As soon as I recognized her from Hawaii, I turned my head away in hopes she wouldn't notice me. Unfortunately, today was not my day.

"Well, well," she said, climbing onto the barstool next to mine with surprising agility for someone who had to be pushing ninety. "If it isn't Sheriff Beefcake."

"Ma'am," I murmured with a polite nod before staring back into my beer.

Alex closed his eyes and shook his head slowly.

"*Ma'aaaaamm.*" She said the word slowly, as if testing it on her tongue. "If we're going to start with insults, *I'll* be the one to throw the first volley."

She opened her mouth to unload, but Alex stopped her before she could begin. "Aunt Tilly, what are you doing here? I thought you were at the lodge with everyone else."

"Why yes, thank you, Alexander. I'd love a drink." She flipped a hand toward the bar like a queen granting an audience. "Whiskey. Neat. The good stuff, not the swill you serve the tourists. And get Biceps of Justice another, too. He looks like he's going to start crying into that beer any minute, and salt never did a craft brew any favors."

I inhaled and let out a breath. "It's domestic. And I'm pretty sure the last time I cried was over a decade ago."

It wasn't true, but I got the sense that if I gave this woman any indication I owned tender human feelings, she'd fillet them and lay them over a clothesline in the town square to bake in the sun.

No, thanks.

Alex handed over the drinks and took one last look between the two of us. "Foster Blake, this is my great-great-aunt Tilly. Aunt Tilly, this is Foster Blake, Sheriff of Majestic, Wyoming, and head of Search and Rescue at SERA."

"We've met," I said. I tilted my hand side to side. "Ish."

"Squat Rack here means I rescued his dignity from the jaws of a slow-motion train wreck starring Tommy, a very suggestive shirt, and several dozen lei-wearing Marians with opinions." She gave me a saucy smile. "Saved him from Granny's walker, too. When the woman's on a tear, she's like a Roomba on Red Bull, bless her."

Alex winced. "Uh. Foster, you should consider calling it a

night," he warned before moving away to help one of his servers.

"Nonsense. Don't listen to him," Tilly said. "I'm only here to buy you a drink for helping to get my girl out of that vehicle last night. I heard you assisted the local first responders." Her eyes met mine. "I'm incredibly grateful, Foster."

I blinked at her while I replayed her words over and over, looking for the trick. She seemed sincere. "Uh... thank you?"

She nodded and took a sip of her whiskey, savoring it before swallowing. "Now, some might say it's the least you could do for ruining my Tommy's wedding..."

And there it was. I gritted my teeth but remained silent.

"But I'm inclined to give you a pass on that," Tilly declared. "I always thought Kari was a bit... dramatic."

I goggled. *This* woman had a problem with people being dramatic? "You don't say."

"And I'm glad Tommy's moving back to California," she went on, eyeing me in a calculated way. "In fact, I have a few people I've been dying to set him up with."

Right. Time to go. I stood and reached for my wallet. "Well, good luck with that—"

"Shame, though," she interrupted. "That Tommy never found out Kari slept with her brother's best friend last summer. I wish that had come out when all the shit hit the fan in Hawaii."

I froze before slowly turning back to her. "Kari cheated on Tommy?"

Tilly pursed her lips and nodded. "You can't tell him, though."

"Why not? He deserves to know! And how do you know Kari cheated if Tommy doesn't?"

Tommy had carried guilt for kissing me—it had been written all over his face, that night in Hawaii, along with his regret at pushing me away. But he'd done the right thing the second it happened. And he'd never intentionally hurt anyone.

The idea that his fiancée might have abused his trust and generosity, letting him think he was the only one to blame for ending their relationship—

"Easy, Tiger." Tilly reached out a hand to pat my arm. I hadn't even realized I'd taken a seat on the barstool next to her again and begun growling under my breath. "I overheard two bridesmaids talking about it at the hotel bar after the breakup. I guess the brother's friend thought he was the reason the wedding was called off."

"Asshole," I muttered, then knocked back some beer to keep from saying more.

Tilly nodded as she sipped her whiskey. "I didn't tell Tommy because I'm not a hundred percent sure if it's true or just a nasty rumor. Besides, Tommy felt bad enough as it was. Never seen him so upset."

I reached for my fresh beer and took another long pull. "He cared about her a lot."

The truth of that burned a hole in my gut. Hell, I was jealous of Robyn and her too-friendly smiles, but Tommy had been *engaged* to Kari. Would have married her if he hadn't met me that day.

"Maybe he did. Probably. Tommy's a caring sort of person."

Tilly shrugged. "But I think he was mostly upset because he had to face some harsh truths about himself."

I swiped a thumb through the condensation on my beer bottle. "Look, I don't care if you're related. I'm not talking about Tommy's truths with you—"

She rolled her eyes. "I'm not talking about his sexuality, Glutes McGraw. I meant the truth that he's not perfect. That he's a human being with emotions, and he can't always follow the script he's written himself."

Her words sounded... well, *fond*. But I felt raw and protective on Tommy's behalf anyway.

"Tommy's a high achiever," I said hotly. "He doesn't like to make mistakes. And who could blame him? In his line of work, mistakes are deadly."

"Mmm." Tilly tapped the rim of her glass with a fingernail. "Did he ever tell you why he got into medicine in the first place?"

I thought back to the night in Hawaii. We'd talked for a few hours before being interrupted by Matthew. "Yeah. He said one of his cousins got hurt on his watch."

Her face softened in memory, and I suddenly realized she'd completely changed while we'd been sitting here. From a provoking, insulting instigator to a provoking, concerned... well, no, she was still an instigator.

"His cousin fell on a hill behind the family's lodge here in Legacy one summer when Tommy was fourteen. All the adults and Tommy's big sisters were in Billings for some... oh, I don't remember now. Tommy was the oldest one at home that day, which meant he was in charge of the motliest crew of Marian kids you've ever seen... outside of their parents, perhaps." She rolled her eyes before continuing thoughtfully. "Every child who was there tells the same story—when poor Cami fell, Tommy flew into action. Assessed the situation, called for help, delegated tasks to the others, and then carried her carefully down the trail to the house. When help arrived, he kept everyone calm while cleaning and treating her scrapes and bruises. His cousins thought Tommy hung the moon. They still do."

If fourteen-year-old Tommy had been even a little bit like the determined, capable man who'd saved Hazel yesterday, I could see why.

Tilly smiled wistfully into her whiskey tumbler. "I find Eagle Scouts to be insufferable, present company included. You're god's gift to emergency preparedness and moral superiority, not to mention perfectionists who think you know everything because you can start a fire with two sticks and a merit badge." She sighed. "But I guess Tommy'd picked up a thing or two at Scouts that came in handy."

I grinned. "You're wrong about me being an Eagle Scout... but I happen to agree with you about the rest."

Tilly eyed me up and down. "Huh. Aged out before completing the badges? Figures. Not everyone has what it takes."

My snort-laugh took me by surprise. It also shocked the hell out of Alex, who gaped at us from the other end of the bar before quickly returning to whatever task he was using as an excuse to stay well away from our conversation.

"If only the rest of us could be as perfect as Dr. Thomas Marian," I said with a reluctant smile.

"Your lips to god's ears." She leaned her elbow on the bar and rested her chin in her hand. "So why don't you want him?"

I blinked at her. "I... I thought we were studiously avoiding this part of the conversation," I admitted.

"I lulled you into a false sense of safety." Tilly winked. "Trap sprung. Also, I stole your truck keys."

I patted my pocket. *Empty.* "The fuck?"

She patted her chest. "In my bra. Where they're safe. And you won't go digging."

That was for sure. Still...

"I'm not talking to you about my love life," I insisted. "And I'm sure as hell not talking to you about Tommy's."

Tilly flicked a hand in the air. "I already know you kissed in Hawaii." When I shot her a look, she continued smugly, "Tommy told Ella, and Ella told her father, and Blue Marian tells me everything. What I want to know is why it can't work."

For a moment, I floundered. Then I countered with, "Who says either of us wants it to?"

Her hand came up to fake a yawn. A ring with giant diamonds caught and scattered the light. "Spare me the denial, Man Candy. I don't have much time left."

The news was surprising. "Are you sick?" That would devastate Tommy. Family was everything to him.

Her face crinkled in confusion. "What? Hell, no. I'm tired and need my beauty rest. So let's skip the conversational gymnastics. Why don't you want my Tommy?"

I ground my teeth together before capitulating. "I do. I do

want him. And if you can figure out how to make it work when we live noncompatible lives, I'll buy you a bottle of whatever whiskey you prefer."

Tilly's eyes lit up. "You'll regret that offer because I *will* take you up on it."

Now it was my turn to shrug. "You talk a big game, lady."

Her eyes narrowed. "Don't get smart with me, boy. I've been managing Marian men since before you were born."

I let out a laugh, unsure why I was engaging with this firebrand. "Tommy doesn't need managing."

He needs loving. And if I could figure out how to be the one to do it, I would.

Before I could respond, Alex's shout rang through the bar. "Another random fire safety inspection? We just had one!"

I glanced over to see an attractive older man I recognized as the fire chief who'd been at the scene of Hazel's accident yesterday. At the time, he'd struck me as being coolheaded and efficient as he'd helped manage the rescue effort.

Now, he was flushed and intent as he leaned over the bar, eyes focused on Alex.

"That's what 'random' means, firebug," he growled. "If you knew when they were coming, you'd get your house in order and pass with flying colors."

Alex threw up his hands. "You're insane, Kincaid! This is harassment! What the fuck is wrong with you? Why me?"

"Do you really want a list, Marian? Because I could give you one."

Tilly giggled softly. She nodded at Alex and shot me a look of extreme satisfaction. "Case in point."

I blinked at her. "What do you mean?"

"Never you mind. Here's what you need to do. You need to find a way to remind Tommy what it is he really wants."

"Pretty sure he knows exactly what he wants. The man is currently in California, interviewing for his dream job. Face it, we're different people with different lives. He belongs in the city, and I belong in Wyoming."

"Says who?" The shrewd intelligence in her eyes was unsettling.

"Says... reality?" I shook my head. "I'm a small-town sheriff who pulls tourists out of trees. He's a brilliant trauma doc who saves lives in ways I can't even comprehend. You should have seen him during Hazel's accident—"

"Oh yeah? What'd you see out there?"

The question seemed simple enough, but something in her tone suggested it wasn't. I thought back to those hours at the accident scene, the controlled chaos of the rescue, the way Tommy had moved through it all with absolute certainty.

"I saw someone who was exactly where he belonged," I said, making my point easily. "Someone who was made for that kind of work. Tommy was in his element. He threw his whole self into getting Hazel out of that car and making sure she didn't..." I stopped before saying *bleed out*.

Tilly studied me for a moment and then shook her head, reaching into her shirt for my keys. "Maybe you're right, Muscles. But if you are, then I must have gotten the story mixed up. Because the way I heard it..." She met my eyes with laser directness as she dropped the keys into my palm. "There wasn't a damned emergency room within a hundred miles of him when he was supposedly 'in his element.'"

I stared at her, both frustrated at not getting my point across and also feeling like she'd somehow judged and found me lacking.

She banged her fist on the bar to get Alex's attention. "Barkeep, put it on my tab. Tilly out."

She stopped to give Chickie a quick pat on the head, and then I watched her saunter away, arms swinging past her designer puffer vest with a *shh-shh* sound.

The woman was a force of nature. Her interference and meddling were enough to make my mother's matchmaking look like child's play by comparison.

I dropped enough cash on the bar to make up for all of our drinks before waving my thanks to Alex and heading out. Once in the truck, I couldn't get Tilly's words out of my head.

You need to find a way to remind Tommy what it is he really wants.

I thought back to our conversation in Hawaii, about how Tommy's face lit up with excitement and passion when he spoke of his time practicing wilderness medicine in North Carolina. About the way he thrived here at SERA, teaching others how to help people in an emergency and improvise when needed.

Once I was on the road out of town with Chickie's ears flapping in the wind on the seat beside me, my phone buzzed with a call from my mom. I clicked to accept.

"Hey, sorry I haven't called you back," I said before she could lecture me. "Things have been crazy around here."

"I figured as much. Just wanted to hear your voice and make sure you're alright up there." Her warm, familiar voice washed over me. I felt my shoulders come down a little from around my ears.

"Yeah. All good. How's it going in Majestic? Everyone okay?"

As my mom launched into her update on local gossip, I smiled to myself. Jo Blake was the social hub of our small town, and if there was news to be had, she had it. She told me about my good friends and their families, my sister's latest achievement in her beginner pickleball classes, and the fact that the new dentist had possibly met his forever match in one of the visiting adventure racers.

"That could have been you," she lamented. "If you'd just let me—"

"I met someone," I blurted, shocking myself possibly even more than my mother.

"You... what?" Her voice carried suspicion, and I could hardly blame her for it.

"Don't get excited. It's not a permanent thing. I just..." I blew out a breath. "I really like him, Mom. And I can't have him."

She was silent for a beat. It had been a long time since I'd confided my feelings for a guy to her, but there'd been a time when I'd told her everything. My dad had taken off when I was eleven, and she'd been a single mom ever since. For as busy as she was running the cafe, she'd always had time for me and Anna.

It was one of the reasons it had been my honor to stay close to home and look out for the two of them in return.

"Baby. Tell me everything. Is he one of your students?" She gasped. "Is it against the rules?"

"Not a student," I said with a laugh. "He's actually an instructor. And no. I don't think Trace would have a problem with it since the woman I'm replacing married another instructor recently."

"Then what's the problem?"

I began to fill her in on Tommy's move from New York to California, the fact that moving to Majestic wasn't even an option for a doctor at his level, and the ultimate agreement we'd made to keep things limited to a summer fling.

It was unlike me to share this much with her, but after talking to Tilly, I was left feeling even worse than I'd felt before walking into Timber. Whether she'd intended to or not, Tilly had painted a picture of Tommy's future, one that could potentially include me. If he decided to pursue wilderness medicine, he could find a job in Wyoming or Montana.

He could be closer to me.

"So what's the problem?" Mom asked. "I still don't get why you're so convinced it won't work."

"Tommy's spent his whole life being a good guy, doing what's right. Trying to be perfect. He's selfless and kind, generous and devoted. There's no way he's going to give up a chance to move back home to be near his parents and grandparents. And he's not going to reject the opportunity of a lifetime if Stanford decides to give him an offer. Guys like him... they don't say no to Stanford, Mom."

Even if it might not make them happy.

"He sounds like a nice man," she said carefully.

My throat was too thick to speak, so I nodded into the dark cab of the truck and made a *mmhm* sound.

"Are you going to be okay, sweetheart?"

I shook my head, glad she couldn't see me. "When am I ever not?" I asked, forcing a smile on my face in hopes she'd hear it.

"Wouldn't hurt you to be a little selfish, you know. You don't always have to be so strong." She paused again, and just when I expected her to press, she changed the subject. "Tell me you heard about Hanson arresting the guy towing a hot tub?"

I was grateful for the opportunity to collect myself. "What? No. Why'd he bring him in? Must have been a good reason, but towing a hot tub itself isn't illegal."

"There were people in it at the time," she said with a snicker. "And apparently, they'd been enjoying their party the whole way from Mammoth Hot Springs."

I let the sound of her laughter and the remainder of her story carry me the rest of the way back to SERA, and for fifteen straight minutes, I wasn't bombarded by thoughts of the golden boy who'd weaseled his way under my skin in such a short time.

But when I opened the door to the cabin and heard Chickie's pitiful whine of disappointment, something felt different. Not just Tommy's absence—I'd been expecting that. It was the way his things were still here, scattered around like he belonged. His book on the nightstand. His jacket on the chair. The lingering scent of that damn shampoo.

For the first time since Hawaii, I let myself imagine what it would feel like if he never came back. If Stanford offered him everything he'd ever dreamed of and he took it. If he left me behind.

The thought hit me like a physical blow. To never share a room with him again, a shower. A bed.

To never sit next to him and share a laugh over a training exercise gone wrong, or strategize a rescue drill, or have him remind me to give a student a fair shake because people could change.

To never run my tongue along the ticklish spot below his ribs and hear the intake of breath half a beat before his soft snort of laughter.

"Fuck," I whispered to the empty room. Suddenly, it was clear to me that if he came back to me, even if only for a few more weeks, I'd take every ounce of him I could.

If he'd give me another chance, I'd grab any opportunity to have a summer fling with Tommy Marian, even knowing it would leave mangled wreckage behind after he was gone.

Better to taste heaven for a few weeks than spend the rest of my life wondering what loving Tommy Marian felt like.

18

TOMMY

My hands shook as I opened the door to Cabin 8. It had been a long two days, and I was dead on my feet. My uncle Jude had insisted on sending me to San Jose in his plane, which meant I'd managed to catch a little bit of sleep on the way there and on the way back.

By the time I'd reached Hazel and Avery's place a couple of hours ago, I'd nearly burst into tears. Hazel was awake and cranky, complaining about all the fuss the family was making over her recovery. Thankfully, she'd allowed me a few minutes to talk about the details of her medical situation and assure me she was following her discharge instructions.

Unthankfully, my mother had taken one look at me and insisted I either crawl into the nearest guest bed or make my way back to SERA in their rental car asap to get some real sleep. While I knew she was right, I bristled at being babied while I was trying to assert my authority as a physician with real concerns over Hazel's recovery.

But now that I was here, only moments away from seeing Foster, suddenly, I *did* want to be babied. I wanted someone—okay, fine, a specific someone—to take care of me. And if he wanted to brush my teeth and tuck me into bed, all the better.

As soon as the door opened, Chickie barreled into my legs, knocking me back until I nearly tripped down the single step to the dirt path beyond.

"Chickie, fuck!" Foster barked.

I gripped the doorknob for balance as several things hit me at once. First, the sheer comfort and familiarity of this man's voice.

Second, the joy of causing someone mind-blowing happiness just by arriving—even if that someone was a canine.

And third, the utter relief of Foster stepping toward me, yanking me into his arms, and crushing his lips to mine in a blinding kiss.

I let out a breath of surprise through my nose and then lurched even closer to him, throwing my arms around his neck and sinking my fingers into his hair.

Thank fucking god.

This welcome was ten thousand times better than I'd expected and even more than I'd hoped. I'd worried he wanted to dial things back, put distance between us to keep us from getting too close. But this? This was the exact opposite of distance.

"Missed you," he said, moving his lips down my jaw and

sucking a spot on my neck. I closed my eyes and relished the attention, even though Chickie was doing her best to get my attention.

"You have no idea how happy I am to be back," I confessed before dropping a kiss into his dark, wind-tossed hair.

He smelled like pine and mountain sunshine, masculine sweat, and faint hints of coffee. For some reason, the combination smelled like the best place on Earth.

"Chickie, dibs," he growled without taking his lips off my neck. "You need to wait in the damned line."

"I smell like ass," I said. "Let me take a shower first."

Foster pulled back and looked at me. His eyes were wild and weary, lips stained with abrasion from my stubble, hair even messier now from my fingers. "I like ass."

I grinned. "Good to know. But I still need a shower."

"If you think I'm letting you out of my sight before morning, Dr. Marian, you're very much mistaken."

Within moments, I was naked and pressed up against the shower wall with a mountain of hard muscles against my back and his lips back on my neck. Foster's hand pulled lazily on my wet cock with a soapy slickness that was more promise than satisfaction.

"Not enough," I begged, reaching my hand down to clasp his. "Just do it already."

He batted my hand away before grabbing it and placing it back on the wall. "Hold still."

I leaned my ass back into his own hard cock, feeling the slight brush of his pubic hair against the tender skin of my ass.

The idea of him back there, cock pressing against my ass, made my stomach flip. Nerves or excitement? Hard to tell, but at this point, I was turned on enough to try anything with Foster, as long as it would get me off.

"Touch me," I begged, pressing back into him again before trying to thrust into his fist.

"Can't decide if you want my hand or my dick, Dr. Marian," he teased. The brush of his lips behind my ear prickled my skin and set all the tiny hairs on my arm standing at attention.

"Whatever it takes," I said on a gasp as he moved his free hand to my ass and brushed a finger between my cheeks.

His low grunt, half acknowledgment and half pleasure, went straight to my cock just before his finger skimmed the rim of my hole.

"Oh fuck," I breathed. "Please."

Foster released my dick, pressed a large hand between my shoulders to bend me forward, and dropped to the floor of the tiny shower. Before I knew what he was doing, a warm, wet tongue began teasing my rim. I sucked in a breath and nearly choked on shower water.

I'd never felt anything like it. The intimacy, the vulnerability, the sheer pleasure of knowing this big, commanding man was on his knees for me, serving at the feet of my pleasure.

My face pressed against the molded plastic wall as I whimpered and begged, needing more, wanting him to stay there like that for hours, just so I could know what it was like to feel this new sensation.

His hands held my ass cheeks as his mouth devoured my ass. Once my sluggish brain finally got its shit together, I reached down to stroke my cock. It didn't take long before I cried out my release, the broken sound deafening in the tiny space.

My knees were jelly as Foster stood and wrapped an arm around my front, pulling me back into his chest and pressing a musky kiss to my cheek. "You like that?" he asked on a low laugh.

"Fuck."

His hard dick rocked gently against my ass cheek. I reached back to stroke it before suddenly wanting to make him feel even a fraction of how good he'd made me feel.

I turned in his arms and sank to my knees, surprising him.

Up till now, we'd mostly jerked each other or frotted until we came, like a pair of teenagers. The time we'd had together had come in snatched moments after a long, exhausting day when neither of us wanted to take the time to do more than share a quick release. I was also pretty sure Foster had been holding back, like he was worried about overwhelming me.

But then Foster had sucked me off for the first time the other day, and now I couldn't stop fantasizing about reciprocating, imagining myself taking his big cock into my mouth and watching his eyes as he came apart.

"You going to kiss and make it better, Doc?" he asked, eyes bright and the edge of his lip curled up.

I rubbed my cheek against his thick, ruddy shaft, reveling in the sight and scent of him. The hair at the base of his cock sparkled with water droplets from the angled light over the vanity shining through the glass door.

"Want to make you feel good." I ran my tongue along the

shaft, from root to tip, imagining all the times I'd received the same kind of treatment, never in a million years imagining I'd be the one on my knees doing the same thing to another man.

I'd never felt so powerful and undone all at once. Knowing I was pulling those sounds from him, that I was the one making his fingers tighten in my hair and his quad muscles bunch.

I pulled his tip into my mouth and suckled it, toying with him but also exploring the feel of him on my tongue, testing the way certain moves made him react.

"Ah Jesus *fuck*, Tommy. Just like that. So good."

I wanted to be good. Wanted to make him happy, make him feel a fraction of what he made me feel. I wanted to drive him to his knees with pleasure. And, yes, maybe there was a small part of me who wanted to show him what he'd miss when he walked away from me.

That thought was enough to spur me on, to double down on dragging my tongue along his shaft, sucking his balls into my mouth, and taking him as deep as I could, even when it caused me to gag.

The noise of my gagging echoed around us, but I didn't let it stop me, especially when it seemed to make his dick even harder and his balls draw up.

"Coming, Tom. Fuck. Coming. *Fuck!*"

The salt hit my taste buds as the sting of his grip in my hair made my eyes smart. I realized belatedly he'd been trying to pull me off of him before his release hit.

Too late and too bad.

I wanted it. Wanted every ounce of this experience with

him. I didn't want to do a damned thing to take any of his pleasure away.

My mouth filled with his release, strange and tangy on my tongue. I choked and sputtered, exposing myself as the neophyte I was. My cheeks heated with embarrassment, but when I saw the look on his face—a mix of dazed bliss and something tender that made my chest ache—I realized I'd take any embarrassment again if it meant seeing that expression.

I wanted more than sex. I wanted permanence, even if I didn't have the guts to say it out loud.

It took me a minute to realize the water had gone cold, but as soon as I did, the exhaustion and overwhelm from my trip and the events leading up to it hit me in full force.

"Hey, hey. Let's get you dried off, okay?" Foster's voice seemed to come through water. I stood up with his help, large hands under my arms. My eyes remained on his cock, enjoying the view of it still ruddy and fat against his damp thigh.

He was so fucking sexy, so powerful and attractive. I couldn't imagine living my entire life without ever having had this experience and this feeling.

In a way, I felt... almost cheated. Like all of my gay and bi cousins, my uncles and friends, had been able to experience this sooner, *know* this part of themselves earlier.

But I was so fucking glad I knew it now.

"Tommy, look at me."

I blinked up at Foster, who was somehow already wrapped in a towel and holding a toothbrush with toothpaste on it.

"My toothbrush," I realized.

"Yes. Your toothbrush. Brush your teeth, baby. You're wiped out. We never should have—*ow*!"

I yanked a hair on his chest. "Don't say that. Don't you dare ruin my first blow job. My first rimming. My first..." I thought back to the sensation of his strong tongue on my ass, *in* my ass. "Lots of things," I finished lamely. Because words would never do it justice.

Foster's face softened. "Okay then. Brush your teeth, Cherry. We'll have to finish your sexual awakening another time."

I shoved the toothbrush into my mouth and began brushing. "Want to have anal sex," I said through a mouthful of suds. "With you."

His eyes darkened. "Better the fuck be with me. Unless you found some pretty boys in Stanford."

I leaned against him as I brushed, grateful for his solid presence. "Lots of pretty boys." When Foster's mouth dropped into a frown, I leaned on him even more and added, "Don't want pretty boys. Want my beefy sheriff."

After finishing my teeth, I rinsed and spit into the sink, taking the hand towel Foster put in front of me. I dried my face, ruffled the towel over my wet hair, realizing it was somehow already towel-dried.

Foster finished his own teeth and herded me into the bedroom, yanking back the covers on my bed. "In."

"You."

The single word was all I had the energy for, but he understood it. He slipped between the sheets first and then yanked me in to lie half on top of him the only way we really fit in the bed together.

Pretty sure I was asleep before he even pulled the covers over us. The only thing I remembered was him saying something that sounded oddly like, "You're as stubborn as your aunt Tilly."

But that couldn't have been right.

19

FOSTER

Tommy had been back for five days, and I still hadn't gotten up the nerve to ask him about Stanford.

I was a total chickenshit, but to be fair, we'd also been busy with training exercises, including an all-day wildfire and missing-person rescue drill, a long search and rescue exercise, and an unexpected request to help provide additional support at an ultramarathon being run through the foothills on the far side of Slingshot.

When we weren't working, Tommy spent as much time checking on his sister as possible. His entire family was in town to see Hazel, and even if he hadn't wanted to visit with the patient, he would have been expected to spend time with his parents and extended family.

He'd invited me to join him a couple of times, but I'd declined with excuses. Chickie needed training, Trace needed help with something, or, in one case, I'd had bad chicken at dinner.

None of it was true—or not true enough to keep me from joining him. The real reason was self-preservation. My only chance at surviving this "fling" was to weld a damned cage around my heart and drive sharp spikes into every inch of the metal grating. Getting to know his family any better would be a colossal mistake, considering there was no future between us.

Which was why my heart rate shot up when Tommy's eyes pierced me across the now empty table in the SERA dining hall and he said, "You're not saying no tonight."

I played dumb, scrambling to come up with another excuse to beg off a Marian family visit. "To...?"

He bounced his eyebrows. "Maybe I'll tell you back at the cabin."

Oh. The lascivious expression on his face made the tension in my shoulders release. *Definitely not a family thing, then.*

I leaned in closer and lowered my voice, even though no one was around to hear. "If it's something that'll take place at the cabin, you have to know I'm not saying no to you."

Tommy's grin jolted something low in my belly. "Then what are we waiting for?"

As soon as we stood up, Chickie scrambled to her feet and fell into a natural heel next to Tommy's leg. The three of us made our way back to the cabin, the low evening sun still plenty bright and the breeze blowing away the heat of the day.

Halfway back to the cabin, I reached down to grab Chickie's collar. A few nights before, I'd caught an elk nosing around our cabin, so I wanted to play it safe.

"Sorry, Chickpea," I said when she gave me her big eyes. "Better safe than sorry."

I kept walking for a couple of paces before I realized Tommy had stopped in his tracks to stare at me.

"What?" I asked, looking around to see what had made him stop.

The look on his face turned melty-sweet, the kind of tender affection that made me wonder what the hell had happened to suddenly make him look at me like that.

"What is it?" I asked again.

He shook his head and continued walking to the cabin without a word. I shook my head and followed. The minute we were in the cabin with the door closed, he shoved me against it and kissed me wildly. His tongue carried the taste of hot fudge from the sundae he'd had for dessert, and I licked into his mouth, seeking more of it.

When he finally pulled back, I asked dazedly, "What was that about?"

His hand was still clutching the front of my shirt. "Chickpea! You got a SAR puppy and named her after my hummus, just like I suggested."

Shit. Since he hadn't put it together in the last four weeks, I'd figured he'd forgotten that part of our Hawaii conversation.

"That's not... no, I..." I blew out a breath and knocked his hand away from my shirt. "Fuck off," I muttered, moving over to my bed to kick my shoes under the edge of it.

Tommy followed me and pressed himself against my back, wrapping his arms around my middle and splaying his hands across my stomach and chest. "Why can't you admit it? It's the nicest thing anyone's ever—"

"Don't." I put my hands over his but didn't pull them off me. Instead, I caressed them with my thumbs. "If you tell me that's the nicest thing anyone's ever done for you, I'm going over to your family's lodge right this fucking minute with some very choice words for every single person there."

His laughter vibrated through my back. "Maybe I'm exaggerating, but I'm still..." He blew out a breath. "I'm touched, okay? Very touched."

This entire conversation made me very uncomfortable. "I can think of better ways to touch you," I growled.

He laughed again and turned me around to face him. "Which brings me to the thing I said earlier about not saying no." Tommy's eyes darkened, but I could also see a sliver of insecurity. "I want to fuck you. Or... or you can fuck me, although I'll probably be a big giant baby because you have a massive bull-cock, but I'm happy to try."

I snorted as my dick suddenly perked the fuck up at the thought of thrusting into Tommy's sexy ass. "Are you missing the tight heat..." I stopped myself from the stupid tease about sex with a woman. "Sorry, that was crude and uncalled for."

He lifted an eyebrow. "Also inaccurate, considering I've had the tight heat of your mouth many, many times the last week or two. And, just so you know, *no*. There's not a single moment I've missed having sex with a woman. The shittiest orgasm I've had with you has still been ten thousand times better than any I've had with women."

Tommy's words shocked me. "Liar," I accused, hoping it didn't sound like the fishing expedition it was.

"Well..." He pursed his lips, considering. "Maybe you're right."

"Mpfh."

A shit-eating grin split his face. "There haven't *been* any shitty orgasms with you." He slid his hands up and down my arms. "In fact, I was just thinking the other day that if this is what being with a guy is like, I've been missing out."

"It's not. Not always," I found myself saying. Looking away, I cleared my throat. "So you really never considered being with a guy before, ah... before Hawaii?"

Before me.

Tommy shrugged. "I thought I *had* considered it. With as many gay and bi men as there are in my family, I couldn't not. And it's possible there's been a long-standing Captain America thing I might have misinterpreted as hero worship..."

"Spandex suit got you?"

"More the muscles under the suit, I think." He ran an appreciative hand over my chest that had me stifling a groan. "But my point is, I've always been open to being attracted to anyone. I've just never been attracted enough to a man to label it. Or to act on it." Those heart-stealing hazel eyes met mine. "Until you."

I grabbed his face and kissed him, hard.

"Want to fuck you so fucking bad," I admitted against his lips before pulling back and meeting his eyes. "But we'll start the other way tonight, okay?"

I could tell from the heat in Tommy's eyes the idea was *very* okay.

We continued kissing and touching, yanking clothes off each other, until we were humping each other on the bed, panting with need. I grabbed a bottle of lube and poured some onto my fingers. "Haven't been with anyone like this since…" I glanced at him from under my lashes. "Ah… New Year's. So. All tests negative."

His cheeks darkened. "Yeah? Um. Same. I had a panel done last month. Negative."

Before I could reach around and begin prepping myself, Tommy took the lube from my hands and poured some into his own. "I've been told I have good hands," he teased. "You should let me do that."

Instead of reaching for myself, I moved my slick fingers to his cock. "Sounds like a plan."

His eyes rolled back as he sucked in a breath. "Wait, fuck. If you do that, I won't be able to… oh fuck, Foster."

We played with each other a little while, teasing and stroking, stretching and taunting, until both of us were rock hard and out of breath.

Tommy pushed me over until I was sprawled beneath him on my stomach, one knee pushed up toward my chest. "You okay?" His voice was insistent as he gently moved the lubed head of his cock across my hole.

"This your way of drawing out the anticipation? Fuck me already. I'm not the cherry here." I reached back for his hip and held on to it, urging him forward.

"If you could cease referring to previous experience while I'm preparing to fuck you, that'd be appreciated," he grumbled.

"Tommy, sweetheart, you're not going to hurt me. Take a breath and soldier on. I promise you'll like it."

He pinched my ass. "Jackass."

When the tip of his cock stretched into my hole, I focused on breathing and relaxing. For all the big talk, it had actually been a long time since I'd bottomed for anyone. I was up for it, especially with Tommy, but it didn't come so naturally to me. And I wanted to make it good for him.

"Oh fucking fuck." The high-pitched edge to his voice as he sank into me was worth every moment of discomfort as my body tried to ease around his cock. "Foster. Oh god. You're so fucking tight and hot."

I squeezed around him involuntarily, making him jolt and groan. "What can I do to make it good for you? Because I'm... oh god... I'm not gonna..."

He moved tentatively in and out, pushing deeper with each thrust into me. The warm dampness of his chest pressed against my back as his lips landed at the base of my neck. "Thank fuck. Thank Christ. Oh fuck." His words ran together, a breathless, incredulous whimper.

I reached back and threaded my fingers into his hair, pushing back with my hips to meet his thrusts and encourage him to keep going.

The shift in angles did the exact right thing to my nerve endings, and on the next pull, his dick dragged across my gland, making me slur, "Just like that."

It was quick, which was probably a good thing, but feeling Tommy inside of me like that—and knowing he'd never done this with another man—made me feel a fierce possessiveness. Like he was mine.

I didn't want him ever doing this with another man.

To be honest, I didn't want him doing this with another soul.

It was sacred. Too much and not enough all at once. I'd never, ever felt this kind of connection and trust with another person before.

His hand came around to grip my chin. "You're mine," he said through his teeth. "Do you understand me? I don't want you letting anyone else inside you like this but me. Please, Foster. Please tell me you won't—" His voice broke on the second *please*.

The way his thoughts echoed my own nearly ripped my soul in two.

I turned and kissed him quickly to keep him from saying anything else. As I held his head with his lips pressed tightly to me, I felt his orgasm crash over him, triggering my own.

Tommy's words had shocked me, not because it was a surprise he wanted more than a fling but because he hadn't been able to keep from admitting it out loud. There was a relief in that. I knew he'd been walking on eggshells to a certain extent, trying to keep his pleas for more than casual to himself. Trying to keep from scaring me off.

So the fact that he hadn't been able to keep from saying it meant he was overcome with feelings.

And he wasn't the only one.

I wished that changed things. Wished it meant I could

respond to his pleas with promises of my own the way I wanted to. But my weak grasp on my commitment to keep it casual was the only protection I had left, and I was trying to hold on to it for as long as possible.

Four more weeks.

20

TOMMY

THERE WERE three weeks left of the summer SERA session. The past week had flown by in a hazy fog of hard work and harder sex. After I'd fucked Foster in the cabin that first night, I'd become obsessed with trying it every which way possible, which had very quickly led to him fucking me.

The first two times had been semi-aborted attempts, the first due to a premature ejaculation situation I wasn't even sorry for. The man had magic fingers, and it turned out... I had a very sensitive prostate. That had led to a sleepless night of trying to repeat the experience as many times as humanly possible until I'd finally passed out, sprawled over Foster's chest for the final hour before sunrise.

The second attempt had been wildly successful. So wild and successful, in fact, I was a convert. Sex with Foster was all I could think about, all I wanted to do, all the time.

I felt like a sex-crazed teenager... which might have

explained why I'd spent the better part of a scouting hike with Foster begging him to fuck me in the woods.

"Not happening," he grunted as he stepped up a steep embankment threaded with thick roots, sending pebbles and dirt chunks down the embankment behind him.

He reached back to lend me a hand, but I batted it away and climbed up after him. "My med kit has lube, if that's what's holding you back."

"It's not." He continued through the trees in search of the right spot to place our search and rescue training target for the upcoming sign-cutting drill. Since the students assigned to medical rotation were stuck in the classroom doing a CPR refresher course this morning, I'd elected to accompany Foster on his hike.

It was proving very frustrating.

We continued moving farther off the trail and deeper into the woods. The air was cooler up here than at SERA, and I enjoyed the break from being around lots of other people.

I also enjoyed the view of Foster Blake's ass in those shorts and the way his hair flicked out around the edges of the backward ball cap he'd stolen from me.

After a few more minutes, it was clear Foster wasn't to be deterred from his mission. So I tried a different tactic.

"You haven't asked me about Stanford. It's been *two weeks*." He was in front of me, leading the way, so I could only see the tensing of his shoulders as he froze for a beat, the gray SERA T-shirt stretched wide over his shoulders.

A twig snapped loudly under his boot as he finally moved again. "I figured if you wanted to tell me, you'd tell me."

"Aren't you curious at all?"

"Not really."

Now, he was just pissing me off. "Why not?"

He stopped and turned. "Because I know you exceeded their expectations. Because I know you charmed the pants off of them, and I know they want you. What's to ask?"

I threw out my hands in frustration. "Oh, I don't know, what *I* thought about it? How *I'm* feeling about it? What it was like to try to impress people and be on the top of my game while sleep-deprived and exhausted and worrying about my sister?"

Foster's face fell. "Tommy, I—"

I held up a hand. "Spare me whatever the fuck too-little, too-late bullshit you're getting ready to fumble, okay?"

He took a step toward me, but I glared at him, freezing him in place. Just as he opened his mouth to speak, the sound of happy chatter broke through the woods from the direction of the trail. By unspoken agreement, Foster and I remained silent until after they'd passed. When he spoke again, it was in a softer voice.

"I'm sorry. What can I do to make it up to you?"

I folded my arms over my chest. "First, you can explain why you care so little about my feelings. It's one thing to want to keep things casual, Foster, and a completely different thing to deliberately not give a shit about the person you're being casual with."

His expression was pained. "I do care. I care too fucking much, that's the problem. And the only way this works is if I keep those feelings to myself." He stopped and blew out a breath, threading the fingers of both hands together over his ball cap. "But you're right. I wasn't even being a good friend, and I'm sorry."

Foster's confession shocked me. I'd suspected he had serious feelings for me, *hoped* he did, but he'd never admitted it out loud. I'd only sensed it in the way he touched me. The way he cared for me when I was in need of comfort or reassurance. The way he'd practically attacked me when I'd returned from California.

"What can I do to make it up to you?" he asked again.

I teetered between two paths. One of them would include forcing him to talk about his feelings, get them out in the open so we could try and figure out a way to be together despite seemingly impossible odds.

The other was to admit the truth to myself. That he was right to keep his feelings to himself. Because there really wasn't a clean solution to this, and he'd made it very clear from the beginning he wasn't interested in a messy one.

The fact was, I'd nailed my Stanford interviews. More than that, I'd loved it there. The people were amazing, the opportunity was top-notch, and the proximity to my family couldn't be beat. I'd grown up only thirty minutes away in Hillsborough. My parents and grandparents still lived there, and several of my high school friends had remained in the area. Accepting a job there would be a no-brainer...

And it was no place at all for a Wyoming sheriff who belonged under this big sky, breathing clean mountain air and remaining king of his castle.

"You can fuck me," I said, sticking out my chin. "Right here and right now."

I might as well have waved a red cape in front of an angry bull. His eyes narrowed as he assessed me for a beat.

Then he began stalking closer. "Yeah? Right here where anyone could see us? See *you*, ass out for any random hiker who comes along?"

My chest heaved as the air got thinner. "If not you, then I really will have to grab a random hiker."

His jaw ticked. "Like hell you will. Open your pants, Doc."

I looked around, the reality of the situation finally sinking in. "Or maybe—"

"Pants. Off."

After dropping my pack, my hands went to my belt, flicking it open as quickly as possible and fumbling for the button and zipper. Foster rifled through my pack until he found what he was looking for: a single packet of medical lubricant. *Score.*

I shot him an *I-told-you-so* grin.

"You're entirely too smug right now," he grumbled, moving closer to me while reaching for his own belt. "When we wind up arrested for public indecency and I lose my career over this, I need you to remember whose idea it was."

I could tell from the tone in his voice he wasn't at all interested in being talked out of it. I batted my eyelashes at him. "But, Sheriff, I was just doing what you said. You said if I walked into the trees and acted like a good boy for you, you wouldn't write me up..."

He laughed and shook his head. "Shut the fuck up before I lose my boner."

I turned to face the tree behind me and waggled my bare ass

at him. "Is this good enough for you, sir? Am I being a good boy?"

Foster moved up behind me, a thick finger with cold gel moving straight to my hole. "Role-playing isn't for you, sweetheart."

I sucked in a breath as he deliberately dragged his fingertip down along my gland. "Dr. Blake, are you sure this... this kind of exam is necessary for a sprained ankle?"

Foster's large hand came around and clamped over my mouth. "How about pretending to be a pain in the ass getting fucked against a tree?" he murmured against the back of my ear. "Can you do that for me?"

I closed my eyes and made a sound of agreement as he pushed his slick cock between my cheeks. I was up on my toes, the rough bark from the tree sharp against my forehead. The intrusion of his giant dick required me panting through my nose as my body stretched to accommodate his.

"That's it, sweetheart," he murmured, making my stomach clench. "*Such* a good boy for me."

My eyes rolled up. Foster's muscled forearm tightened around my front as he began thrusting into me, continuing to murmur dirty encouragement in my ear as his other hand tightened over my mouth.

The breeze blew across my skin, but I hardly felt it. I did feel the familiar scratch of his happy trail on my skin, the softness of his lips on my ear, and the solid anchor of his larger frame around mine.

I knew without a shadow of a doubt that if anyone came upon us like this, he'd do anything within his power to hide me from view, even if that meant sacrificing himself and his entire career.

Foster was rock solid. Dependable. Loyal. *Kind.*

And I was gone for him.

As he continued to fuck me against that tree, giving me everything I wanted, I felt euphoric, like I was high on the very best pain meds.

Unfortunately, even the best highs only end in one of two ways.

And neither one of them was enjoyable.

21

FOSTER

I HAD TO ADMIT, I was feeling pret-ty good when I walked out of the woods after the trail sex. My legs were nice and loose, my brain was calmer than it had been in days, and I was even grateful one of my students had volunteered to keep Chickie back since she'd be involved in the search and rescue exercise later in the day.

So maybe that was why I didn't have my guard up when the attack came from an unexpected angle.

"You're expected at the cookout tonight," Trace said as my team huddled around the table in the makeshift command tent during the exercise.

"What cookout?"

"Over at the Marian lodge. The family's celebrating Hazel's recovery, and they wanted to include everyone who had a hand in her rescue. I told them you'd be there."

I scrambled for a reason I couldn't go, but he was onto me.

"I told them you'd be there," he repeated more slowly, giving me a flinty look as if challenging me to argue with him. "And since the Marian family donated the land we're standing on for the establishment of SERA, I would consider it a kind of... oh, let's say *command performance.*"

I breathed out through my nose. "Yes, sir. Looking forward to it, sir. Sounds amazing."

He rolled his eyes. "Simmer down, asshole. No one ever died from a backyard burger."

I chose not to tell him about the time I had to respond to a natural gas fire at the Majestic River campground. "Sure. Sounds safe as fuck," I said instead. "My kind of event."

At least that got a laugh out of the man. "Thanks. I'd offer to keep the pup, but I'm sure you'll want to use her as social lube."

I shuddered. "Don't make it sound nasty."

He shrugged. "It's either that or alcohol, and I don't recommend getting drunk around some of those folks. One time, Teddy Marian got drunk and woke up with a tiny tattoo of a squirrel nestled in his pubes. Almost ruined his marriage. Oh! And stay away from anyone over the age of eighty. They're the ones you need to watch out for."

I stared after him as he sauntered away.

Tommy's voice appeared low in my ear. "Staring at another man's ass already? It's only been an hour since you had your—"

I spun around and clapped my hand over his mouth again, making his eyes flare hot enough to harden my cock again. I quickly yanked my hand away, glancing around to see if anyone had seen. Thankfully, everyone was too busy focusing on the exercise.

"I need you to stay here tonight," I blurted.

His eyes widened even more. "I can't. I'm due at my family's place for a dinner thing. I'd invite you, but I know you—"

"I'll come!"

"You will?" The surprised expression turned suspicious. "Why?"

My breathing was coming fast. "You sure you don't want to stay here?"

"With you?"

"No, I..." I blew out a breath. "Your family invited me to the cookout."

Comprehension dawned on his face. "And you're freaking out."

"Pfft. *Pffttttt*. Pft."

Tommy's grin was offensively wide. "Oh man, this is going to be incredibly fun."

IT WASN'T FUN. Not one single bit of it was fun.

"Your great-great-aunt is going to give me a tattoo in my private places," I whispered as we walked around the back of the giant log building that had been in their family for several decades. I'd already known the family was wealthy based on things I'd heard from Trace and around town, but seeing the scale of it still took me by surprise and didn't help one bit with my nerves.

Tommy snapped his head around. "I'm sorry, *what*?"

"She's going to call me Sergeant Man Meat or Thigh Mountain. And she's going to fix you up on dates, probably in front of me. She's been dying to set you up with people, and she definitely doesn't like me. I'm guessing she already has someone here to set you up with. The fire marshal, maybe. He's good-looking, if a little mature for you."

"The... fire marshal? Is too mature for me? Are you saying I'm immature?"

"Tommy," I urged. "Focus, okay? We need a plan. Like, a signal or something. If Tilly starts asking me about my feelings, I'll make this sign."

I tapped two fingers on my forearm. "You know this one, right? It means I need help."

He laughed. "It means *medic*."

"Same thing. And if you need rescuing, all you need to do is —*oh hi!*"

I forced a grin at Tommy's cousin Ella, who approached us as soon as we rounded the corner of the lodge. People were standing in clusters across a low, wide deck and the stone patio beyond. Music played from hidden speakers, and lit tiki torches wafted the faint scent of citronella into the evening air.

The sun hadn't dropped behind the mountain yet, and it lay fat, golden stripes on the grass between the trees.

"So, I take it this means we've progressed past the 'room-mates who only kissed that one time in Hawaii by accident' stage?" Ella asked, her gaze darting between us.

"Twice," I said without thinking.

Tommy closed his eyes and groaned. "She did that on purpose to get you to correct her. It's her favorite trick."

Ella snapped her fingers and pointed at me. "Gotcha."

I shot a pleading look at Tommy. "See? See why I keep saying no? I'm outgunned."

Ella frowned in sympathy. "You brought a knife to a nuke fight. Listen, I get it. It must be intimidating to walk into a group of forty to fifty people who saw you wearing Tommy's shirt in Hawaii and would literally murder anyone who made Tommy cry, but—"

Tommy muttered an apology before grabbing Ella and dragging her a few feet away. While they spoke, I glanced around to see if I could find any friendlies in the crowd.

Tilly was making a beeline for me with a red Solo cup in each hand. Following behind her at a more dignified pace was an elegant-looking older man who looked familiar, but I couldn't place him.

"Chest Almighty," she said, shoving a cup of draft beer in my hand. "Here ya go. Liquid courage. Don't say I never gave you nothin'. Come find me later."

As soon as she was there, she was gone again.

I took an appreciative sip of the beer and relished the crisp coolness as it slid down my throat.

An older guy with strawberry blond hair approached and reached out a hand to shake. "You must be Foster Blake," he said. "I'm Blue Marian, Ella's dad. Nice to meet you. I've heard good things about you."

Before I could say a word, a stream of people joined him. First, another attractive older man appeared and slid his arm around Blue. "I'm Tristan. Whatever Blue is telling you, ignore him. We're happy you're here."

A tall guy with a beard and a flannel open over a tee that

said, *Only Hunt with a Zoom Lens*, eyed me up and down. "This him?"

I stood up a little straighter and tried to remind myself I was a Wyoming sheriff. I didn't get intimidated; I did the intimidating.

"Thank you for having me. It's nice to take a break from SERA. Trace said you serve a mean burger."

A shorter man I recognized as a famous country music singer shot me a friendly smile. "We also have a lovely beet salad and a giant fruit bowl."

I felt like a bug, not under a microscope but smashed flat on the windshield of a vehicle doing a hundred miles an hour in a speed zone.

"How's Hazel?" I asked, looking around in hopes of finding her somewhere nearby, beckoning me over with a wild wave of her hands.

A woman with reddish hair streaked with gray came barging through the crowd, elbowing people out of the way. "Everyone give the guy a break, alright?" She met my eyes and beamed. "You must be Foster?"

Before I could finish nodding, she threw herself against me and hugged me tight. "Thank you so much for saving my daughter."

Her voice was full of emotion and gratitude. I realized I had Tommy's mother in my arms, and I carefully hugged her back, suddenly wanting to thank her for gifting the world, gifting *me*, the miracle of her son's existence.

"You're very welcome," I said instead. "I didn't do much. Honestly, it was your son who—"

She pulled back and held on to my shoulders, eyes full of unshed tears. "I already thanked him, too, don't worry. But he said without you keeping a cool head, you might not have gotten there before someone made a mistake."

I shook my head. "It's my job. And I was proud to be there to witness Tommy in his element."

She squeezed my arms before throwing herself into me for another quick hug. "I'm so, so happy you're here. Ignore all these idiots and come with me. I'll find you something to eat. Tommy says you like tomatoes on your hamburger, so Avery and I saved the best from their garden just for you."

I let her lead me away, shooting one last look over toward Tommy, who was done talking to Ella but was now standing off to the side, talking on the phone.

Once I'd been seated among the scattered outdoor sofas and chairs, Hazel wheeled over in a mobility scooter. She still looked pale, but she was obviously feeling much better.

"How are you doing? It's good to see you out of bed."

She reached over and squeezed my arm. "I'm only allowed to stay out here for an hour, but I'm very happy to thank you in person."

"Everyone keeps saying thank you to me. I didn't do anything but get Tommy there safely so he could help."

Avery came up behind Hazel and rubbed her shoulder. "Don't listen to him, babe. He worked side by side with the firefighters to get the door off the car. I was there, I saw everything. He was amazing. Foster also kept the media away."

Out of desperation, I did what my mother and cousin had always taught me never to do. "When are you due?" I asked them. Thankfully, I had solid proof Avery was actually pregnant, so I figured the question was justified.

They both beamed. "Four more weeks."

That was enough to get the subject fully off me. Everyone around us began talking excitedly about the baby. I was able to pitch in every now and then since I'd recently become a kind of uncle to my cousin Sheridan's baby.

Tommy finally joined me, sitting down with his own plate of food and a muttered "I'm starving."

As he ate, I realized this big group of Marians reminded me of home, of my cousin Way and his group of friends. I'd envied Way the family he'd accidentally married into, the group of guys and their husbands who'd formed a brotherhood of sorts in Majestic.

They'd done a good job of including me in most things, but I'd still never truly felt a part of the group. I was usually good at getting along with most people, and I felt like I was doing a fine job of it here, too. Everyone was friendly and kind. I appreciated watching the little moments of teasing, flirtation between spouses, and snarky banter between siblings. As I watched the family dynamics play out, I was struck by how amazing it was to be among this many examples of happy marriages between two men.

Tommy had grown up surrounded by gay men, and yet he'd never dated one before. Why in the world had he picked me?

I glanced over and caught him looking at me. "What?" I asked.

"Making sure you don't bolt and leave me without a ride back to SERA."

I reached into my pocket and pulled out my keys, handing them over easily. "I go when you go, Doc."

As my fingers brushed his hand, he clamped his around them, pulling me in so he could whisper something in my ear. I tried not to look around guiltily to see if anyone had noticed the intimacy.

"I've been watching for the international distress signal," he teased, the breath warm against my ear. "So far, so good."

I patted my chest and gave a thumbs-up, the SAR signal for "I'm okay."

He grinned. "Gotta admit, I enjoyed seeing the big, bad sheriff intimidated by my family."

"Intimidated? Pfft. Hardly. Oh shit." I spotted Tilly making her way toward me. This time, she was flanked by the other old ladies from Hawaii. "Abort, *abort*."

I didn't wait for him, only mumbled something about finding a men's room and took off. Unfortunately, Tilly was lying in wait for me when I came out of the hall bathroom.

"Major Denial," she said, eyeing me up and down.

I couldn't determine whether it was another nickname or simply a statement of my current emotional situation.

"Ma'am."

Her eyes narrowed. "You worked things out yet? And before you answer me, I can already tell it's a big fat *no*."

"Nothing to work out," I said, way more easily than I felt.

She nodded. "Alright then. I guess it's a good thing he accepted the job offer this evening. Nothing more to say." She patted me on the chest. "Take care of yourself, Foster."

Instead of sticking around to provoke or needle me further, she simply walked away.

I didn't know what bothered me more: hearing that Tommy had taken the job in California or hearing Tilly call me by my actual name.

Both things were devastating.

But only one made me feel like I'd lost something irrevocably precious.

I spent the rest of the evening trying to figure out how to be happy for Tommy. How best to support him. If he'd made his decision—and after seeing him at the scene of Hazel's accident, I could understand why he had—I wouldn't stand in his way.

22

TOMMY

FOSTER WAS quiet on the drive back to SERA. I figured he was experiencing a Marian hangover, so I left him to it. Maybe by the time we returned to the cabin, he would have put the trauma behind him.

In the meantime, I replayed the phone call from the chief of emergency medicine at UC Davis that had come in just after we'd arrived at the lodge. He'd caught wind of my availability and was eager to bring me in for an interview—practically pleading with me not to commit elsewhere until they'd had a chance to make their case.

After I'd hung up, I spotted a video conference invite from Stanford's HR department for tomorrow morning. It seemed unlikely they'd go to the trouble of setting up a meeting just to let me down gently... but stranger things had happened.

I glanced over at Foster. The evening air caught the ends of his hair as the dashboard lights threw a cool cast over his skin. He flicked his eyes over to me and back to the road.

"Y'okay?" he asked softly.

"Thanks for coming tonight," I said, feeling truly grateful. "Everyone loved meeting you."

He shrugged. "You've got a great family. It was nice to see you among your... people."

There was something off about the way he said it, but I couldn't put my finger on it. "And you were able to avoid Tilly, I noticed. Not so much Granny and Irene, though."

He winced. "That little one's a fireball. Offered me five American dollars if I'd lift her over my head."

I couldn't help but laugh. "What'd you say?"

"Told her if I started picking up random women at parties, I'd lose my gay card. She frowned and nodded. Seemed to think that made sense."

Chickie tried to nudge my shoulder from the back, insisting on her share of the conversation, even though a moment earlier, she'd been so hard asleep there'd been snores coming from the back seat.

I reached back to pet her through the partition. "You ready for bed, Chickpea?"

Foster shifted in his seat but didn't say anything about the name. Meanwhile, I'd been carrying it around all day like a bright, flawless little pearl hidden deep in my pocket. That kiss in Hawaii hadn't just changed *my* life; it had left a mark on Foster, too.

"Long day," Foster said after a few more minutes on the road.

I glanced over at him. "Yeah?"

He shrugged. "The hike to set the target. The SAR exercise and medical response. Dinner with your family—I mean, not... not like that. I just meant dinner at the lodge. Where your family happened to be."

I bit my lip against a smile. "It's my family's lodge."

"Right."

"And they were the only ones there."

"Yes."

"So... technically, you had dinner with my family, Foster."

He nodded but didn't take his eyes off the road. "And I already told you it was nice."

"Fine," I said, letting him off the hook. Suddenly, I was tired of the games. Tired of being the only one in this supposed "fling" who seemed to want to push past it like two grown adults, even if the solution wasn't neat or easy.

I was tired of Foster getting moody instead of talking to me about his feelings. One day, he was cold as ice, putting up his "physical only" walls, and the next, he was holding me tight and telling me how much he missed me. Making fucking love to me like I was precious. Like he never wanted to let me go.

Maybe this was a sign. Maybe this was exactly what I needed to see before receiving the official offer and making my decision.

It was time to stop wishing Foster would fight for us when he'd told me all along he wasn't interested in that.

"You're right," I said as he turned off the highway onto SERA's gravel drive. "Long day. I'm exhausted."

After he threw the SUV into Park, he turned to look at me. "Everything okay? Anything you want to talk about?"

I glanced at him, wondering if this was an opening to discuss my potential job offer. To ask his advice. To feel him out about the possibility of trying to make a long-distance relationship work.

The engine ticked quietly as I turned to face him. "If Matthew hadn't cheated on you, would the two of you have ended up together?"

Foster's eyebrows dipped in confusion. "Me and Matthew? What do you mean?"

"Were you in love with him? Would the two of you have ended up together?"

He tilted his head. "Those are two separate questions, Tommy."

I shot him a look, forcing him to give me a real answer.

Foster sighed and sat back against the door. "I *wanted* to love him. I wanted to settle down, have a partner I could come home to. Share my life with. I fantasized about the little things. Having a warm body waiting in my bed after a long shift. Spending lazy afternoons in front of a football game or getting up early for a hike in summer."

He blew out a breath and forked his fingers through his hair. "My friends all have partners now, and I see them at the grocery store or grabbing a quick breakfast at the cafe before work. That's what I wanted. The everyday companionship."

"But Matthew moved to New York," I said. "He wasn't there with you. So that's why you didn't stay together?"

He met my eyes. "The only reason Matthew and I were

together at all was because I was an idiot with more hope than practicality. He obviously needed something more. Something bigger. And I had no desire to hold him back or tie him down."

My stomach dropped like a sack of bricks. I pressed my lips together and nodded. "Understood."

We moved through our nightly routine by rote, slipping into our own beds automatically. Apparently, our sleeping arrangements were clearly defined based on the unspoken mood between us.

I slept fitfully—so fitfully that Chickie jumped up in my bed at one point and lay down on top of my chest, nuzzling her cold nose in my neck until I relaxed.

The next morning, I awoke to an empty cabin. Foster and Chickie were already gone, so I was able to shower and dress without walking on eggshells or, worse, staring at his body in a way that might lead to something physical.

I made my way to the dining room for breakfast, where Robyn cheerfully waved me over to a spot at her table. "Tommy! Over here. We've got room for you, and I wanted to ask you about today's certification exam for your students."

While she spoke, I picked out Foster's and Trace's voices as they entered the dining room from the direction of Trace's office. Robyn must have seen me watching them because she glanced over and back to me. "Good news, I think. Foster has a lead on a new medical director for the program."

It took me a moment to comprehend what she was saying. "A new medical director? Like, my replacement?"

Robyn frowned. "Well, you're only here for the summer session, right? I guess Foster heard from a guy he knows down in Colorado. They worked on some SAR jobs together, and Foster thinks highly of the guy. He knows Trace needs someone killer to fill your shoes. "

And he'd mentioned it to Trace instead of me?

A thousand questions piled up behind my teeth. I started with just one. "What's the rush? The next session doesn't start until mid-August, right?"

Her forehead crinkled. "Yeah, but that's in five weeks. This is kind of the time we need to be looking, depending on how much notice our ideal candidate needs to give to their current employer." She leaned in and placed a hand on my arm. "Are you sure you wouldn't consider staying on for another session? You know we'd love to have you. We're so lucky you chose to come here this summer!"

I watched Foster and Trace, heads together over steaming mugs of coffee. Neither spared me a moment's glance, which was galling if they were considering the best person to be the medical director of SERA.

Who better to consult on the topic than the current one? Who better than the only medical professional on-site?

"I know, I know, you can't stay," Robyn went on, still talking despite my lack of participation in the conversation. "I think it's because Foster told Trace you were for sure taking the job in California, that Trace realized he needed to do something—"

"I'm sorry, he what? Foster told Trace...?"

She nodded and shot me a warm smile, teeth flashing as her ponytail bobbed in excitement. "Congratulations, by the way. I didn't know it was official yet, even though I'm not surprised they made you the offer."

It was on the tip of my tongue to correct her, to inform her no one had made me any offer yet and it was for damned sure *not* official, but for all I knew, it was only a few hours before it would be true.

I politely excused myself and headed outside, if only to keep from murdering Foster Blake with a butter knife.

He thought I'd gotten and *accepted* an offer but hadn't told him about it? And he hadn't said a word to *me* about his assumption?

Anger coursed through my veins. I strode to Cabin 8 and dialed my cousin Ella.

"Hey, babe. How'd it go last night?" she asked.

"Can you come get me?" I tried to keep my voice steady so my anger didn't show. "I have a video call in an hour I'd like privacy for."

In true Ella fashion, she read the room and agreed without asking a single question. Within twenty minutes, I'd informed Robyn of my need to leave campus for the morning, thanked her for proctoring the exam for my students—which she'd offered to do anyway—and grabbed a nicer shirt for the video meeting.

As Ella was backing the car out of the spot in front of the cabin, Foster and Chickie walked by and noticed me leaving.

"Want me to stop?" Ella asked softly.

"No," I said, looking anywhere but at Foster fucking Blake.

My anger toward him only grew and festered throughout the morning until I was an overfull pot on a roiling boil.

Stanford offered me everything I asked for and more. They made me feel wanted and appreciated, respected and recognized. I felt the full benefit of the professional and academic achievements I'd made leading up to now. Getting hired at St. Ignatius had been an honor, but landing the job at Stanford? It was serendipitous.

Everything I'd ever thought I'd wanted for my career. For my future.

So the fact that I felt hollow inside instead of excited made me even angrier. And that anger had a clear target.

When my mother ran me back to SERA, I considered confronting Foster, asking him why he was spreading lies about my job situation. I thought about confessing my feelings for him and begging him to be honest about his own. Begging him to consider a future for the two of us.

But I'd already tried talking to him multiple times about moving past our "summer fling" agreement, and he'd shot me down every single time. A relationship between us was never going to be a possibility if it was always me pressing for it.

Foster had tried to tell me he wasn't interested in more, over and over, and I hadn't listened because I didn't want to hear it.

"Hey, Tommy," Trace called from the path leading to our cabin. "Wait up."

"I'm headed back to the classroom as soon as I change out of these clothes," I said, indicating my button-down.

He waved a hand through the air. "No rush. The instructors stole all the students for a helo thing up on Pronghorn Ridge anyway. They won't be back until four at the earliest, unless the weather turns. Monroe said if you want to join, just catch him on the radio. Otherwise, consider yourself with a few hours off. Although I'd love your help assessing candidates for the medical position later, if you have time." He smiled. "Congratulations, by the way. Foster told me your exciting news, not that it's a surprise. Stanford is lucky to have you."

I considered correcting him, but I wasn't sure I could do it without saying something scathing about Foster Blake. Instead, I thanked him and headed into my cabin to change. After yanking on my boots, filling my hydration pack, and stuffing a few necessities into it, I took off on a long hike in hopes of exercising and exorcising my demons—one tall, hard-headed, muscly demon in particular.

And I headed in the exact opposite direction from Pronghorn Ridge.

23

FOSTER

We called the helo exercise when the wind advisory came with an added warning of sleet. The low front expected from Canada had moved much faster than predicted, sending us back to SERA.

After stowing our gear in the increasing darkness from heavy cloud cover, I set out to find Tommy. Despite my hurt feelings at him not telling me about Stanford, I knew I needed to congratulate him rather than let this fester any longer.

He wasn't in Cabin 8, and he wasn't in the classroom or instructors' offices. I poked my head into Trace's office. "You seen Tommy?"

He shook his head. "Not since midday, but Robyn said she saw him take off on a hike. I assumed he was back by now."

I shook my head and glanced back out at the darkening sky. Water droplets were beginning to fall. "I'll call him and check the cabin again. If he's nearby, I'm sure he'll head back now that the rain is coming."

Trace frowned and pulled out his phone to check the weather report again. "Let me know what you find out. They're predicting snow at elevation. Possible we get flurries here, too."

I nodded and jogged back to the cabin, Chickie hot on my heels and happy to stretch her legs after I'd had to leave her behind for the helo drill.

The fact Chickie had been in the cabin when I'd arrived led me to believe Tommy was back from his hike. He most likely would have taken her with him if he was going for a long walk in the woods, if only because he was a sucker for her big puppy eyes.

The cabin was still empty. His boots and hydration pack were gone. I quickly dialed his number, knowing cell reception wasn't great on the hill behind campus. The ring trilled from somewhere in the room, sending a slither of dread down my spine.

Sure enough, his phone was in the pants pocket of the pair slung across his bed. I pulled it out and stared at the screen. There were multiple missed calls and texts, indicating he hadn't checked it for several hours.

"Fuck."

I glanced outside. The rain wasn't heavy, but it was steady and cold. The wind blew through the trees, turning leaves silver in the odd light.

"Fuck," I said again. My rational brain tried its best to remind me that Tommy was experienced in wilderness survival.

He knew all the rules about watching the weather and taking shelter when necessary.

But my rational brain wasn't the one in charge of my body.

I raced through my supplies, hauling out warm, dry layers as well as rain gear, extra socks, and the few remaining packs of trail mix in the box on the little table in our room. After shoving several more things in my pack and filling up an extra water bottle, I took off for the office to grab a radio before heading out.

Trace looked up at me in surprise as he caught me striding into the building, dripping water from my rain gear onto the wood floors. "You find him?"

I shook my head. "I need to find Robyn to see what direction he took. He's not back yet, and he doesn't have a phone."

Trace's eyebrows winged up. "Doesn't have his phone? Did he take his beacon?"

I shrugged. "He took his hydration pack, and I think he keeps the beacon in there along with basic med and survival gear. I'm sure he wouldn't have gone off alone without taking any precautions."

"Well he didn't fucking tell anyone he was going, and that alone is grounds for fucking dismissal. He knows better than that." I could tell his anger masked concern.

"I'll find him," I said, "I'm sure he'll be fine. He knows how to take care of himself."

Trace met my eyes. "If you really believed that, you wouldn't be getting ready to go off half-cocked."

"I'm not. I'll take plenty of gear, including my beacon and a radio. You know as well as I do he could be hurt. I'd rather find him now than after the sun goes down and he has to spend a night in freezing temps without proper equipment."

He reluctantly nodded. "Keep us updated. If I have to send a SAR team out for my SAR director, there'll be hell to pay, do you understand me?"

When I found Robyn, she was wringing her hands. "I think Tommy might be stuck on the mountain. He told me he was going for a long walk, but I never saw him come back, and now he's not answering his phone."

I didn't bother asking why she hadn't said anything to anyone. "Did you see which trail he took?"

She explained where she'd seen him, next to one of four trailheads scattered across the back and side of SERA's compound. I thanked her and made my way out, calling to Chickie, who didn't need any encouragement to follow.

I strapped Chickie's raincoat on her and we hiked for twenty minutes in the wind and cold rain before my radio crackled.

"Base to Blake. You copy?"

I reached for the handset on my pack strap. "Blake here. Go ahead."

"Storm's coming in faster than expected. We're getting gusts over 40 down here already—any sign of him?"

Unfortunately, even the best tracker would have trouble differentiating any sign of Tommy this close to the trailhead on a popular route. Hundreds of hikers had most likely already been up this trail in the past month or so, but no one was still out to give me any idea of whether or not he'd been spotted. I didn't expect to see any signs of him until I got a little farther along the trail, past the meadow that featured the popular lookout point this trail was known for.

"Wind and rain are picking up. Visibility's down. I'm about a half mile below Devil's Backbone, heading northwest along Elk Fork Trail. No sign of him yet."

"There's a cave just under the ridge on the southeast approach from your location. Be sure and check it on your way past. There's also an abandoned hunting shack just over the saddle between Devil's Backbone and Slingshot. He could be there waiting out the weather."

I thanked him and assured him I'd check in again once I got to the cave.

Another fifteen minutes later, I was almost to the base of the ridge when he called in again.

"Base to Blake."

"Go ahead, base."

"We've got reports of a rockslide on the southwest side of Devil's Backbone. Repeat: rockslide reported near your location."

My stomach dropped, and I felt a strange kind of numbness. "A rockslide?" I asked stupidly, forgetting to click my radio first.

I glanced up in hopes of seeing any sign of what he was reporting, but visibility was way too low. Could Tommy have been caught in a rockslide? It would have explained why he'd never returned, why he hadn't been able to get back before the weather turned.

I needed more information and scrabbled for the button on the radio. "No way to see from here. Cloud cover too low. What do we know?"

The radio crackled with static before his response came through. "Local climbers in the area almost didn't make it out. Said half their gear was covered, and one of them reported a leg injury."

My ears perked up. "They need medical attention?" Maybe Tommy had witnessed the incident and had made his way over there to help.

"Negative. They helped out their injured friend and headed straight to the clinic in town to get her checked out. They reported no sign of anyone else in the area."

Damn.

"Let me know if you hear anything else," I said.

"Foster... I know I don't have to tell you this, but don't do anything stupid. I know you care about him, but use your head."

I knew the only reason he wasn't commanding me to stand down was because he knew how much experience I had in situations like this. Threat assessment was my job. I'd just spent four weeks telling others when to take shelter and not be stupid.

"Copy that."

After a few more minutes of slogging through the mud on the trail, there was a brief thinning of the cloud cover, enough to see the wet, rocky mess down the west side of Devil's Backbone. I stared at it, horrified at the sight. It had shoved full-grown trees over and left others with broken branches. Rocks, mud, and other litter were strewn all over the hillside in a path leading away from town.

Fuck. Those climbers were damned lucky to have survived

being anywhere near that devastation.

Please let him be okay.

The swath of destruction was wide enough that he could have easily been caught in it without the other witnesses seeing anything. Before I had a chance to catch my breath from the sight, Chickie took off like a rocket up the east side of the ridge.

"Chick!" I cried after her. "Come!"

She ignored me, leaping across downed trees and bushes, straight in the direction of the saddle between Devil's Backbone and the main peak of Slingshot Mountain.

That area was above the tree line and would be exposed to lightning, not to mention another rockfall risk. "Chickie!" I called again, racing after her.

I slipped up the trail as fast as I could, grateful when the muddy trail ended and I caught the rocky grass under my boots instead. Cold rain pelted me from all sides, whipped up by the howling wind. The bright orange of Chick's coat made her easier to see through the thick fog around us, but it wouldn't take much longer for her to outrun the visibility.

"Chickie!" I continued to call before realizing there might be a very good reason for her failure to listen. The only other times she'd been this disobedient had come when she'd ignored me in favor of Tommy.

Hope threaded through me like a thin, shimmering wire. Please, *please.*

When I began carefully picking my way over the slick boulders and scree toward the top of the saddle, I saw a thin plume of smoke that seemed a little darker than the fog around it. I hoped it was coming from the hunter's shack Trace had mentioned.

I quickly thumbed the radio. "Blake to base."

"Base here."

"Smoke coming from hunter's lodge. Approaching now."

"Thank fuck. Let us know when you have confirmation."

In my excitement to get to the shack and hopefully find Tommy in it, I didn't pay attention to where I stepped. When my boot hit the next rock at a funny angle, the giant rock shifted, sending me sideways toward the sharp edge of another boulder. I cried out in surprise as I scrambled to catch myself. The ground underneath me continued to slip as the rocks began tumbling one over the other down the side of the mountain.

"Rock! Rock! Rock!" I shouted out of habit from my years of SAR and rock climbing. "Rockslide! *Fuck.*"

The entire ground below me was moving back down in the direction I'd come from, and if I didn't act fast, I was going with them. The sound of Chickie's barking came through the thick fog, along with a muffled shout.

"Foster?"

Tommy's voice barely made it to my ears as I scrambled forward toward the thin plume of smoke and away from the sliding rocks below me.

"Stay there!" I shouted. "Stay back!"

The sound of his voice brought with it a new urgency to get to him, to make sure he was okay. To... to, I wasn't sure. Keep him safe. Tell him how I felt. That the past four hours had been some of the worst of my life, thinking he was alone and hurt in a storm.

I moved as quickly as possible from one boulder to the next in search of stable ground, but I was being carried down the slope, almost in slow motion.

Thankfully, the side of the saddle with Tommy on it, with safety and a warm fire, was out of the path of the rockslide, but the side I was on seemed hell-bent on creating the same path of devastation and broken trees that I'd seen west of here. I felt like a lumberjack trying to stay on a spinning log in the river without being flung into the icy depths.

"Foster!"

The ground continued to shift under me as I tried to determine the safest way forward. I clawed at the rocks higher on the mountain and tried climbing up them. Smaller rocks hit others and bounced into my legs and feet. My hands slipped on the slick granite as I scrabbled to keep hold.

"Tommy!" I cried, hoping to god Chickie didn't try and come to me. "Find Chickie and hold her! Stay back!"

His safety was the last thought I had before the ground disappeared beneath my feet.

24

TOMMY

IT WAS like a scene out of a horror movie. One minute, Foster was there, fighting for his life as the rocks tried their best to fling themselves down the mountain, and the next, he was gone.

"*Foster!*" My panicked shriek seemed to fill the entire canyon as I raced as close as I could without losing my own footing. Chickie's collar dug into my palm as I struggled to hold her. All the hair on her back stood on end, and she barked in Foster's direction. "Wait, baby," I pleaded, unsure whether I was asking it of the dog or the man. "Wait."

My eyes watered as I refused to blink, scanning the spot where I'd last seen him. Suddenly, I saw movement and raced forward just in time to see the dark green tip of his rain jacket hood appear.

"Please," I whispered. "Foster? What can I do? Should I find some rope?"

I didn't have any rope, but I would cut off the straps from my pack and yank out the water tube from my hydration system if I needed to.

His hands appeared, reaching for another handhold on a large, wet boulder. I edged closer until I could reach him safely, clasping his wrist in one hand while trying to control Chickie with the other.

"Got you," I said, finally seeing his face. There was a laceration on his eyebrow and cheek, the blood mixing with rain to form a pink stream down into his stubbled jaw. His hands seemed to be protected by gloves, but the gloves were definitely trashed.

When he reached the side of the boulder closest to me and realized he was finally on solid ground, he stumbled into me and grabbed me in a filthy, wet hug, burying his cold nose in my neck.

His entire body trembled with adrenaline, but the first words out of his mouth were "Are you hurt?"

I didn't dare loosen the arms I had tight around him. "No. I was safe and warm until I heard you cry out. I didn't even realize Chickie was scratching at the door."

At the reminder of the little hunting shack, I pulled back and yanked Foster toward it. "There's shelter and a fire. Come on."

Foster was bruised and filthy, soaking wet and freezing. His radio squawked with increasingly panicked voices, but he didn't seem to notice. When I got him inside. I began pulling his wet outerwear off, starting with the radio on his jacket.

With my free hand, I thumbed the radio. "Marian to base.

Blake and I are safe. Repeat. Tommy Marian and Foster Blake are safe."

"Thank fuck," Trace said. "Location status."

"There was a rockslide on Devil's Backbone saddle. Current location is hunter's shack just north of the saddle. Will shelter in place for now. Over."

There was a pause before he came back over the radio. "We heard about the rockslide. Is it impeding your return? Over."

Foster seemed to come to clearer awareness. He pulled the radio out of my hand. "Blake to base. There was a second rockslide on the west side of the ridge. The two of us and Chickie are on the other side of it. Will need help with extraction when the storm is over."

"Copy. Stay tuned while we work up a plan. Probably won't be until morning if you're good there."

I took the radio back and finished up with Trace before setting the radio aside and reaching over to take off Chickie's rain gear. There were wooden pegs lined up on each side of the door, so I hung up as much of the wet gear as possible to keep it off the floor in the tiny space and away from the old woodstove.

Chickie immediately curled up on the floor in front of the stove and lay down with her head on her paws, like this particular adventure had used up even her boundless energy.

After nudging Foster onto the little wooden cot built into the side of the cabin, I reached into my pack for an emergency blanket and my med kit. "Take off your shirt. It's wet and covered in blood."

He looked down at himself in a daze, hands shaking and

clothes ruined, before looking up at me with concern on his face. "You okay?"

I squatted in front of him and reached out to push dirty, wet strands of hair off his forehead. "Baby. I'm okay. You're the one who's hurt. You're a med student's dream for suture practi—"

"I'm in love with you."

I stared at him. "I... I think you might have a head injury."

Foster's eyes filled with tears, a sight I would have been happy to spend my whole life without seeing. "I'm in love with you, and I can't fucking stand it."

"Oh, Jesus." I lurched forward and kissed him again, holding on to his face carefully to keep the worst of the cuts from being impacted.

Hot tears mixed with blood and cold rain on my cheek and lips. "I would apologize, but I'm not sorry," I whispered, pulling back until our foreheads were still pressed together. "I'm in love with you, too."

He shook his head, another tear escaping his eyes as he squeezed them closed. "No, that's just it. You can't be. It won't work. I've tried to figure it out, Tommy, and it just won't fucking work."

"I need you to shut up about that for right now and let me take care of you. Just set it aside for a little while, okay? Let me play doctor. I promise I'll fulfill all your fantasies; it just might involve a very long and medically accurate lead-up."

The edges of his lips quirked up. "Promise it has a happy ending?"

I pressed a kiss to the edge of his lips. "Promise."

He let me take care of him then, cleaning up the blood on

his face and tending to the lacerations. I added another piece of wood into the stove and mentally thanked whoever had left this little shelter stocked with it last.

"Take off your clothes," I said, bouncing my eyebrows.

"Aw, yeah. Now we're talking." He reached for the hem of his shirt and winced in pain.

"That's what I thought would happen," I said, moving closer and pulling up his shirt to reveal red areas of bruising. "You want to tell me how bad it really was?" He'd already tried to tell me he "slipped on some rocks," but it was clearly more than that from the state of his gear and body.

He blew out a breath as I carefully removed his shirt. "The whole thing was my fault. I stepped wrong, and the rocks started moving."

I ran gentle fingers over his skin, prodding just enough to make sure the damage wasn't serious. "Thank god you found your footing."

Foster's hands came up to rest on my hips before moving to my belt and fiddling it open. "I wanted to get to you. I *needed* to get to you."

I fussed a little bit more over him while he pulled my clothes off, but it didn't take long before we were sprawled out on the built-in bed platform with nothing but a Mylar blanket between us and the splintered wood.

We kissed for what seemed like hours, slow and gentle explorations with our lips, tender caresses with our hands. There were no more words spoken, just soft moans and pleas, the breathy call of a name or the sweet murmuring of an endearment.

For the first time since I met him, Foster let me see his true feelings without trying to hide them. His eyes didn't flick away. His touch didn't hesitate. Everything about the way he moved against me, held me, kissed me—it was all stripped bare of pretense.

It was careful. Reverent. Like he was trying to memorize the way we fit together, like this moment might be all we'd ever have.

And I let him. I let him map my skin with his hands, let him lose himself in the shape of me. I met him kiss for kiss, sigh for sigh, until the only thing I could feel was the slow, sweet ache of falling.

When we finally moved together, his body under me, *inside* of me, it wasn't about release. It was about being known. Being chosen.

Afterward, tangled in the quiet with the cool drafts through the log walls mixing with the heat from the stove, I felt the rise and fall of his breath beneath my cheek and knew.

I wasn't alone anymore.

No matter how stubborn this man could be. And no matter how much he might try to backtrack when the cold light of reality burst into our little fantasy world on top of this mountain.

He was mine, and I was his.

No matter what.

25

FOSTER

IT HAD BEEN a long time since I'd taken a punch. Long enough that I'd forgotten what it was like waking up the day after.

The radio squawked, waking me from a dead sleep, but it was my attempt to jolt upright that truly got my attention.

"Fucking fuck!" Every muscle ached. My body felt like it had been pummeled by boulders—which, of course, it had.

"Radio," Tommy murmured next to me. I glanced down at him and noticed he was wearing a comical amount of the warm clothes I'd brought in my pack. I vaguely remembered waking up during the night to take a piss and deciding to bundle him up before stepping outside.

Now that I was freezing and mostly naked, I wondered at my reasoning. Chickie's judgmental eyes said she wondered the same.

"Radio," he said again without moving or even opening his eyes.

I reached for the radio hanging on one of the pegs.

"Blake here."

"Helo inbound to your location. Ten minutes out. No need to scout a landing spot. I'm not taking any chances. Hoist or hover depending on the wind when they get there."

"Copy that. We'll be ready. Request K-9 harness if possible."

I could rig Chickie to me with the webbing I had on me, but it wouldn't be pretty.

"Already loaded. Will be good practice for your students. Let's hope they like the two of you. Over."

Tommy's warm body moved against my back as he sat up and leaned forward to place a kiss on the back of my neck. "You got any extra clothes? Because I'm not willing to share. The comfy fairy visited me in the night, even though I didn't do a damned thing to deserve it."

I turned around and pulled him in for a real kiss. "I might beg a visit to that big family lodge of yours later just so I can soak in a deep tub with the hottest water I can stand."

He shook his head and *tsk*'d. "No submersing those lacerations for several days, Sheriff. But I promise to find other ways to warm you up. Deal?"

"Mpfh."

He pressed a final kiss to my cheek and stood, moving to my pack to dig around for more clothes.

In the end, I was able to put my original clothes back on, surprisingly warm and dry from being hung near the stove. While I yanked on a clean pair of socks, Tommy fed Chickie pieces of his protein bar.

"She's going to start begging at the table," I grumbled. "People food is a bad idea."

"Maybe if you'd packed some dog food instead of five pairs of socks, we wouldn't be in this situation."

The whir of rotors reached us through the drafty door and walls. We finished packing up, leashed Chickie, and made our way out to the scree field in front of the hut.

Monroe and his bird appeared within seconds, hovering a hundred feet above us. His voice came over the radio as he commanded the scene. I could see the excitement on the faces of the students as they worked together to bring down the harnesses and get us and our gear hoisted up.

"Fucking sick, dude!" Cody said, reaching out to fist-bump me.

"Easy with the victim," Tommy said over the noise of the blades, grabbing my jacket and shoving me down onto a nearby seat. "Strap in."

Once he fell into the seat next to me, I leaned over. "What happened to going easy on the victim?"

He grinned, his face golden in the morning sunlight. "Who said you were the victim?" He ruffled Chickie's ears where she was tucked safely between us, scanning the inside of the heli-copter with her sniffer working a million miles an hour.

When Sierra finally slid the door closed, the wind stopped stinging the skin on my face.

The ride back to the landing pad at SERA went by quickly. Trace was waiting for us when we landed and tried insisting I head to the medical clinic in town "just in case."

Tommy shook his head. "He's fine. Already treated him and

assessed him for a head injury. All he needs is a hot shower, a decent meal, and sleep."

As we started moving toward the main building, a large SUV pulled up, and Marians began pouring out. Ella took a flying leap at Tommy, who stumbled back as she hugged him.

I watched to make sure he was okay, but then I was quickly overtaken by my own Marian entourage. "You look like shit, Muscles," Tilly said, frowning up at me.

Granny squinted at me. "Scars are sexy. Black eyes… not so much. Tell 'em it was a bear. Makes for a better story."

Irene just tutted, licking her thumb and reaching for my eyebrow. I ducked out of the way before her germs made contact with my open wound.

Tommy glared at them with an anger that surprised me. "Ladies, let the man go. He's hurt and tired. Tilly, *back off*."

I suddenly remembered what she told me about Tommy's job offer at the cookout. Had it only been the night before last? How was that possible?

Exhaustion returned with full force, causing me to feel unsteady on my feet. I locked my knees and plastered on a smile. "This is too much for me," I murmured. And then I turned and walked away.

The rest of the walk to Cabin 8 passed in a blur. I remembered the heat of the shower on my sore muscles, the long gulps of cold water from the sink tap after I brushed my teeth… and then nothing but the soft comfort of my small bed.

I slept for twelve hours. When I woke up, it was dark outside, and there was no sign of Tommy or Chickie. I texted him, half-worried I'd hear the phone ping here in the room, but there wasn't a noise or vibration. Neither was there a response.

I blew out a breath. I'd managed to go nearly the whole day without thinking about our confessions in the cabin the night before—a dramatic rescue followed by hours of unconsciousness were handy that way—but now that I was alone and feeling human again, Tommy was all I could think about. The shock on his face when I'd confessed that I loved him. The warmth in his eyes as he'd said he loved me, too. The way my whole body trembled with the need to hold him. The fact that I still didn't know how the fuck we could be together without one of us taking a huge leap and giving up... well, everything.

I made my way to the SERA dining room in search of them, but I only found Jasper sitting and eating a bowl of pasta while reading a dog-eared paperback. Chickie lay quietly at his feet until she saw me.

I squatted and gave her some love before looking up at Jasper. "Hey, man, you seen Tommy?"

Jasper glanced up and gave me a hesitant smile. "Dr. Marian went on a callout with Monroe and Sierra. He asked me to watch Chick."

"A callout?" I frowned. "For what?"

He shut his book and set it on the table. "From what I could gather, some kids were goofing around while on a trail ride, and one of them got thrown and kicked by the horse. They were pretty deep in the backcountry, so they called for a medevac. SERA's on the list if they're the closest team and time is an issue."

I was upset I'd missed the chance to go, but I also knew that it was way more important for the helicopter seats to be filled with medical and helo specialists than a SAR guy.

"That kid's in good hands," I murmured. "Hope they're okay."

Jasper nodded and poked at his pasta. "I hate that someone got hurt, but I'm glad Tommy got a chance to get out of here." He made a face. "Trace was kinda ripping into him all afternoon about going out alone during a storm. He was, ah... loud."

I winced as I took the seat across from him. "I'm sure Tommy already feels bad."

"I'm sure he does. But I get why Trace was upset, too. You've got to own up to your mistakes and try and do better." He gave me a half smile. "That's maybe the most important thing I've learned at SERA. Definitely worth the four times I had to apply before I got picked."

His words surprised me—not that he hadn't gotten in on the first try, since Trace was incredibly selective, but that Jasper had tried again, and again, and again. When the program had started, he'd been cautious to the point of being evasive, ducking responsibility and deferring to louder voices. I hadn't been impressed. But Tommy had encouraged me to give him a chance, and Jasper had stepped up. A lot.

"I'm glad you stuck with it," I said after a beat, keeping my voice even. "You're a rock-solid student."

"Yeah?" Jasper gave a short laugh and rubbed the back of his neck. "Shit. That means a lot. I, um... I know I wasn't when I first got here."

I raised an eyebrow, inviting him to continue.

"I've wanted to come to SERA forever. Dream thing, you

know? But then about seven months ago, just after I got accepted for the summer cohort, I was the first EMT on scene at this really bad multi-car MVA just outside Golden. Woman's car flipped down an embankment. Kid strapped in the back." He exhaled, his eyes fixed on a point over my shoulder like he was seeing something beyond the dining hall's wood paneling. "The mother was screaming at us to save her kid. She seemed to be shaken but mostly okay. Kid was nonresponsive, so he's the one we focused on. We didn't realize that the mom was suffering massive internal injuries, and..." He broke off and shook his head. "I let a mother's fear dictate my response instead of protocol, and because of that, she died."

"I had no idea," I said quietly.

"Nah. Didn't exactly volunteer that info." Jasper hesitated, then added, "I was scared, you know? Not to talk about it, just... scared I wasn't good enough, I guess? Like, if I couldn't save her, did I even belong here? SAR's the only thing I ever wanted to do, but it felt like my own brain was sabotaging me. Like it was safer not to try than to fail and have someone get hurt. Not logical, I know, but..." He tapped his temple and screwed up his face. "Messed me up anyway. I wanted to curl up in a ball and just stay small and safe."

Like it was safer not to try than to fail and have someone get hurt. His words hit a little too close to home.

"What changed?" I demanded.

"Well. Couple things." Jasper smiled, slow and sure. "Remember the missing kayaker drill, back at the beginning of the course? I told you I didn't want to be in charge of nav. I was freaking out and hoping you'd hand it off to someone else so I wouldn't mess it up. But you said, 'I trust you to do it.'" He looked up at me, eyes bright. "And I thought, well, okay, then. I don't trust *me* right now, but I trust *him*. So if he thinks I can do it, maybe I can."

I blinked. I'd had no fucking clue he'd take anything I said so seriously. "And you did."

"Yeah, I did. And then the second thing… After the crash with Dr. Marian's sister, he came to talk to me. Thanked me for organizing the gear and said it helped." He grinned. "He's a good guy."

"The best," I agreed, my voice scratchy. "The very best."

"Right? So, I asked him, 'How were you able to handle that, Doc? How'd you learn to keep it together?' And he told me, 'Training. Courses like SERA help you learn not to react out of fear, to trust yourself and the people around you. Every time a drill goes right, your brain realizes you can handle it, and that builds confidence. You can't always control the outcomes, but your job is to show up, do the right thing to the best of your ability, and *keep* showing up, even when it's hard.' And I was like, *shit*, he's right. I realized if I kept reacting out of fear, if I let it make me hide away and stick to what was safe, I might not be there for the next person who needs me." He shrugged. "I did the best I could for that family that day, and I know that I made the choice that mother would have wanted."

I swallowed. Hard. Because all I could think about was Tommy.

Tommy with his steady hands in a crisis.

Tommy, who came apart crying my name.

Tommy, who'd called off his wedding and walked away from

a life that didn't fit because it was the right thing to do. Even though it was hard.

Who'd showed up, and kept showing up... even after I'd tried to hold him at arm's length and pretend this thing we were building was something I could bear to throw away in a couple more weeks.

Maybe I'd been doing the same thing Jasper had. Maybe the fear of being hurt had made me want to stay safe in my familiar small town. In my comfortable job. *Alone.*

I looked over at Jasper and nodded. "Thank you. For telling me."

He shrugged, but his smile stayed in place. "Sure. You helped me when I really needed it, Foster. You're a good guy, too."

And damn if that didn't make something shift in my chest.

"Thanks for looking after this punk," I said, nodding at Chickie. "I owe you one."

"No worries. Oh, hey, Trace said to tell you to come find him after you got a bite to eat. There's leftover pasta in the fridge."

It was late, but my brain was buzzing, and I knew I wouldn't be able to sleep for a while, so I reheated the pasta and sat down near Jasper. He'd gone back to reading his book, so while I ate, I took out my phone and checked my messages.

To my surprise, I had three new ones just in the past few minutes.

MOM

Can't wait to see you for Anna's birthday dinner.

WAY

You didn't hear this from me, but your
sister wants tickets to see Femme
Theory in Bozeman in August. It's a
band. Here's the link for tickets.

MOM

If you happen to have any friends at
SERA you'd like to invite, we have
plenty of room.

I huffed out a laugh. *Smooth, Mom.*

After taking another bite of pasta, I sent a response to my
cousin.

I forgot Anna's birthday is tomorrow.
What time is dinner?

WAY

6pm. We're having it at the ranch and
everyone's coming. Bring your new
boyfriend.

I bit back a curse.

Who said I have a new boyfriend?

WAY

Your mother and now half the town.
Said he's a SERA instructor. I'm
picturing hiker's ass, climber's calves,
and rope-callused hands. Tell me I'm
wrong. Better yet, send proof in a pic.
Or three.

Pretty sure your husband would take
issue with you lusting after another
man.

WAY

Pretty sure my husband would ogle him
with me. Besides, my husband is hotter
than any man you could land. Bet.

I snickered.

Not a chance in hell.

WAY

Prove it.

I cleared my plate back to the kitchen and cleaned up after myself before thanking Jasper again and making my way to Trace's office. He wasn't there, so I headed to his cabin.

"Just the man I wanted to see," he said from his spot on a battered porch swing. His cabin was larger than the instructor cabins, maybe about four times the size, and it was clear he'd made it a home over the last few years.

I propped my ass against the porch railing and crossed my arms. "I want the job," I said firmly. "Permanently."

Trace's eyes widened in surprise. "Well, shit. If I'd known you were interested, I would have hounded you sooner. Hell, I would have hounded you, period." He grinned.

I took a breath and let it out. "I obviously need to know what the details are. Compensation, time off, all that. But I really like what you're doing, and I want to be a part of it. I think I can make a difference here. I've admired the work you're doing for a long time; I just never considered moving up here to be a part of it before."

He peered at me. "Why now? What changed?"

I thought about Tommy's dedication to his work, the difference he made in saving people's lives. More than that, I thought about my encouraging him to follow his dreams and about how hypocritical it was when I wasn't pursuing my own.

Was there a small part of me that hoped to see more of Tommy when he visited his family in Legacy? Maybe. But even if he never came back here, if his job kept him in California all the time, I would still want to do this work year-round.

"I love Majestic," I said. "My friends and family are there. My career. I take pride in being the sheriff. It's been part of my identity for a very long time. But more and more, it's about politics and regulations, paperwork and permits. The higher up I go, the duller it gets."

"You want excitement?"

I shrugged. "I want to be challenged. I want to innovate. Law enforcement is law enforcement. I was never in it because it spoke to me on a deeper level. You know my heart has always been in Search and Rescue. And I did as much of it as I could in Majestic in the best way I knew how. When my dad left, I vowed to stay and take care of my mom and sister."

I ran a hand through my hair and straightened. "I've done my job for my family. And now, I'd like to work for this family. The SERA family."

Trace's face split into a wide grin. "Well, hot damn. I just landed myself my top candidate without having to lift a finger." He stood up from the swing and stepped closer, holding out a hand to shake. "I'll make sure and put together a compensation package that'll work for everyone. I'd sure as hell like to have you here. When can you start?"

After talking a few more minutes, I left Trace's cabin feeling a combination of hopeful and nervous. Hopeful about a more exciting and challenging career path but nervous about such a big change.

It hadn't been a spur-of-the-moment decision. It was something I'd wanted forever.

Well, *one* of the things I'd wanted forever.

But this one was going to be a huge change, and I was going to have to break it to my friends and family back home.

I debated about calling Tommy again to tell him about my decision, but I wanted to see his face when I gave him the news. I hoped he'd be happy, hoped he'd see this was at least a small step in the direction of the two of us having a future beyond this summer, hoped he'd see that I was willing to set my fear aside and *try*.

The job at SERA came with two-week breaks between every eight-week session, which meant I could spend ten weeks a year with him in California. If he was able to come to Legacy for weekends and holidays here and there, maybe we could make it work. At least until we came up with something better, something more permanent.

When I got back to Cabin 8, I texted him again while trying to juggle Chickie's leash and open the cabin door at the same time.

> I'm headed to Majestic in the morning.
> Be safe.

I didn't realize until later how a simple text could have been so utterly misinterpreted.

26

TOMMY

If I'd known how long it would be before Foster and I got to talk, I would've followed him back to Cabin 8 yesterday.

Since I hadn't, I'd stayed behind to calm my family. Once they'd left, there'd barely been enough time for me to shower, kiss Foster's sleeping forehead, and retrieve Chickie before rushing back to the main building to meet with Trace about "the future of my job at SERA."

That convo, which had also included an epic—and, yeah, well-deserved—dressing-down for being an idiot, had been interrupted by an emergency call, and the next thing I knew, I was in a helicopter on my way to the far side of Slingshot Mountain for a medical assist. There hadn't been time to tell Foster I was leaving, even if I'd wanted to chance waking him with a text.

The following twelve hours had been nonstop, to the point that I'd finally collapsed in one of the on-call room beds at the hospital in Billings so I could catch enough sleep to make my way back to Legacy safely. I'd woken hours later to the gentle nudging of a hospital admin handing me the keys to a rental car they'd arranged for me.

By the time I slid into the vehicle's cool leather seat and pulled out my phone, it had been nearly eighteen exhausting hours since I'd spoken to Foster, and I decided I couldn't wait another minute.

Which was when I saw the text that had come in last night.

FOSTER

I'm headed to Majestic in the morning.
Be safe.

Maybe it was the long shift and all of the stress. Sleep deprivation. A muddled head from having just woken up. But this seemed weirdly like a brush-off.

I quickly texted Trace.

Leaving Billings now. Did something happen with Foster?

I sipped shitty coffee from the hospital while I waited for a response, but it didn't help my brain fire any better.

TRACE

You mean about him leaving?

I stared at the text, trying to figure out what the hell was going on.

Was there a family emergency?

TRACE

Not that I know of.

Did he quit?

TRACE

I think so.

Jesus fucking Christ.

Had Foster seriously left SERA in order to get away from me? He'd told me he loved me—

Actually, no. He'd said *I'm in love with you, and I can't fucking stand it.* This had seemed incredibly romantic at the time. Now, combined with the last thing he'd said before walking away from me and my family—*This is too much for me.*—it felt like something else entirely.

My hands gripped the steering wheel so tightly they hurt.

How *dare* he chicken out without even talking to me? Was he really that immature? I didn't like to think so, but he was undeniably on his way to Majestic, and if it had been a previously planned thing, wouldn't he have mentioned it?

I was pulling out of Billings before I knew it, and with each mile that passed, my anger grew more wild and feral, a volcanic eruption that could level entire cities.

I was fucking furious.

Furious enough to take Hwy 310 instead of 212 and head straight for the Wyoming border.

Like any sane person did when they wanted to commit murder.

Thankfully, it was hard to fall asleep at the wheel when you were contemplating violent death.

That motherfucker.

I thought about calling Foster, lighting him up with all of my thoughts and feelings as soon as humanly possible, but if I did that, I ran the risk of him shutting me down. Telling me not to bother coming.

I needed to see his gorgeous, awful face.

When I pulled into Majestic, I realized I recognized it from a day trip to a rodeo when I was a teenager. We'd been on our way to Yellowstone in a camper, and Mom and Dad had given in to Hazel's insistence that we stop in Majestic to see a rodeo star named Avery Hart. Hazel had been in her mid-twenties, and Avery had been her semi-famous crush for a year already.

The two of them hadn't actually met until two years later when the rodeo came to Legacy during another summer vacation, but now that I saw the fairgrounds on my way into town, memories flooded in. Majestic was charming. I could see why Foster took so much pride in his role as protector of this place.

Flower baskets hung from street lampposts along the main road through town. A cycle store, boutique clothing store, and ice cream and chocolate shop lined one side of the road while the other hosted a green park with a playground, flanked on either side by more businesses and restaurants. On one end of the street was a bright stone building with City Hall stamped into the polished stone above the large double doors.

I parked nearby, googled the sheriff's office, and started walking. When I saw Foster's SUV parked out front, my walk became a stomp.

Inside, the front desk was deserted, but I heard a man's

voice through the open doorway to the offices beyond, so I followed the sound.

"Who's the guy you told your mom about?" the guy asked, a laugh in his voice. "Is he hot? Does he have anything to do with you acting like a complete jackass all fucking winter?"

My heart rate picked up as his words hit me.

"Because I've never seen you meaner and more pathetic than you were after your so-called hookup trip in Hawaii. Hell, I was on the verge of joining your mom's matchmaking team just to see if I could get you laid. Silas and I placed bets on it."

Foster's voice was calm and teasing. "Who wins the bet if I murder you?"

"Considering the bet is for a deep-throated face-fucking, I'm gonna say we both win no matter how it plays out."

I stepped into the office space on the word *fucking*, and felt my face heat immediately.

Both men looked up at me in surprise, but for some reason, my eyes went right past them to the wall behind Foster...

Where a very familiar photo was pinned front and center by a handful of darts and what looked like hundreds, if not thousands, of tiny holes.

My breath caught in my throat as I stared at my own face, enlarged and printed in grainy black and white. The photo from St. Ignatius's website—the one with my professional smile and neatly combed hair that now looked absurdly formal compared to the battle-worn dartboard surrounding it.

"Holy shit," I whispered, taking a step closer. The paper was curled at the edges, worn soft from months of... what? Anger? Obsession? The dart holes formed a constellation around my face—some clustered near my eyes, others scattered across my cheeks and forehead. It looked like a crime scene.

"Oh," I said stupidly. "Well, then."

Foster and his friend turned to see what had caught my attention, and it seemed like all the oxygen was sucked from the room.

"Wait," Foster said. The only thing that kept me from bolting or throwing something at him was the thread of absolute panic and fear in his voice. He walked toward me slowly with his hands out, as if trying to approach a wild dog. "Tommy, I can explain."

I couldn't look away from the dartboard. Six months. He'd been throwing darts at my face for six fucking months. "You can explain why I'm the face of your workplace rage?" My voice came out strangled. "Jesus Christ, Foster. How many times did you—" I gestured helplessly at the punctured remains of my professional headshot.

The other guy, who I'd guessed by now was his cousin Way, from everything I'd heard as well as an obvious family resemblance, breathed, "Ho-lee fuck. It's... it's you." He looked from me to the dartboard and back again. "I thought this was just some picture Foster found on the internet. Like maybe he had a bad experience with doctor porn or something."

"Doctor porn," I repeated flatly, finally tearing my gaze away from the dartboard. "That's... actually not too far off, I guess." The laugh that escaped me sounded slightly unhinged. "Though I'm pretty sure most people don't print out photos of their porn to use for target practice. Especially after they kissed them on a Hawaiian beach."

Way's eyes went wide. "Oh, dude. You're the reason—"

"Waylon," Foster warned, his voice deadly quiet.

But I was already piecing it together. The way Foster had looked at me that first day at SERA. The careful distance he'd maintained. The walls he'd built between us. "You hated me," I said, and it wasn't a question. "Before you even knew me, you hated me."

Foster didn't take his eyes off me or crack a smile. "Tommy, what are you doing here? I thought you were headed back to SERA."

"That's funny because I thought you were at SERA, too."

Way's grin was so wide it bordered on shit-eating. "Soooo, Foster... if you need me to help you figure things out the same way *you* helped *me* when Silas first came to town, I could—"

Foster didn't take his eyes off me. "Waylon, get the fuck out. And so help me if you pretend to flirt with me, I will beat the shit out of you right here, right now."

Way's laughter followed him out until the sound of the door closing ended it.

The silence stretched between us, heavy and loaded. I walked closer to the dartboard, studying the damage. Some of the holes were small and precise—clean hits that spoke of careful aim. Others were jagged tears where darts had been yanked out in frustration.

"How often?" I asked quietly.

"Tommy—"

"How often did you throw darts at my face?"

Foster's shoulders sagged. "Every day. Sometimes... sometimes multiple times a day."

I traced a finger along one of the larger tears, right through where my left eye would be. "Were you imagining revenge or something?"

"No." His voice was raw. "I was imagining forgetting you."

Suddenly, I realized my eyes were filling with stupid-ass tears. I gritted my teeth against them. "Why did you leave without saying goodbye?"

His eyebrows crinkled together in confusion. "You were in Billings. I sent you a text."

"You sent me a 'Have a good life' text!" I snapped.

Now his eyebrows nearly shot up into his hairline. "What? No I didn't. Why would I do that? I fucking love you! I have since... Hawaii! I had to come home for Anna's birthday dinner, but I was going to drive back as soon as it was over. Slide into bed with you, even if it meant waking you up—"

"You love me?" I spun around to face him fully. "You love me, but you've been throwing darts at my face for six months? That's not love, Foster. That's—"

"Torture," he finished quietly. "It was torture. Every single day, seeing your face and knowing I couldn't have you. Knowing you belonged to someone else."

"I broke up with her!" The words exploded out of me. "I called off my wedding because of you! Because one kiss from you was worth more than ten years with her, and you—" I gestured wildly at the dartboard. "You turned me into your personal punching bag."

Foster stepped closer, and I saw something give way in his expression. "I didn't know you'd broken up, Tommy. I thought you were married. I thought you'd used me for some pre-wedding experiment and then went back to your perfect life. And I *still* couldn't stop myself from wanting you. I looked up your picture because I thought you couldn't be as gorgeous as I remembered, but you were." He gestured at the dartboard. "Then I thought maybe if I could destroy it, I might destroy the hold you had on me, but that didn't work either." His big hand reached out and cupped my cheek. "I fucking *ached* for you. Day and night."

I took a deep, shuddering breath and turned into the warmth of his palm.

"Because deep down, I didn't want to let you go, no matter how angry and hurt and heartbroken I was," he went on in a voice so tense it cracked. "I kept your T-shirt, just so I could touch it. I got a dog, just like I'd told you I would, and the minute I saw her, I thought about how damn happy you looked when you were eating that damn hummus dip and teasing me to name her after—"

"Hummus." A laugh wanted to bubble up, but I was too scared things were still too precarious. "I can't believe you named her after hummus because I made an offhand joke."

Foster nodded, his gaze warm and a little wary. "Every time I said her name, I'd think of you, even when I thought I'd never see you again. And then I showed up in Legacy... and there you were. Even smarter, and funnier, and kinder than my memory. A hundred times more compelling than that damn picture." His eyes bored into mine, like he was willing me to believe him. "If you think I could walk away from you with a 'have a good life' text, Tommy Marian, think again."

I stared at him, trying to make sense of what he was saying. "But... Trace said you quit."

Foster scowled. "Bullshit he did. I didn't quit. I hired on!"

I stepped back and rubbed my hands over my face, trying to make any of this make sense. "What do you mean, you hired on? I asked him if you quit, and he said..." I stopped and replayed the words. "He said he thought so?"

That didn't make any sense. How could Trace not know if Foster quit SERA?

Foster's eyes closed, and he let out a breath before stepping toward me again. "Baby. He probably thought you knew. He probably thought you were asking if I'd quit my job yet."

Before I could respond, he added, "Quit my job *here*. In Majestic. I accepted a permanent position at SERA."

The words hit me like a physical blow. An impossible gift. "You... what?"

He gestured to the desk, which was neat and mostly bare, with the exception of a single, white business envelope. "My letter of resignation. I took the job Trace offered. Permanent SAR director. I'm moving to Montana."

I felt like the world had tilted sideways. "When did you decide this?"

"It's been in the back of my mind for a while, but I decided for good the other night, when we were stuck in the hunting shack. After I almost lost you on that mountain." He ran both hands through his hair. "I realized I could have it all, my dream SAR job and maybe a chance to build something with you, too. If I live in Legacy and you live in California... well, I'll have two weeks off between every SERA session to come see you. And when you come to Legacy to visit your family…"

It was too much. Too good to be true. "I thought you'd decided I was too much trouble. Too much drama. Too much… Marian."

Foster's face crumpled. "Christ, Tommy. You're not too much of anything. You're *everything*. You're the reason I'm here turning in my resignation instead of running from you again."

I felt like I couldn't catch my breath, like there were too many questions and not enough answers. "You accused me of running, when really… it was you."

"Yes."

"Because you'd already fallen for me."

His smile was tender and sweet. "On the airplane that very first day. I didn't believe in love at first sight, but I think I knew you were The One, even then. I guess you could call it… *kismet*."

I huffed out a laugh that sounded almost like a sob. "Real, like daisies in sunshine?"

"Exactly." His smile faded, and he stepped forward, taking my hands in his. "And it turned out you had the answer all along. You remember what you told Matthew that night at the bar? You said, 'When you find The One, you hold on to him and find a way to make it work.'" He pulled me closer. "So if long distance doesn't work for us and you want me to come to Stanford with you instead… I will."

I blinked at him. "But…"

"Your great-aunt Tilly told me at the cookout that you'd accepted the position," Foster said with a little eye roll. "And she'd already told me she planned to set you up with every available person in Northern California. But we're *never* letting on that her shenanigans helped me get my ass in gear and realize what was important, okay? Because it's bad enough I'm going to be called Sheriff Muscles for the next two decades—"

"Foster," I interrupted. "I turned down Stanford. And I told UC Davis I wasn't interested." I took a deep breath and admitted, "I already accepted a different job."

"Oh." His mouth fell open, and I saw the rapid calculations happening behind his eyes as he tried to recalibrate. "Okay. Right. Well, we'll make it work. If it's further away from SERA, we can—"

"Actually," I interrupted, wrapping my arms around his neck, suddenly needing there to be no distance whatsoever between us. "It's closer."

"Closer?" He blinked. "How close?"

I grinned. "About... three feet away from you? Possibly four. But I really think I need to bite the bullet and get a decent-sized bed, so—"

"Tommy." He gave me a light shake that said he wasn't in the mood for teasing. "Where?"

But I saw the hope blossoming in his gaze, and I could tell he already knew.

"SERA." The look in Foster's eyes was so happy, so vulnerable, I couldn't help but lean in and press a kiss to his mouth. "I love you," I whispered.

"I don't understand," he croaked. "Jasper said Trace was ripping you a new one before you left."

"He was," I said ruefully. "He told me he would only hire me if I swore never to do something that stupid again. I don't blame him."

"Fuck, baby." Foster's voice was barely a whisper, his eyes seeking mine. "Are you sure? You'd be giving up—"

"Nothing that I truly want." I threaded my hands through the hair at the nape of his neck. "I figured out what I really want. And it's not a prestigious job in California. It's not impressing my colleagues or making my parents proud or any of the things I thought mattered."

"What do you want?"

"You," I said simply. "I want morning coffee with you complaining about compliance paperwork. I want to argue about training techniques and fight over who gets the bigger half of the bed. I want to watch you work with Chickie. I want to teach students and save people's lives in ways that matter."

Foster's hands came up to frame my face. "You have to be a hundred... no, a *thousand* percent sure. Because I can't—I can't do this if you're going to change your mind. I can't watch you leave again."

"I'm not leaving." I covered his hands with mine. "I'm staying. I'm staying for the job I actually want, I'm staying for the family I chose. I'm staying for you *and* for me."

Foster grabbed my face with both hands, crushing our mouths together in a bruising kiss. I threw my arms around him and held on as tightly as I could.

"What can I do to make this good for you?" he asked, pulling back and meeting my eyes. "I don't want you to have any regrets."

"Mmm, let's see," I said, tapping my finger to my chin. "I *was* considering some cost-cutting measures."

His eyes caught the light as he laughed. "What did you have in mind, Dr. Marian?"

"I figured I'd need to find a roommate. Someone who knows the area. Someone who's good with his hands and doesn't mind sharing a bed."

Foster's lip quirked up in a smile. "I thought room and board were included at SERA. But maybe if we agree to continue sharing, the program will save on housing, and they'll be able to use that to bump your salary a little," he teased.

"Ahhh, see there? You're solving my problems already." I clutched the front of his shirt and yanked him until his nose brushed mine. "You, sir, are awfully convenient to have around."

"Tommy." Foster's voice was serious now. "I need you to understand something. I'm not going anywhere. Not anymore. If you stay, if we do this, it's not a summer fling or a temporary thing. It's forever. I'm talking about building a life together. A real life."

"Are you threatening me with a good time, Sheriff? What does this life look like, exactly?"

"It looks like coming home to each other every night. It looks like planning SERA's programs together and arguing about curriculum and probably driving Trace crazy with our bickering. It looks like weekends at your family's lodge and holidays in Majestic with mine." He paused. "It looks like maybe getting a house together when we're ready. Maybe getting married. Maybe adopting a whole pack of rescue dogs because I know you're going to fall in love with every single one and give them all ridiculous names."

My heart felt like it might explode. "That sounds perfect. But you forgot something."

"What?"

I gestured toward the dartboard. "It looks like you taking down that photo and burning it."

Foster laughed, the sound rich and warm. "Nah, I think I'm having it mounted on a real dartboard because surely there'll be times I'll need it again in the future."

I squinted at it again. "Those are very precise holes, Foster."

"I was imagining them as acupuncture points." He grinned. "Trying to cure myself of wanting you."

"I was just as obsessed," I admitted softly. "I've never jacked off quite that much before. You weren't the only one who found a photo online. Only, I used yours for good, not evil."

He hooted. "Meaning you jerked off to it?"

I shrugged and tried to look unaffected. "So I have a thing for men in uniform, sue me."

His eyes darkened. "And you're taking a job where you'll be surrounded by cops, EMTs, firefighters, pilots..."

"I might have joined SERA for you, but I didn't say there weren't other perks," I teased.

He growled and kissed me again, rough and wild, just the way I liked it.

"I love you," I breathed.

Foster cradled my face in his hands. "I meant what I said. I fell for you, head over heels, that first night. I'm sorry it took me so long to admit it, but I will love you until the end of time. You're it for me, Tommy. I'm yours."

I couldn't believe this was my life, that I was on the cusp of stepping into a new chapter, one in which I would get to live authentically, pursuing my dream job next to the man of my dreams.

"And I'm yours. Always."

Foster's shoulders dropped, as if he'd somehow been worried about my response. "Damned right you are."

"Now what?" I asked with a watery laugh.

I looked around his office—at the neat desk with his resignation letter, at the dartboard, at this man who'd just turned his entire life upside down for me.

"Now I introduce you to my friends and family," he said. "Because it's time you learned the Marians aren't the only... *colorful* family around."

I let out a laugh. "Shall we place bets? On whose family gives us the most trouble in the years to come?"

Foster's own laugh rang out in the nearly empty office. "Nah. I'll still give that to your side. I don't have a Tilly."

As we walked out of the sheriff's office together, Foster's hand warm in mine, I caught a glimpse of our reflection in the glass door. We looked like what we were—two men who'd found their way to each other despite every obstacle, every misunderstanding, every dart thrown in frustration.

We looked nothing like the future of ticked boxes and empty accomplishments I'd planned for myself—the future Foster Blake had rescued me from.

We looked like everything I'd never known I wanted.
And more than I ever imagined.

EPILOGUE ONE

FOSTER – AN HOUR LATER

I WALKED into Way and Silas's house that afternoon like I was ten feet tall and walking on fairy bubbles. After the last few years of watching one friend after another find their soulmate, it was finally my turn.

And I'd found the most amazing man on the planet.

When my mom caught sight of the beautiful doctor on my arm, she screamed and burst into tears. "I knew it! I knew you weren't throwing darts at a stranger."

Tommy snorted inelegantly beside me and shot me an accusatory glance. "You know the dart thing will never be over, right?"

I shrugged. "You have your coping skills, I have mine." I met my mom's eyes and nodded my head in Tommy's direction. "Mom, this is Dr. Tommy Marian. Tommy, this is my mother, Jolene Blake."

Mom's cheeks were wet with tears. If it had been with

anyone other than Tommy, I would have been embarrassed by what this display of emotion meant—namely, that I was such a lost cause that even bringing a guy around was huge progress—but I wasn't. I was too happy for any other emotion right now.

"Call me Jo. I'm so happy to meet you, Tommy." She gave him a quick hug before pulling back and beaming at him. "And I'm happy you're not pockmarked in real life."

Tommy smiled. "You aren't the only one. It's nice to meet you, too, Jo. Thank you for…" He swallowed, and I noticed his ears turned a little pink at the tops. "Well, thank you for this guy. He's one of the best people I know."

More tears as Mom glanced over at me with pride. "Same. I couldn't have asked for a better son and friend. Or business partner!"

"Alright, alright," I said quickly. "Can we skip this part, please? Where's Anna?"

I glanced around in hope of finding my sister, but instead, I found the shit-eating grin of Way's husband, Silas.

"Well, well, well. It's finally time for the tables to turn," he began. "And who's this tasty morsel?"

"Touch him and die," I warned in a low voice without losing my friendly grin.

Silas barked out a laugh and introduced himself to Tommy. "I hope you know your boyfriend is the world's biggest flirt. He takes great pride in causing trouble between other couples. Don't be surprised if people dish it all back out tonight. Welcome to Majestic."

I felt the heat of Tommy's eyes on me. "A flirt, you say? That doesn't sound like Foster. He's so quiet and meek, like a baby bird afraid to leave his own nest."

I leaned over and pressed a kiss to his forehead. "Exactly. See? You get me."

Tommy sucked in a breath. I turned to see what he was reacting to when I noticed him staring at my sister from across the room. "Holy fuck, who is that?" he breathed. "She's fucking gorgeous. Can you introduce me?"

I stood in shock, reeling from his pronouncement before hearing the sound of men's laughter and realized he was in on some kind of joke.

They'd somehow set me up.

"You don't even know these guys!" I accused, catching the teasing light in his eyes. "How the fuck did you know that was Anna?"

Way clapped me on the shoulder and grinned. "You were so busy staring at the good doctor here, you didn't see Silas gesture to Anna and mouth her name."

Way, Silas, and all of their friends, *my* friends, laughed and teased me as they swarmed around to meet Tommy properly. I could tell they were all genuinely happy for me, with Way the happiest of all, other than my mom, of course.

Finally, Anna walked up. "You must be Tommy. I've heard a lot about you from Foster's office wall."

That was all it took for everyone to start laughing again. I pulled her into my arms and gave her a hug. "Happy birthday, asshole."

Tommy poked me in the back. "See! I knew it. I knew you

called your family names, too. And you got mad at Hazel for doing it to me."

I turned and winked at him. "I'm the only one who can call you names. No one else."

He slid his hand into mine and threaded our fingers together. I noticed a faint tremble in his hand and suddenly realized this was the first time he'd held a man's hand in public. First time he'd been claimed by another man to anyone.

I met his eye and mouthed, "Okay?"

He smiled and nodded before leaning into my shoulder and pressing his face into my neck for a quick kiss below my ear. "I didn't know it could be like this," he whispered. "Very okay."

I pressed a kiss into his hair and straightened back up, catching my mom looking on wistfully. Anna began peppering Tommy with questions about what it was like to live in New York since she'd always wanted to go and see a show on Broadway.

My friend Tully came over with his young daughter on his hip. She immediately gasped with excitement and babbled, "Fossa!" as she lurched at me with arms spread wide. I had to let go of Tommy to catch her, and when I gave her a big raspberry kiss on the cheek, I caught my guy flashing moony eyes at me.

Suddenly, I remembered our conversation in Hawaii. About how he wanted kids and a family. I met his eyes and grinned. "This is Lellie. She's two and a half. And these are her dads, Tully and Dev. Guys, this is Tommy."

Tommy greeted Lellie first, instantly winning over her two proud parents. Within moments, she'd jumped ship for

Tommy's more interesting antics, and Tully and Dev were pulling Tommy away to get him a drink from the collection of beer and wine in a nearby cooler.

Way surprised me with a huge hug, the tight, back-slapping kind that he was famous for. "So fucking happy for you," he said, emotion in his voice. "Nobody deserves a good guy more than you."

When he pulled away, I gathered my courage. "I didn't get a chance to tell you this back at the office, but, uh..." I sucked in a breath. "I'm moving up to Legacy and joining SERA full-time."

Way's face fell. In addition to being my cousin and best friend, Waylon Fletcher was also the mayor of Majestic. While my news might be acceptable on a personal level, since I wouldn't be all that far away and he'd married into enough money to travel it in style, professionally, I was dealing him a significant blow.

"Oh. Shit," he murmured.

I caught my mom's eye a few feet away. She pressed her lips together in an understanding smile. I'd called her on the way to town to tell her everything, so she'd already had a chance to come to terms with it. And she was thrilled I was finally doing something for myself after spending so long looking after her and Anna.

"I think Hanson's ready to take on the role, but obviously, that's up to the people to decide. I'll certainly back him if he wants to run."

"Shit, Foster," he said again, blowing out a breath. "That's... unexpected. I'm... *fuck*. I'm going to miss the hell out of you."

"Likewise. You have to promise not to be a stranger, and

maybe… well, maybe you'll take one look at Legacy and decide to move all the horses up there. It's awfully pretty."

He gave me another hug as he let out a laugh. "I'll bet ranchers are a dime a dozen in Montana. In fact, I happen to know Lennon Mar—wait. *Marian*." His eyes widened. "Is your doctor related to Jude Marian?"

Our friend Zane's ears perked up from nearby, and he meandered over to find out what we were talking about. As the conversation moved like popcorn popping, in quick, noisy bursts all over the place, I looked around at the life I'd built here in my hometown.

Friends and family. Warmth and welcome. A place and people who'd helped me be who I needed to be. And who would support me as I continued doing that exact same thing up in Legacy.

After a while, when we'd gathered around several large tables out back and the sun was just starting to set behind the peaks of Three Daughters, Zane's boyfriend, Ryan, tilted his head and looked at Tommy funny.

"Hey… weren't you in that commercial with the dog and the…" His face crinkled. "The thing?"

Zane's eyes lit up. "That was you?"

Tommy shook his head sadly, though his hazel eyes danced as they found mine. "Nah, I get that a lot, though. Guy's name was Wade Brown. Passed away."

"Ah, shit," Zane said. "Is that right?"

I held up my beer bottle to clink against Tommy's glass of wine. Happiness bubbled in my chest like fizzy champagne.

"To Wade."

"To Wade," he said with a grin. "And kinsmin."

EPILOGUE TWO
TOMMY – SEVERAL MONTHS LATER

"Relax, it's not about you," I said for the millionth time.

Foster yanked at the collar of his shirt. "This thing is choking me. Pretty sure *that's* about me," he said.

"The wedding is over. Take the tie off if you want. No one cares." I glanced around the vineyard lodge. The familiar wood-beamed walls and large stacked stone fireplace made the perfect backdrop for my cousin Mattie's wedding in Napa. She and her new spouse stood in the open doorway leading out to the terrace, accepting well-wishes from their guests as they filtered through the lobby out to the wedding reception. "Everyone's eyes are on the happy couple anyway."

"Forgive me if the last wedding I attended was my boyfriend's," he muttered, eyes darting around. It was only because I knew him so well that I assumed he was making sure Tilly, Granny, and Irene were not within striking distance.

"Huh. I didn't realize your boyfriend was married. Weird."

He shot me a look. "You know what I mean. That was the last time I was surrounded by this many Marians. It's a lot."

He wasn't wrong. Last night at the rehearsal dinner in the barrel room, my cousins, aunts, and uncles had all given Foster the third degree, peppering him with questions about search and rescue, his old sheriff job, and what it was like to "turn a guy gay."

"We've heard about it from gay lore, but we've never seen it in real life," my cousin Rosie had teased.

Foster had looked right at her with a straight face and said, "I have a magical—"

"Okay!" I'd cried, slapping a hand over his mouth.

He'd laughed and pulled my hand away, not without kissing my palm first, and finished, "—way with men. Baby, what did you think I was gonna say?"

They'd all loved him. He'd charmed the pants off them, as usual, which meant his insecurity today made no sense.

"What's gotten into you?"

Foster grabbed two champagne glasses off a passing server's tray and handed one to me before taking a healthy swallow from the other. "Nothing. Well, other than *you* getting into me this morning in the shower. That what you mean?"

"Definitely not. You've been acting strange all day."

I suddenly realized what it could be and pulled him over to the edge of the room for a little privacy.

"Are you feeling pressure to get married?" I asked, trying not to laugh at the idea. "Is being at a wedding with me making you squirrelly because you think everyone's going to put you on the spot about *us*? Baby, we've only been together for four months. Nobody's thinking about that right now."

His eyes pierced me with the same intensity he always seemed to get when he told me he loved me, like it was the most serious declaration he'd ever make for the entirety of this life and all the lives that came after it.

My throat thickened with emotion. *Fuck*, I loved him.

"Thomas Marian, you will be marrying me when we're ready to take that step. It's not a question of *if* but *when*. And, listen, I'm not in a hurry. You know that. But if you think for one minute the idea of marrying you would make me squirrelly, you haven't been paying attention."

My heart tripped into its usual rapid pace whenever Foster got like this. "Not if but when, huh?"

He grabbed my tie and yanked me in for a bruising kiss. "That's right. Notice I didn't ask your opinion."

A laugh bubbled up. "Duly noted. But for the record, I concur."

"Mpfh."

"So then why are you acting weird? It's not about..." I glanced at the couple exchanging longing glances in the corner and lowered my voice. "It's not about the Robyn thing, is it? Because I swear, until two days ago, I had no idea the best man had even *met* her when he was in Legacy last month, let alone hooked up with her and invited her to the wedding as his plus—"

"Of course not. You know I like Robyn a lot." Foster winked. "And I like her even better now that she's not swinging her ponytail in my boyfriend's direction."

I rolled my eyes. "Then I'm officially out of ideas as to why you—*oof*."

He pulled me over to one of the nearby leather sofas and sat, yanking me down practically on top of him. His arm immediately came around me, holding me close, and his lips brushed my ear.

It took me a minute to realize he was preparing to tell me a secret, not seducing me at a family wedding.

Damn.

"I saw something I shouldn't have, and now I don't know what to do about it."

"Continue."

The warm breath of his huff tickled the skin on my neck, but I tried to stay focused.

"Okay, I was sitting next to Tilly last night at the rehearsal dinner—"

"I remember. She swapped out my place card with her own," I grumbled. "And claimed it was to 'thank Commander Quadzilla for the lovely bottle of Macallan he sent me.'"

"Right. But apparently, she was in the middle of a scheme with her fellow evil-doers. She needed to sit next to Alex so she could steal his phone when he went to the buffet."

I snorted. "Babe, Tilly's gonna Tilly. She once stole my phone to put herself on my Amazon Prime account, but then she loaded a two-hundred-dollar gift card on it to cover the fees. Don't ask me why. She said it had something to do with governmental spy agencies, but I honestly think she was just being lazy."

He gave me a meaningful look. "She was in the *Flint* app."

I blinked at him. "I don't know that one."

Foster's warm bark of laughter surprised me. "Jesus fuck. Sometimes I forget you're a little baby bisexual with literally zero experience in the gay world."

"I beg your pardon." I poked a finger between his ribs and lateral thorax—jackpot tickle territory, medically speaking. "You weren't complaining about my lack of gay experience in the shower this morning."

He grabbed my hand to stop my assault. "It's a gay hookup app. *Flint.* Was started by a group of firefighters in California, actually, during the Granite Hollow fires a few years ago. Anyway, doesn't matter. I just remember hearing about it at the time because I was called in to help find a missing kid."

"Did you find the kid?" I asked, already knowing from hearing many of his SAR stories that he had good ones and horrible ones.

"Safe and sound, asleep at a friend's house," Foster confirmed. "But back to Flint. Tilly used Alex's profile—or, hell, maybe she made him a profile, I don't know—and started conversations with people." He looked around and lowered his voice. "*Sex* conversations."

I bit my lip to keep from howling with laughter. "Okay? Why are you so upset about this? Do you want to tattle on my great-great-aunt? Or do you maybe want to leave it alone and let Alex reap the benefit of a little old lady's sexual fantasies?"

We both stopped and winced at the notion before Foster's body was wracked with a shudder. "I'd rather forget the entire thing."

"Sounds like a plan, big guy. Let's go get some food." I started to move off his lap, but he held me tighter.

"Not so fast. I didn't tell you the intriguing part yet."

I gaped at him. "Tilly pretending to sext a stranger as my cousin Alex isn't the intriguing part?"

He glanced around before brushing my ear with his lips again.

"Sheriff, those lips are doing things to me," I breathed.

"They're going to do things to you later if we can find a moment alone," he promised.

"Continue." I was hoping he'd continue the lips more than the story, but I was out of luck.

"I think the guy she was messaging was Chief Kincaid."

I whipped my head around so fast I nearly knocked noses with him. "No!"

Foster looked smug as shit as he nodded. "Yes. Pretty sure, anyway."

"Alex hates the chief! They're mortal enemies."

He shifted me on his lap until I was straddling the man. It might have been a little embarrassing if we hadn't been at a wedding with a thousand horny young queer people... and if I hadn't been one of them who seriously didn't give a fuck as long as I was pressed against my favorite person in the world.

"I know," he said. "But it reminded me of something Tilly told me last summer."

He closed his eyes as if he needed to replay the tape of his memories to get it right. "She said something about how she's been managing Marian men since before I was born..."

I nodded. "That tracks."

Foster opened his eyes and met mine. "Then she nodded at Alex and the chief, who were arguing as usual, and said, '*Case in point.*' Don't you find that fishy? The woman is up to something. She's meddling again."

"She's a meddler. Meddling is what she does."

Foster's face suddenly split into a bright grin. "You know what? She meddled in our relationship, and we turned out just fine. Maybe I'm overthinking this."

I leaned in and kissed his impossibly beautiful lips. Lips that sang funny, made-up songs to Chickie about how good dogs don't chase bad rabbits. Lips that tasted every terrible dish I tried to cook for us. Lips that murmured sweet reassurances to me in the middle of the night when I woke up from a bad dream. And lips that had told my parents three days ago in secret that he wanted to propose to me during the holidays.

"I'm not asking you for permission. I'm giving you the courtesy of advanced notice," he'd said, according to Ella, who'd overheard it and hadn't been able to keep her trap shut. *"Because he's already mine, and nothing you could say will change that."*

"I love you," I said, the scope of what I felt for him stealing my breath away.

His grin softened. "Promise?"

I nodded emphatically. "Forever."

"Mmm, that's a good promise," he murmured against my lips. "Say it again."

So I did. And a year later, I said it again in front of a crowd of our friends and family.

While we stood on a South Carolina beach with bare feet in the sand... and Foster wearing a suspiciously familiar T-shirt.

Looking for a little more of Tommy and Foster? Sign up for my newsletter to read their bonus story, "Rescuing the Proposal", available here → https://readerlinks.com/l/4907476

Check out Hashtag Holidate, *a fake dating, forced proximity, holiday romance full of cameos from both Made Marian and Made Marian Legacy characters! Get it here → https://readerlinks.com/l/4947976*

The legacy continues in the next book in the Made Marian Legacy series, Burning for Alexander. *Get more info and your copy here → https://readerlinks.com/l/4968333*

A LETTER FROM LUCY

Dear Reader,

Thank you for reading *Rescuing Dr. Marian*. I am thrilled to be back in the Made Marian world! Up next: watch sparks fly as Alex Marian and the grumpy fire chief cross swords in *Burning for Alexander*.

I knew as soon as Foster Blake showed up on page in *Marrying Mr. Majestic* that I wanted his story. I deliberately made him a search and rescue guy because I wanted to see him outside searching in the wilderness for his lost love.

When I thought about which Marian to pair him with in this new series, I knew it needed to be someone who would be a complete fish out of water in the wilderness. But the more I got to know Tommy Marian, the more I realized I had it wrong. He didn't need to be a stranger to the wilderness. He needed for it to be his long lost passion. I wanted to see him return to his heart. I wanted to see him find himself while falling into love. I hope I did their story justice.

Along the way, I fell in love with Hazel Marian. By the time I finished *RDM*, I knew I wanted to tell her love story. You can find "Saddled With Feelings" for free on my Patreon (*https://read erlinks.com/l/4938232*). If you like Hazel and Avery's connection, you might also like reading about MJ and Neckie in the Forever Wilde series. Their story is told in the background of *His Saint*.

On my Patreon, you can also find a minific about Tommy as a teen, handling an outdoor emergency with grace and maturity. "Hearts in Overdrive" was written as Tommy's medical origin story, the reason he wanted to become a doctor. It's a sweet little short that features some of this new Marian generation as kids, as well as some of the original Made Marian characters learning how emotionally-challenging parenthood can be.

Finally, there is a bonus short for this book called "Rescuing The Proposal". If you purchase new releases directly from my shop, the bonus comes in the back of the book. If you purchase or borrow from a retail site, you can get access to the bonus in my newsletter, here → https://readerlinks.com/l/4907476. (Unfortunately, retailers have rules about bonus content.)

Be sure to sign up for my newsletter to get bonus content, sales announcements, and more, including discounts on the next releases!

You can also follow me on your favorite retailer site to be notified of new releases, and look for me on Facebook for sneak peeks of upcoming stories. You can also join me right now on Patreon for exclusive content and behind-the-scenes glimpses.

Please take a moment to write a review of *Rescuing Dr. Marian*. Reviews can make all the difference in helping a book show up in searches.

Feel free to stop by www.LucyLennox.com and drop me a line or visit me on social media. To see inspiration photographs for all my novels, visit my Pinterest boards. The Pinterest board for *Rescuing Dr. Marian* can be found here → https://www.pinterest.com/lucy_lennox/rdm/

Finally, I have a fantastic reader group on Facebook. Join us for exclusive content, early cover reveals, hot pics, and a whole lotta fun. Lucy's Lair can be found here → http://www.lucylennox.com/l/1437683.

Happy reading!
Lucy

ABOUT LUCY LENNOX

Lucy Lennox is the USA Today bestselling author of over fifty gay romance titles including the GoodReads Hall of Fame winner Wilde Love. Born and raised in the southeast USA, she is finally putting good use to that English Lit degree she earned before the turn of the century.

Lucy enjoys naps, pizza, and procrastinating. She stays up way too late each night reading romance because it's simply the best.

For more information and to stay updated about future releases, sales and audio news and to grab some free and bonus reads, please sign up for Lucy's author newsletter on her website at LucyLennox.com or to stay in the know, join her exciting reader group, Lucy's Lair on Facebook.

facebook.com/lucylennoxmm

instagram.com/lucylennoxmm

amazon.com/Lucy-Lennox/e/B01N0IOYPT

bookbub.com/authors/lucy-lennox

patreon.com/lucylennox

pinterest.com/lucy_lennox

ALSO BY LUCY LENNOX

Find me online → https://www.lucylennox.com/links/

Read my books:

Made Marian Series

Forever Wilde Series

Aster Valley Series

The Billionaire Brotherhood Series

Made Marian Legacy Series

After Oscar Series (with Molly Maddox)

Twist of Fate Series (with Sloane Kennedy)

Licking Thicket Series (with May Archer)

Champion Security Series (with May Archer)

Honeybridge Series (with May Archer)

Find a complete list of my stand alone romances and novellas at www.LucyLennox.com along with audio samples, freebies, suggested reading order, and more!